ASPHALT COVEN

WITCHES OF KIRRA CROSS BOOK 1

GWEN DEMARCO

CHAPTER 1

Oh my god. This place is a dump.

Darby Hendricks stood in the doorway of what the landlord generously called a "cozy one-bedroom apartment," trying not to let her horror show on her face. Water stains bloomed across the ceiling like diseased flowers, and the hardwood floors sagged in places that made her wonder about the structural integrity of the entire building.

"It's got character," the landlord said, his voice echoing slightly in the empty space. He was a thin man in his sixties with yellowed teeth and the kind of nonchalance that came from knowing desperate people had limited options. "Original 1920s fixtures."

The sound of shouting erupted from somewhere beyond the thin walls, followed by what sounded like something heavy hitting the floor. Darby flinched.

"Don't mind the neighbors," the landlord continued, as if domestic disputes were just another charming period feature. "They keep to themselves mostly."

Darby looked at the sagging ceiling. "Is that... is there a leak?"

"Nah, old tenant left some water running upstairs. Been fixed for ages, nothing to worry about." He watched as Darby gave the ceiling another wary look. It still looked slightly damp to her eyes. "I could knock a little off the rent for that," he added quickly.

Well... that's kinda tempting.

Darby could make any savings stretch, but even with a discount, she'd still be paying for a place that looked like it was one heavy rainstorm away from growing its own ecosystem.

Darby walked deeper into the apartment, her footsteps hollow on the warped floors. The kitchen consisted of a hot plate, an ancient fridge that hummed unevenly, and a sink with a faucet that dripped steadily into a stained basin. Through the grimy kitchen window, she'd hoped to at least catch a view of the Taskequan River, but all she could see was the industrial landscape of Medeon stretching out in shades of gray and rust – abandoned factories and empty lots interrupted by the occasional fast-food sign.

This was the fifth apartment she'd toured this week. She'd been really hopeful that this place would be the one because it was in the Argos borough, the next neighborhood over from Kirra Cross where she worked. She would only have to take one quick bus ride to get to work instead of the complicated transfers she currently dealt with from Maya's place. But she'd bet her next paycheck that there was black mold lurking behind those water stains, and she wasn't desperate enough to risk that. Even if the rent was actually in her price range for once.

The other apartments she'd looked at had been either significantly worse or so far beyond her post-divorce budget that she'd laughed out loud at the rent prices. She knew starting over would be expensive, but she hadn't grasped just *how* expensive until she'd tried to find a decent place on an entry-level accountant's salary – especially with a decent chunk of every paycheck going toward the debt Roy had racked up during their marriage.

Maybe she needed to find a place with roommates. She'd

wanted to strike out on her own – to prove she could make it without depending on anyone else – but that was looking more and more like an impossibility.

"I need to think about it," she said finally, the words coming out more tired than she'd intended.

"Don't think too long. Places like this go fast."

Darby almost asked him where exactly they went fast *to*, but bit her tongue. The landlord was already walking toward the door, clearly ready to move on to the next desperate soul on his list.

She followed him out into the hallway, which smelled like cigarettes and something sour she didn't want to identify. The fluorescent light above pulsed intermittently, casting everything in a stuttering yellow glow.

This is what starting over looks like, I guess.

Standing at the bus stop outside the apartment building, Darby watched a group of kids playing in a lot filled with broken concrete and weeds. Behind them, a faded mural on the side of a building depicted Greek gods on Mount Olympus overlooking a harbor below – some long-ago civic pride project that nobody had bothered to maintain. The children seemed happy enough, laughing and chasing each other around the debris. Maybe there was something to be said for making the best of what you had.

Her phone buzzed with a text from Jessica, an old friend from her hometown: *How's the apartment hunting going? Found anything nice?*

Darby stared at the message for a long moment. Jessica was nice enough, but they'd been friends through Roy first, which made everything feel slightly off-balance now. They had perfected the art of surface-level conversations that skirted around too much honesty.

She typed back: *Still looking. Medeon has a lot of character.*

It wasn't entirely a lie.

She'd chosen to move to Medeon partly for the job opportunity – a small accounting firm willing to hire someone whose resumé was heavier on retail experience than accounting credentials – but mostly because it was far enough from Granville that she wouldn't run into her ex-husband and his new girlfriend at the grocery store. The problem was, she barely knew anyone here.

During her marriage, she'd let most of her friendships wither away, too absorbed in trying to fix something that had been broken from the start. Now she found herself in a strange city where her deepest conversations were with landlords showing her increasingly depressing apartments. She had coworkers at the firm – pleasant enough people – but she was still too new, too careful about making the right impression to really open up to anyone. That left Maya, the only college friend Darby had kept in any real contact with, as the closest thing to a friend she had here. But they'd both changed since college in small, imperceptible ways that added up. Conversations felt like they required more effort than they used to, filled with polite catch-up questions rather than the comfortable shorthand they'd once shared.

Maya had been generous to let her stay, but Darby could feel her welcome wearing thin. The apartment was small, Maya had her own life, and after three weeks of awkward morning conversations and feeling like a burden, she needed her own place and her own space. Hell, she needed a life.

The loneliness was the worst part. What she really craved was human contact beyond those awkward morning conversations with Maya about whose turn it was to buy toilet paper. Real conversation. Something to remind her that she still existed as more than just a divorced woman taking up space on someone else's furniture.

She couldn't fix all her problems right now, but she *could* get a caffeine fix.

Darby pulled out her phone and googled "coffee shops near me." She skipped over the first few options, as she was not interested in a chain shop. The first result to catch her eye was a place called The Golden Apple. The photos showed exposed brick walls, local artwork, and people who looked like they might have interesting conversations about something other than rent prices and security deposits.

It was worth a shot.

CHAPTER 2

Twenty minutes later, the bus dropped Darby in the center of Kirra Cross, her favorite neighborhood at the center of Medeon. Like a lot of Michigan cities, Medeon had sprawled outward over the decades, but Kirra Cross had held onto its walkable, slightly scrappy charm.

Darby approached the glass doors of The Golden Apple.

She paused just outside, her attention snagged by the row of boxwood shrubs lining the sidewalk beneath the large glass front. They looked stressed – leaves turning brown and brittle, probably from the early frost they hadn't been protected against. Without thinking, she crouched down and brushed her fingers along one of the branches, imagining she could feel the plant's quiet distress. *Poor things.*

She straightened and pushed through the glass doors. The contrast from the traffic-clogged city outside was immediate and striking. The space was warm and inviting, with high ceilings, industrial light fixtures, and the kind of mismatched furniture that managed to look curated rather than accidental. The air was filled with a symphony of sounds: the chatter of voices, the gentle clink of ceramic mugs, and the rhythmic hiss of steam from the espresso machine.

The place was surprisingly busy for the early evening period. The space was crowded with people hunched over their laptops wearing serious expressions, a group of art students clustered around a corner table covered in sketchbooks, and what looked like a business meeting happening near the window. Everyone seemed to belong here in a way that Darby envied.

She ordered a medium iced coffee with oat milk – her accountant brain calculating the cost against her tight budget – and found a seat at a small empty table near a tiny stage that held only a stool, a microphone stand, and a couple of pots with fake plants.

Darby sipped her coffee slowly, savoring it as she pulled out her phone and scrolled through apartment listings. The same depressing options she'd been looking at all week appeared on her screen: decent apartments that would eat her entire salary, claustrophobic studios with one tiny window facing a brick wall, or shared housing situations designed for twenty-year-olds who didn't mind living like they were still in a dorm. Now that Darby was closing in on thirty, she wasn't interested.

A figure swept past her peripheral vision, jolting Darby back to her surroundings. She looked up to see a woman with a guitar case approaching the small stage. The woman moved with easy confidence, stepping up onto the platform and pulling her guitar from its case. She had striking features with high cheekbones, olive skin that suggested she might be descended from the Greek founders of Medeon, and purple-streaked hair pulled back in a messy bun. She wore a vintage band t-shirt layered under an oversized cardigan, dark jeans with strategic rips at the knees, and worn leather boots that looked like they'd walked through a dozen cities. Silver rings adorned her fingers, and a collection of delicate necklaces caught the light as she moved. Darby found herself watching as the woman settled onto the stool and began tuning her instrument, her fingers moving over the strings with practiced ease.

The woman began a sound check, adjusting the microphone stand. As she loosened it to lower the height, the whole thing suddenly slipped through her hands as the mechanism failed to catch. The heavy base swung down, striking her knuckles before she could pull her hand away. The woman sucked in a sharp breath, cradling her hand against her chest.

Darby half-rose from her seat, ready to help if needed. Their eyes met and something passed between them; not recognition exactly, but something familiar in the woman's dark eyes. A kind of weariness that Darby recognized in her own reflection, the look of someone who had learned that life didn't always go according to plan.

The woman gave her a small nod of acknowledgment before tightening the mic stand and returning her attention to her guitar.

Darby realized with regret that she needed to leave. Rush hour meant that her bus ride back to Maya's would take twice as long. She stood reluctantly, gathered her things, and gave the woman a small smile. She grinned back, warm and genuine, before returning her attention to her guitar.

Darby walked over to the counter area and placed her empty cup in the plastic tub. She was about to head for the door when something caught her eye. It was a bulletin board covered in colorful flyers and handwritten notices. Dog walkers advertising their services, bands looking for drummers, yoga classes, tutoring services – the usual community board fare. She leaned closer, hoping that maybe someone had posted a flyer looking for a roommate, scanning the offerings with the desperate hope of someone running out of options.

"Not staying for the show?"

Darby turned to find the woman from the stage standing beside her. Up close, she was even more striking, with the kind of presence that seemed to fill more space than her physical body occupied.

"I'd love to, but I need to catch my bus," Darby said.

"I'm Topaz," the woman said, extending her hand.

"Darby. I'm an accountant. Not nearly as interesting as a musician." She immediately felt foolish for adding that last part.

Topaz smiled, and the expression transformed her entire face. "Everyone's interesting if you know how to look. What brought you to Medeon?"

Darby wondered how Topaz could tell she wasn't local. Was it something about the way she carried herself, or how she'd been studying the bulletin board like a newcomer searching for connections? The question was asked casually, but something in Topaz's tone suggested she actually wanted to hear the answer. Darby found herself being more honest than she'd planned.

"Divorce. Fresh start. The whole cliché."

"Nothing cliché about it. Starting over takes guts. Real courage."

Darby felt an unexpected warmth spread through her chest. When was the last time someone had called her courageous? Her ex-husband had certainly never used that word. Neither had her family, who'd spent the past year treating her divorce like a personal failure rather than an escape from a relationship that had been slowly suffocating her.

"I don't feel very courageous," Darby admitted. "I feel like I'm barely keeping my head above water most days."

"That's exactly when courage counts most." Topaz's voice was warm and steady. "When everything's falling apart and scary, but you choose to keep going anyway."

They talked for a few more minutes, and Darby found herself opening up to this stranger in a way she hadn't expected. When Topaz glanced at the bulletin board behind them, she asked, "So what were you hoping to find up there? You looked pretty focused."

Darby felt heat rise in her cheeks. "Honestly? I was looking for apartment listings or maybe someone advertising for a roommate. I'm staying on a friend's couch right now, but that's not exactly a long-term solution."

Topaz's entire face lit up, her eyes widening with excitement. "No way. We were clearly meant to meet today." She grabbed Darby's arm gently. "My neighbor and good friend Kara is actually searching for a roommate right now. She's got this amazing apartment in a refurbished canning factory just a few blocks from here, and she's been struggling to find the right person. We both live on the sixth floor."

"Really?" Darby felt a flutter of hope mixed with wariness. Things that seemed too good to be true usually were.

"Really. Kara is fantastic – she's a librarian at the local library, super laid-back, and she makes the most incredible herbal teas. The building is rent-controlled, so it's not crazy expensive, and the apartment has these amazing huge windows." Topaz was practically bouncing on her toes. "I was just over there yesterday helping her vet applicants online. Most of them seemed like weirdos or scams. This is perfect timing."

"I don't know," Darby said slowly. "I mean, I appreciate the offer, but she doesn't even know me. I could be a terrible roommate."

"Kara has good instincts about people, and so do I. Plus, anyone brave enough to start over in a new city after a divorce is exactly the kind of strong, independent woman she'd want to live with." Topaz pulled out her phone. "Let me text her right now. Are you free this evening? She could show you around the place."

Darby felt a familiar anxiety creep in. "I don't know. This feels too fast. I mean, I just met you five minutes ago, and now you're setting me up with your friend?"

"But this could solve your housing problem," Topaz argued. "Come on, what's the worst that could happen? If it doesn't work out, you're no worse off than you are now."

The logic was sound, even if Darby's cautious nature wanted to resist. "Okay," she said finally. "If she's open to it, I'm willing to meet her."

Topaz was already typing on her phone. "This is going to be perfect. I can just feel it." She looked up at Darby with a grin. "Sometimes the universe puts exactly the right people in your path at exactly the right time."

As Topaz sent the text, Darby wondered if she was being foolish to trust a stranger she'd just met. But then again, staying on Maya's couch indefinitely wasn't exactly a sustainable plan either. Maybe it was time to take a leap of faith.

"She says she can meet you after work if you want to come check out the place," Topaz announced, reading her phone. "I can give you the address, and if you want, I can meet you there to make introductions."

"That would be really helpful, actually," Darby admitted.

"Perfect." Topaz rattled off an address that was indeed just a few blocks away. "You know what? Why don't you stay for my set? Then we can walk over to Kara's together. That way you don't have to worry about finding it on your own."

Darby checked the time on her phone. If she stayed, she'd definitely get stuck in the worst of the rush hour traffic, but if this housing opportunity was real, it might be worth a crowded, uncomfortable bus ride. "You know what? Yes. I'd like that."

"Excellent." Topaz started walking back toward the stage. "Make sure you cheer loudly, okay? I always get better tips when the crowd is lively."

As Topaz returned to the small stage, Darby found a seat with a good view and pulled out her phone to text Maya that she might be late. For the first time since arriving in Medeon, she felt like something might actually be going her way.

CHAPTER 3

By the time Topaz finished her set, Darby was amazed by how the coffee shop had transformed. What had been a moderate crowd had swelled to standing-room-only, with people packed around the small stage and others listening from the doorway. Topaz's voice was rich and haunting, and her lyrics spoke to something deep and universal about loss, hope, and finding your place in the world. During one particularly moving song about chosen family, Darby found herself wiping away tears.

As the audience applauded and began to disperse, Topaz packed up her guitar and joined Darby at her table.

"So? Ready to meet your potential new roommate?" she asked, slinging her guitar case over her shoulder.

"Ready as I'll ever be," Darby replied, gathering her things.

* * *

THEY WALKED in silence for a block, passing a vintage clothing store and a yoga studio, their windows bright with tasteful displays. The wind picked up, biting and sharp, and Darby adjusted her knit cap to cover her ears. As they walked, the neighborhood started to shift. The storefronts became a laundromat with a buzzing neon light and a corner store with bars on the windows. Warehouses with broken windows lined the street, a chemical plant belched steam into the charcoal sky, and chain-link fences bordered loading docks where nobody seemed to be loading anything anymore. The sidewalk cracked and buckled under their feet.

"I know a shortcut," Topaz said. "Beats walking past the Anchor on Porter Street."

"The Anchor?"

"Dive bar a few blocks over." Topaz kept her voice casual, but her pace quickened slightly. "It can be dangerous. Some gang members use it as their spot – I try to avoid it if possible."

Topaz led her down an alley between a defunct paper mill and what looked like an old water treatment facility, its concrete walls streaked with rust and crowned with barbed wire. At the back of the alley, partially hidden behind a tangle of chain-link fence covered in wild vines, was a gap – a section where someone had peeled back the fencing.

"Through here," Topaz said, slipping through sideways.

Darby hesitated at the gap, eyeing the torn metal edges and the darkness beyond.

"Come on," Topaz called back, a hint of amusement in her voice. "You gotta be bold, take life by the balls. Can't rebuild yourself if you're playing it safe all the time."

There was something in her tone; not quite mocking, but close. Like Topaz was pushing to see if Darby would rise to the challenge.

Darby felt a flush of embarrassment, followed quickly by gratitude. Topaz was right. This was exactly what she needed – someone to push her out of her comfort zone, to help her shed that timid version of herself who'd let her ex-husband walk all over her for years. Topaz was helping her be braver and more adventurous. A better friend than she'd had in a long time.

She pushed through the gap, feeling a small spark of pride at her own daring.

Of all the things Darby had imagined finding behind that fence, a cemetery hadn't made the list. And yet here it was, tucked impossibly into the dead center of the city.

The cemetery spread before them, crumbling and forgotten, hemmed in on all sides by darkened industrial buildings that towered over it like indifferent giants. Headstones tilted at drunken angles, half-swallowed by dead grass and the withered skeletons of vines. Many tombstones had toppled completely, their inscriptions worn smooth by decades of neglect. A massive elm stood sentinel near the center, its gnarled trunk twisted with age. The roots had grown relentlessly over the decades, pushing up through the earth and knocking headstones askew like chess pieces on an abandoned board.

A stone angel knelt in prayer beyond the elm, one wing broken and the left arm missing entirely, crumbled bits of stone littered around its kneeling form. Lichen covered everything in shades of green and gray, softening the edges of death into something almost organic. The air smelled of damp earth and moss, ancient and undisturbed. Thick vines grew rampant over a mausoleum, clinging to the crumbling stone façade of the small building.

The place was utterly silent except for the distant hum of machinery from the surrounding plants. No traffic noise penetrated here. No voices. Just the wind moving through the grass and the creak of the old elm's branches overhead.

"No one knows this place is here anymore," Topaz said, picking her way along what might have once been a path. She stumbled suddenly, catching herself with one hand against a tilted headstone. "Shit. Watch your step. There are roots everywhere."

Darby looked down and saw what Topaz meant. The elm's roots had broken through the surface like arthritic fingers, snaking across the ground and creating a maze of trip hazards hidden beneath the overgrown grass.

"The treatment plant closed in the seventies, the mill not long after," Topaz continued, brushing dirt from her palm. "They just... built around it and forgot." She glanced back at Darby. "The city probably has it on some old map somewhere, but I've never seen another soul here. It's completely forgotten."

Darby stood among the decrepit graves, feeling the weight of the place settle over her like a shawl. The modern city pressed in beyond the walls, but this place was a pocket that time had overlooked, stuck somewhere around 1940, judging by the dates she could still make out on the nearest stones.

"Wow," she whispered. "This is so cool."

Topaz grinned. "Thought you might think so. I come here sometimes when I'm having writer's block."

They wound their way through the cemetery in silence, following a single worn path between the graves. At the far end, another section of compromised fence led them back out into the world – into another alley, and then suddenly they were on a city street again.

"There it is," Topaz said, pointing to a massive brick structure halfway down the block. "Home sweet home."

Darby looked up at the converted canning factory, taking in its industrial architecture. The building had clearly seen better days. The brick was weathered and stained in places, and some of the original factory windows had been replaced with modern ones that didn't quite match. Fire escapes zigzagged up the sides like iron branches, and the entrance was marked by a simple glass door with peeling paint around the frame. It wasn't fancy, but it had character, and more importantly, it looked like the kind of place she might actually be able to afford.

"It's not much to look at from the outside," Topaz admitted, "but wait until you see the apartments. Those huge factory windows let in amazing light."

The lobby was small and utilitarian, with mailboxes lining one wall and an old freight elevator with heavy metal doors. Topaz stopped at her mailbox and groaned as she pulled out a stack of envelopes.

"Bill, bill, credit card company telling me I'm wonderful and should borrow more money, bill..." She waved the pile dramatically. "The glamorous life of a starving artist."

"You're incredibly talented," Darby said as they waited for the elevator. "You should be famous. That crowd was completely captivated."

Topaz grinned, her whole face lighting up. "That's the plan. And then I won't have to worry about these anymore." She waved the envelopes like a white flag of surrender.

The elevator creaked and groaned as it carried them up to the sixth floor, clearly a relic from the building's industrial past. When the heavy doors slid open, they stepped into a narrow hallway with worn carpet that was clean and well-lit.

"That's my place," Topaz said, pointing to 6A as they approached 6C. She knocked on Kara's door and called out, "Kara! It's me, and I brought that person who's interested in the room."

The overhead lights flickered briefly, and Darby glanced up as they settled back into a steady glow.

When the apartment door opened, Darby found herself face-to-face with a woman who looked like she color-coded her closet. She wore a neatly pressed button-down tucked into slacks, and her brown hair was pulled back in a tidy low ponytail. Wire-rimmed glasses framed intelligent hazel eyes that studied Darby with quiet wariness.

Topaz and Kara hugged quickly before Kara turned to Darby with a warm smile.

"You must be Darby," she said, extending a firm handshake. "I'm Kara Winters. Topaz texted me all about you. Come in, let me show you around."

"Darby Hendricks," Darby replied, grateful for Kara's straight-forward manner.

The space immediately impressed Darby. The main living area was open and airy, with those promised huge factory windows. Even in the fading evening light, they filled the space with a soft amber warmth that made the apartment feel welcoming and lived-in. The kitchen was small, but everything was clean and organized in a way that spoke to Kara's practical nature. Books were everywhere – stacked on shelves, piled on the coffee table, tucked into corners – which made perfect sense for a librarian. However, what really caught Darby's attention was a small balcony accessible through sliding glass doors. She could already imagine filling it with plants, creating her own little green sanctuary.

"This would be your room," Kara said, opening a door off the main living space. "Fair warning – my last roommate disappeared without any notice about two months ago and left some stuff behind that I haven't gotten around to clearing out yet."

The room was a decent size with another of those wonderful tall windows. A simple bed frame with a mattress sat against one wall, and a small dresser occupied the corner. Nothing fancy, but it was furniture. And it certainly beat the couch in a living room she was currently using.

"You can keep what's here or toss it, whatever works for you," Kara said. "I was planning to donate it all eventually, but honestly, I've been too lazy to deal with it."

Darby felt a wave of relief wash over her. She had practically nothing in terms of furniture – just her clothes, books, and a few personal items. The bed and dresser alone would save her hundreds of dollars she didn't have to spare.

Darby's eyes were drawn to the window, where she noticed a small flower box attached to the exterior sill. The few plants inside had clearly seen better days, shriveled and brown from neglect, but the sight of it filled her with unexpected hope. She could already envision starting a little window garden with herbs or maybe some flowers.

"This place is perfect," she said, and meant it.

Kara smiled, and some tension Darby hadn't noticed seemed to leave her shoulders. "You know what? I think this might actually work out."

"I told you!" Topaz looked downright smug. "I could just tell you two would click."

"Come on," Kara said, gesturing toward the kitchen. "Let's sit down and go over the boring stuff – rent, utilities, house rules – all that fun adulting nonsense."

* * *

BACK ON MAYA'S couch later that evening, Darby couldn't stop thinking about the day's unexpected turn. The meeting with Kara had gone better than she'd dared hope. The apartment was beautiful, the rent was affordable, and Kara herself had been warm and welcoming. Even better, Kara had said she could move in right away and would only charge her a prorated amount to cover the remainder of the month instead of the full rent. That small gesture meant Darby could actually afford a few basics like new sheets and a lamp for the nightstand.

She sat with a bowl of ramen, doom-scrolling on her phone to distract herself from how surreal the day had been.

Her phone buzzed with a text from Topaz: *So glad we met today! Kara is already texting me about how excited she is to have you move in. This is going to be amazing!*

Topaz's enthusiasm made Darby grin. When was the last time someone had been genuinely excited about spending time with her?

Darby texted back: *Thank you so much for today. I owe you big time.*

She plugged her phone in to charge and noticed the light under Maya's bedroom door was turned off. Taking the hint, she decided to go to sleep as well.

Please let this work out, she thought as sleep took her.

CHAPTER 4

"*Y*ou sure you don't need help carrying anything else up?" Topaz asked, surveying the modest pile of belongings Darby had managed to transport in two trips on the freight elevator.

"I only have one more load of things to bring up," Darby said, looking at the boxes she'd already carried up which included the discounted mint plant she'd bought at the grocery store. When she'd seen it, she'd remembered Topaz mentioning that Kara liked to make tea. Mint grew easily – it was basically a weed – but it was cheap, and she thought Kara might like having fresh mint around.

"Perfect," Topaz said. "Why don't you go grab the rest of your stuff, and I'll order some cheap pizza and open a bottle of even cheaper wine. By the time you get back and finish unpacking, dinner will be ready. Consider it your official housewarming party."

As they exited Darby's new home together – Darby heading down to get her last load and Topaz going to her place to order pizza – they encountered a teenager and an older woman in the hallway who were clearly in the middle of a heated discussion.

"Thank god," the teenager said, spotting Topaz. "Topaz, can you please tell Abuela to chill?"

"What's going on, Jazmin?" Topaz asked with the weary patience of someone who'd clearly mediated this type of conversation before.

"She's freaking out because my friend Celia is dating this guy who's twenty-five. But Celia's eighteen, so he's not that much older! I mean... Seven years isn't even that big of a deal. Seriously, wasn't Abuelo like five years older than you?"

The older woman's expression softened but remained firm. "I was twenty-seven when I met your grandfather, mija. I'd already lived on my own, had a career, traveled. I had *experience*. Your friend is still in high school."

"Jazzy," Topaz said calmly, "would you be willing to date a thirteen-year-old?"

"Ew, no. Gross." Jazmin's face wrinkled in disgust.

"Why not?"

"Because... because that's weird and gross. They're like... children."

"So why do you think a twenty-five-year-old guy would want to date an eighteen-year-old?"

Jazmin opened her mouth to argue, then closed it, her expression thoughtful.

"Did this guy tell Celia she was mature for her age?" Topaz continued. "That she's not like other girls?"

Jazmin's face fell. "Yeah, actually. He did."

"That's right out of the creepy older guy playbook," Topaz said gently. "He's not dating women his own age because they have the life experience to recognize problems with his behavior. They'd see through his lines and call him out on his BS."

Jazmin huffed but nodded reluctantly. "Fine, I'll talk to Celia. But she's not going to want to hear it."

"That's what good friends do," Topaz said. "Tell her to dump him. And if she needs help with that, I'm happy to have a conversation with him. Or we could always set his car on fire. I'm kidding, Ivette," Topaz said at the sharp look the older woman gave her. Then Topaz winked at Jazmin. "Mostly."

Ivette huffed and rolled her eyes, but Jazmin was grinning.

Topaz gestured to Darby, who had been standing quietly beside her during the conversation. "This is Darby, by the way. She's moving in with Kara. You two want to come over for pizza? We can all get to know each other properly."

Jazmin gave her grandmother a hopeful look, and the older woman smiled. "That would be lovely."

"This is Jazmin Vargas," Topaz said with obvious affection. "About to graduate high school, aspiring artist, and according to her grandmother, a professional pain in the ass."

"Hey!" Jazmin protested, but she was grinning.

"Darby Hendricks," Darby replied, charmed by the girl's good humor. "Recent divorcée, accountant, and apparently, your new neighbor."

"And I'm Ivette Vargas," the older woman said with a slight Hispanic accent. She was compact and energetic, with graying hair pulled back in a neat bun and laugh lines around her eyes. "I keep this one in line. Most of the time."

Jazmin rolled her eyes at her grandmother's words. The three of them headed into Topaz's apartment, and Topaz called back over her shoulder, "Just grab Kara and head over when you're done with your last load!"

Darby headed downstairs to retrieve her remaining belongings. When she returned, she knocked on Kara's bedroom door to let her know about the pizza invitation – and to present her with the mint plant as a thank-you for taking a chance on a stranger as a roommate. Kara was delighted by the gift and excited for pizza with the neighbors.

The two of them headed to Topaz's apartment. The layout was similar to Kara's but composed of one-bedroom instead of two, which made the main living area feel smaller and more intimate. Topaz had nearly filled every inch of it. A futon couch sat against one wall, a basket of clean laundry taking up half the cushions and a crocheted blanket spilling onto the floor. Two acoustic guitars leaned in one corner beside a keyboard, while a mandolin hung on the wall like artwork. Sheet music and spiral notebooks filled with notes covered the coffee table. The bedroom door stood open, revealing an unmade bed piled with more clothes and a wooden milkcrate filled with vinyl records.

"Sorry about the mess," Topaz said, hastily gathering sheet music and making a haphazard stack on a tiny desk in the corner. She grabbed spare clothes from around the room, stuffing them into the laundry basket before carrying it into her bedroom and setting it on the bed. "I've been working on some new material."

"Don't apologize," Darby said, looking around with genuine interest. "This place has so much personality."

Once they'd all settled onto Topaz's mismatched furniture, Darby chose a chair next to Jazmin, staying at the edge of the circle rather than inserting herself into the middle. From her spot, she could watch Jazmin and Ivette volley jokes and quips back and forth, their close bond evident in every exchange.

Jazmin, now that she was over her argument with her grand-mother, was vibrant and funny, full of opinions about everything from music to politics to the best places to get tacos in the city. She pulled out her phone to show Darby her digital art portfolio, and Darby found herself impressed by the intricate character studies from Jazmin's favorite anime.

"These are incredible," Darby said, genuinely impressed. "You have real talent."

"That's what I keep telling her," Ivette said proudly. "She's starting at community college in the fall to study art. Two years there, then she'll transfer to the university."

"That's smart," Darby said. "Your parents must be proud."

Ivette's smile didn't fade, but something shifted in her expression. "I've been raising this one since she was three," she said. "Her mother had some problems with drugs. Overdosed when Jazmin was little."

Darby's chest tightened with embarrassment. "I'm sorry," she said softly. "I shouldn't have assumed."

"It's okay," Jazmin said with the matter-of-fact tone of someone who'd long since processed their grief. "Abuela's been more of a mom to me than my actual mom ever was."

Darby nodded, grateful for Jazmin's easy acceptance, but eager to move past her social blunder. "What do you do for work, Ivette?"

"I'm a freight dispatcher," Ivette continued. "Not glamorous, but it pays the bills and lets me keep an eye on this troublemaker."

"Hey!" Jazmin protested, but she was grinning.

The door buzzer announced the arrival of the pizza. Topaz jumped up to answer it, calling over her shoulder, "Kara, can you open the wine? And Jazzy, I've got that orange Fanta you like in the fridge."

Jazmin hopped up and rushed to the kitchen to grab a soda, calling back, "Topaz, you're the best!"

After paying the delivery person, Topaz carried the pizza boxes into the kitchen and set them on the counter. She reached up to grab wine glasses from the cabinet above. As she pulled the door open, it swung wide on a loose hinge, the edge flying toward her face. She jerked back just in time, barely avoiding it.

"Jesus!" Topaz steadied herself against the counter.

"You okay?" Kara asked, looking up from where she was searching for a corkscrew.

"Yeah, fine. It's an old apartment. I swear… everything's falling apart." Topaz carefully retrieved the glasses and shut the cabinet door gently. "I really need to tighten those hinges before they actually take me out."

"That could've really hurt you," Kara said with concern.

"Eh, I hurt myself all the time. No big deal," Topaz said with a shrug. "That's the life of a klutz. I'm surprised I'm not just one big walking bruise at this point."

Once they had pizza distributed and drinks in hand, Kara suggested they do something fun to celebrate Darby moving in.

"I'm up for anything," Darby said, "but it'll need to be something cheap or free. I'm still pretty broke from the divorce and the move."

"Actually," Kara said, exchanging a look with Topaz, "we've been thinking about starting a book club. That could be fun, right?"

Jazmin groaned dramatically. "With school, I already have enough assigned reading. Please don't make me analyze the symbolism in something written by some dead guy two hundred years ago."

"Who says it has to be written by a dead guy?" Kara laughed. "We could all go to my library and pick something together. We'd only meet once a month – plenty of time to finish a book without it feeling like homework. And I could give you guys the grand tour – the library is actually a pretty cool building. We could make it like a little sightseeing adventure."

"That sounds perfect," Darby said, surprised by how much the idea appealed to her. "I haven't been in a library just for fun in years."

"See?" Topaz said, raising her wine glass. "This is going to be the start of something amazing. I can feel it."

CHAPTER 5

*D*arby was staring at a spreadsheet that seemed determined to remain unbalanced when her phone buzzed on her desk. She glanced around the small accounting office – her coworkers were all absorbed in their own end-of-day tasks – before checking the message. After nearly a week of group texts debating which day worked best for everyone, tonight was finally the first official book club meeting. It felt strange to be this excited about something as simple as a book club, but it had been a long time since she'd had anything resembling a friend group. The group chat had taken on a life of its own – book recommendations spiraling into debates about movies, then food, then whatever random thing crossed someone's mind. She'd learned that Topaz didn't just perform at the Golden Apple, she actually worked there. Darby had found herself checking her phone more than usual, smiling at messages from people who were quickly starting to feel like more than just neighbors.

Topaz: *Hey! Want to stop by the Golden Apple on your way home? I'm working till 6 and we could head to the library together for book club.*

Darby smiled and quickly typed back: *Sounds good! I'll head right there once I get off work.*

The response came quickly: *Perfect. See you soon!*

Darby looked at the clock on her computer screen. Just one more hour left in her workday. For once, time seemed to cooperate with her plans, and it passed quickly as she wrapped up her current project and organized her desk for tomorrow.

At five-thirty sharp, Darby gathered her things and joined the stream of office workers flowing out of the building. The sidewalk was crowded with the usual rush hour chaos – people checking phones, hailing cabs, or hurrying toward the metro station. A man sat against the building's concrete façade, a cardboard sign propped against his knees with a paper cup held out. Darby dug out some quarters and dropped them in without breaking stride.

She let herself be carried along with the crowd, descending into the underground station where the familiar smells of stale coffee, exhaust, and unwashed bodies mingled in the recycled air. Someone had set up camp in the corner by the ticket machines – there was a pile of blankets and some empty food containers, though the person was gone now. Darby managed to snag a seat on the train just as the doors closed, settling in for the ride to Kirra Cross and trying not to notice the suspicious stain on the floor by her feet.

As the train pulled away from the platform, Darby's attention was caught by graffiti on the tunnel wall – a spray-painted flame with the words "Their blood will be on their own heads" scrawled underneath in jagged letters. The ominous message sent a chill down her spine, and she found herself staring until the train's movement carried the graffiti out of sight.

She shook off the unsettled feeling as the subway rumbled through the underground tunnels. Probably just some angry person with a spray can and too much time on their hands. The city was full of random graffiti – most of it meaningless.

A few stops later, Darby emerged from the underground and walked a few blocks to The Golden Apple. The early evening crowd was lighter than it had been during lunch, with only a handful of people scattered at tables with laptops and books. She immediately spotted Topaz behind the counter, her purple-streaked hair caught up in a messy bun and a green apron tied around her waist.

"Perfect timing," Topaz said, breaking into a grin when she saw Darby approach. "Pick something out – my treat."

Darby scanned the pastry case, automatically calculating prices. "Just a blueberry muffin, thanks."

"Come on, live a little. How about a drink to go with that?"

"The muffin's perfect, really." Darby appreciated the offer, but she wasn't comfortable with charity. She didn't want to take advantage of Topaz's generosity.

"One blueberry muffin coming up." Topaz wrapped the muffin in a paper napkin and handed it over. "Grab a table and I'll join you in just a sec. I need to clock out and grab my stuff."

Darby chose the same table where she'd sat during her first visit to The Golden Apple – the one with a view of the small stage. It felt like a lifetime ago that she'd been sitting here desperately scrolling through apartment listings, when in reality it had been barely more than a week. Amazing how quickly life could change.

A few minutes later, Topaz appeared with her messenger bag, having traded her work apron for a denim jacket over her flowing peasant blouse.

"You're an accountant, right?" Topaz asked, settling into the chair across from Darby.

When Darby nodded, Topaz continued, "Do you like that job? I couldn't imagine working in an office every day. I'd be climbing the walls and possibly committing homicide if someone asked me for a report in triplicate."

"It's not so bad," Darby said with a small laugh. "It's a small firm, so everyone's pretty laid-back. I'm mostly just doing basic bookkeeping and tax prep, nothing too exciting." She broke off a piece of her muffin. "So, you're not the office type?"

"God, no. That's why I work here, and sometimes I wait tables at a restaurant down the street. When I need some extra cash, I pick up a few fares as an Uber driver." Topaz gestured around the coffee shop. "I need to stay busy, and I can't stand monotony. Same thing every day would kill me."

"How long have you been working here?" Darby asked, finding herself genuinely curious about Topaz's approach to work and life.

"Mm... About six months. The owner's pretty cool about letting me switch shifts around when I have gigs. And I get first dibs on open mic nights. Plus, free coffee." Topaz glanced at her phone. "We should probably head over to the library soon. Kara said she'd meet us there with Jazmin and Ivette around seven."

"I'm excited to see where Kara works," Darby said. "I've never been a part of a book club. I'm a little nervous."

"Don't be. It's going to be fun. Kara has been wanting to start one for ages, and now we finally have enough people to make it work." Topaz's eyes lit up with the enthusiasm that seemed to be her default setting. "Plus, I have a feeling this is going to be the start of something really special."

As they gathered their things to leave, Darby found herself hoping Topaz was right.

* * *

WHEN THEY STEPPED out of The Golden Apple into the early evening air, Topaz linked their arms together in an easy, natural gesture that made Darby's heart lift. They strolled down the sidewalk toward the library, and the simple contact brought back memories of childhood friendships – those magical moments when you'd just gel with another kid on the playground and within minutes, know you'd be best friends forever.

Having someone who seemed so sure of their place in the world want to be her friend made Darby feel stronger and more like herself than she'd felt in ages. She felt cool again, fearless in a way she'd almost forgotten was possible.

"So," Topaz said with a mischievous grin, "tell me about your dickhead ex-husband. What'd he do?"

"You don't know if he was a dickhead," Darby protested, though she was smiling. "Maybe *I* was the problem in our marriage. We've hardly known each other for a full week."

Topaz scoffed. "I don't need to know you more than five minutes to know that he was a dickhead if he let you get away. I got eyes," she said with a grin.

Darby giggled – actually giggled, like she was sixteen again. "You're right. Roy was a dickhead. A complete and utter dickhead with a gambling problem."

"Oh no," Topaz said, her expression shifting to genuine concern.

Darby nodded, staring but not really seeing the street and crowds around them. "Yeah, he pissed away most of our money. Do you know how embarrassing it is to be an accountant and not realize that your husband lost all of your savings? I thought he was being kind by offering to take over the bills and finances and let me concentrate on my career. But it turned out that he was hiding what he was doing." Her voice rose with suppressed anger. "We had to sell the house. And the cars. And the stupid ATV he just *had* to have for weekend fun with his asshole friends."

By the time she finished ranting, Darby was practically panting, but it felt good to finally say all the thoughts she'd been thinking about Roy and what he'd done to their lives.

"Fuck Roy." Topaz cackled – a delighted, infectious sound – at Darby's shocked gasp.

The casual profanity made Darby bite her lip, but then she found herself saying, "Yeah. Fuck Roy."

Topaz grinned and yelled out, "Fuck Roy!"

She tilted her chin encouragingly at Darby, who took a deep breath and bellowed, "FUCK ROY!"

From somewhere down the street, a voice called back, "FUCK ROY!" making both women dissolve into uncontrollable laughter.

As the library came into view, Darby felt like a million bucks. Like a weight had been lifted off her chest. Like she could take on the world.

CHAPTER 6

The Lyceum Public Library rose before them, an impressive stone facade nestled between towering glass and steel skyscrapers that made the classical building look like a dignified elder surrounded by ambitious grandchildren. The limestone had weathered to a soot-edged gray, and while some of the ornate details showed signs of urban wear, the building maintained its stately presence. Figures in togas were carved into the stone above the entrance, flanked by massive Corinthian columns.

Darby found herself slowing to stare up at the building's grandeur when Topaz grabbed her arm.

"Come on, you can gawk later," Topaz said with a laugh, dragging her up the wide stone steps. "Kara is probably wondering where we are."

Inside, the library was bustling despite the evening hour. People wandered between the tall stacks, worked at public computers, and gathered around long wooden tables for study groups or quiet reading. The space hummed with the productive energy of a community resource in constant use.

Topaz steered Darby toward the circulation desk in the back

corner, where Ivette and Jazmin stood chatting with Kara. Behind the desk, Kara looked completely at home, her sensible cardigan and efficient manner fitting every librarian stereotype Darby could imagine. She had to hide an amused grin.

"Perfect timing," Kara said, stepping out from behind the desk. "Ready for the grand tour?"

She led them through the main floor, pointing out the architectural details with obvious pride. "This building was commissioned by Medeon's founder, Alexandros Makris. He was a Greek immigrant who became quite the robber baron. He made his fortune as a shipbuilder on the Taskequan River."

Darby looked around with new appreciation, noticing the Greek influence Kara highlighted – the fluted columns carved with curling leaves, the geometric patterns in the mosaic floors, the frieze work depicting scenes from Greek mythology that ran along the upper walls.

"Makris wanted to create something that would rival the great libraries of Athens," Kara continued as they walked. "He spared no expense on the details. Look at those ceiling medallions – all hand-carved by artisans he brought over from Greece."

"It's incredible," Darby said, craning her neck to take in the ornate plasterwork above them.

"And the best part," Kara said with a conspiratorial grin, "is that I have permission for us to use the basement archive room for our book club meetings. Much more private than trying to find space up here."

She led them toward a staircase marked with a small sign reading "Staff and Authorized Personnel Only." Kara opened the restricted door and gestured for them to follow her down into the basement level. The lower floor was silent, with tall metal shelving units filled with banker's boxes and bound volumes, and administrative offices lining the corridors.

Being led into the restricted area made Darby feel like a VIP, as if she'd been granted access to some exclusive club. The basement maintained the building's classical dignity even in its utilitarian spaces, with the same attention to architectural detail carried through to the lower levels.

"This is perfect," Topaz said, looking around the archive room Kara showed them – a cozy space with built-in bookshelves lining the walls, worn leather chairs arranged around a faded Persian rug, and the warm glow of table lamps creating pools of light in the windowless room. Even with the metal shelving units lining one wall, filled with archival supplies, old microfilm reels, and storage boxes, it felt cozy. Darby wandered over to a series of glass-fronted cabinets that displayed rare books and historical documents from Medeon's early days.

"So," Topaz said, "how should we choose our first book? I think we should all look around and each pick out a book to suggest for the book club, and then we can take a vote."

"That sounds like fun," Kara said immediately. "I know exactly what section I'm going to look through first."

"Can I browse with you, Topaz?" Jazmin asked. "Help me pick out something good?"

Topaz looked thrilled at the prospect of having a browsing partner. "Absolutely, Jazzy! We'll find something good."

As the group began to disperse to explore different sections, Darby headed back toward the stairs that would take her to the main floor, where she thought the Young Adult section was located. Behind her, she caught Topaz's voice saying to Jazmin, "Let's figure out where they keep the 'banned' books. Those are always the most interesting."

* * *

DARBY WANDERED through the main floor of the library, enjoying the peaceful atmosphere as she browsed the YA section. Her fingers trailed along the spines until a cover caught her eye – a stunning illustration of a rose encased in a glass dome, with thorny vines spiraling around an ornate frame. She pulled it from the shelf and read the back cover. A Beauty and the Beast retelling.

Perfect.

Despite all the problematic elements – the imprisonment, the Beast's temper, the troubling message that a woman's love could fix a broken man – she'd always had a soft spot for Beauty and the Beast. Something about the idea of transformation, of people being more than their worst moments, had resonated with her, even as a child. And maybe this retelling would appeal to Jazmin. Darby had deliberately chosen something from the YA section to make sure the youngest member of their group would feel included, but she also believed Beauty and the Beast was the kind of story that worked for all ages. Plus, it might be an interesting topic to dissect together. Perhaps if Darby had had wiser, older women in her life to discuss red flags in romance when she was younger, she would've picked up on the issues with Roy before she'd made the mistake of marrying him.

Book in hand, Darby made her way back down to the basement archival room. She was the first to return, so she settled into one of the worn leather chairs and waited, flipping through the pages of her selection.

Ivette arrived next, clutching a book with a bright, colorful cover, followed shortly by Kara carrying what looked like a well-worn copy of a classic mystery novel.

"Good choices?" Darby asked.

"I mean... *I* think so. We'll see what everyone else thinks," Kara said with a smile. "Agatha Christie is a classic for a reason. I love a good whodunit. I believe that the best book club books are page-turners that give you plenty to discuss without feeling like a chore."

They arranged the chairs in a circle and had just settled in, when they heard footsteps echoing from the administrative wing.

Jazmin and Topaz turned the corner into the large room, both of them grinning, their eyes bright with mischief.

"You two look as if you've just pulled off a heist," Ivette observed dryly.

"Better than that," Jazmin said, practically bouncing on her toes. She held a book pressed against her chest, shielding it from view. "We found something amazing."

"Should we be worried?" Kara asked, though she was smiling.

"Not at all," Jazmin said with an excited grin, dropping into one of the remaining empty seats and still hugging the mysterious book against her chest. Topaz settled beside her, looking thoroughly pleased with herself.

"So how should we do this?" Topaz asked, looking around the circle. "Maybe we could each take turns showing our book and describing it, then vote on which one to start with when everyone's done?"

"That sounds like fun," Ivette said, and the others nodded in agreement.

Darby went first, holding up her selection. "I found this in the YA section. It's a Beauty and the Beast retelling – I know, I know, problematic fairy tale – but the reviews say it's really good and puts a fresh spin on the story. I thought it might appeal to Jazmin's love of fantasy and art."

Jazmin leaned forward to examine the cover. "That looks cool, actually. I love the illustration."

Ivette went next, holding up a book with a coral-colored cover featuring a stylized illustration of a woman's profile. "Crazy Rich Asians," she announced. "One of the other dispatchers at work wouldn't shut up about it, so I chose this one. She said it's fun, glamorous, and has family drama that'll make you feel better about your own relatives."

Kara held up her mystery novel. "This is a classic Agatha Christie. I thought we could start with something that's stood the test of time – it's smart, engaging, and not too heavy."

Then it was Jazmin's turn. She stood up dramatically and produced her book with a flourish. "Topaz and I found this with the banned books!"

The book she held was unlike anything Darby had expected. It was bound in worn, faded maroon leather, and stamped on the cover was a circular design that looked almost like a compass rose, though Darby couldn't make out the details clearly from where she was sitting.

"Wait, what?" Kara's eyebrows shot up. "There *are* no banned books in this library. Where exactly did you find that?"

"Behind a desk in one of the offices," Jazmin said proudly. "It was on top of a stack of books that looked like someone had tucked them out of sight."

"In an office?" Kara repeated, her tone shifting from amused to concerned. Her eyes narrowed slightly, but Darby noticed she didn't press further about why they'd been snooping in offices. Instead, she stood up and held out her hand. "Can I see it? That looks antique. It definitely doesn't look like something that should be on the regular shelves. I'm wondering if it's someone's personal belonging or maybe something that should be in the historical archives."

Jazmin bit her lip but handed it over carefully. Darby found herself on her feet, drawn to get a better look at the strange book. She noticed the others crowding closer as Kara opened the cover.

The pages inside weren't printed but handwritten in various inks – some faded brown, others still dark and bold. The writing was cramped and dense, flowing in tight cursive that would take patience to decipher. Drawings and symbols filled the margins and spread across entire pages. It looked almost like a field journal; the kind a naturalist or explorer might keep, except the symbols were nothing Darby recognized. Geometric shapes, spirals, circular patterns with lines radiating outward like compass points.

Darby felt something stir in her chest – a strange magnetic

pull toward the book. Her breath caught, and she pressed closer without quite meaning to, jostling shoulders with the others as they all leaned in to see.

"What the..." Kara breathed, carefully turning pages. "What is this?"

She flipped back toward the front of the book, and Topaz suddenly reached out, stopping her hand.

"Wait," Topaz said, pointing at the first page. "What does that say? It looks like... like the stanzas of a poem." She hesitated, then reached out. "Can I see it?"

Kara handed the book to Topaz. The handwriting was elegant but difficult to read, written in what appeared to be English but with strange flourishes and archaic spellings. Topaz squinted at the text, then began to read aloud, her voice taking on an oddly formal cadence.

"By blood and bone, by choice and will,
Those who seek shall find the way.
Circle formed, the power still,
Sleeping magic wakes today.
Bound by thread invisible spun,
Each to each and all to one.
What was lost shall be restored,
Ancient gifts by words outpoured.
Spoken here where witches are gathered.
Let the coven's bond be tethered."

As the final word left Topaz's lips, pure electricity surged through Darby's body, jolting her heart and radiating outward to her fingertips and toes. It even felt like her hair was crackling with energy, each strand standing on end.

A wind erupted in the windowless basement room, whipping around them in a circle. The pages of the maroon book began flipping wildly, a blur of parchment and ink, and then the book jerked out of Topaz's hands.

It hung in the air between them, suspended at the center of their circle, glowing with a faint golden light.

And then Darby's feet left the ground. She gasped, her stomach lurching as if she'd just dropped on a roller coaster. Around her, the others were also lifting off the floor – Kara's mouth open in shock, Topaz's eyes wide, Ivette reaching instinctively for Jazmin, who looked both terrified and exhilarated.

Power flooded into Darby like a river breaking through a dam. It was wild and ancient and *right*, filling every cell of her body with warmth and light. She looked at the others and saw that they were glowing – actually glowing – with the same golden luminescence that surrounded the book.

The power surged stronger, building like a wave. Golden threads woven with black smoke connected all five of them – not just to those beside her, but to everyone in the circle. Each woman was linked to every other, the lines of energy forming a star pattern within their circle like the compass rose on the book's cover. The energy pulsed faster and faster, building in intensity.

It was magic. Real, wild, impossible magic.

The power crescendoed, becoming almost too much to bear. Darby's back arched involuntarily, her mouth opening in a silent scream as the energy coursed through her with overwhelming force. The connections between them blazed bright as stars.

She couldn't think, couldn't breathe, couldn't do anything but feel the raw power burning through every nerve.

Then everything went dark.

CHAPTER 7

*D*arby opened her eyes to the plaster ceiling of the library's basement, momentarily confused about why she was on the floor. Her body felt strange – like bees were buzzing through her veins, a constant hum of energy thrumming beneath her skin.

Sitting up slowly, she saw the others doing the same. Kara, Ivette, Jazmin, and Topaz all looked as overwhelmed and confused as Darby felt. They exchanged wide-eyed glances, nobody quite willing to be the first to speak.

"What the hell was that?" Topaz finally asked, her voice shaky.

Ivette muttered something in Spanish, making the sign of the cross with trembling fingers.

"No, there's no way this has anything to do with Satan, Abuela," Jazmin said. "You don't even believe that stuff! That was magic. But I think it's, like, the good kind. It felt..."

"It felt right," Darby finished, her voice quiet but certain. "It felt... amazing."

The rest of the women nodded in agreement, and something in Darby's chest loosened at the shared understanding.

Gingerly, Kara crawled over to the maroon book from where

it had fallen and started flipping through the pages. Jazmin scooted next to her, peering over her shoulder.

"Is it a spell book?" Jazmin asked. "Are those spells?"

"I think it is," Kara said slowly. "I think it's a grimoire."

Everyone crowded closer, drawn once again to the mysterious book. Kara squinted at one page, tracing the cramped cursive with her finger. "Look. I think this is a spell to speed up the healing of a wound."

She flipped to the next page. "And this one seems like it creates fire."

Jazmin leaned in, her eyes bright with curiosity, and began to read the words aloud.

"Flame awaken, fire bright —"

With the first couple of words, Darby felt a surge of power starting to build like a warmth in her chest, spreading outward. Without thinking, she pressed her hand over Jazmin's mouth.

"I don't think we should cast a spell for fire inside a library," Darby said firmly. "Especially not until we understand better what the hell is happening."

Jazmin nodded behind her hand, and Darby slowly removed it.

"This is insane," Topaz said, running her hands through her purple-streaked hair. "Nothing like this has ever happened to me before. Nothing magical has ever happened to me, period."

"Me neither," Kara agreed, still clutching the grimoire.

"Same," Darby added.

Ivette got a thoughtful look on her face. "There were rumors that my great-grandmother had the 'gift,' but I never met her. I always assumed it was just a story, you know? Something the family told people to make her seem more interesting."

Kara turned to Jazmin. "Can you show me exactly where you found this book?"

They all trooped down the hallway, following Jazmin to a small, cluttered office. Filing cabinets lined one wall, and two desks sat back-to-back in the center of the cramped space, both piled with papers, book carts, and the general chaos of a shared workspace.

"This is a clerk's office," Kara said, frowning. "There's no reason why a book like this would be in here."

They searched through the office carefully but found nothing else unusual. Jazmin showed them where she'd found the grimoire – on top of a stack of books behind one of the desks.

"But the rest of the books in that stack were just pulled because of low circulation rates," Kara explained. "The two librarians who work in this office run the yearly sale where we sell books the library doesn't want to stock anymore. Nothing to do with magic, banned, or restricted books."

Kara flipped through the grimoire again, examining the binding and pages. "The library always stamps its books," she said. "This one doesn't have a stamp anywhere."

She closed the book and turned toward the stack of discarded books, reaching out as if to place the grimoire back where Jazmin had found it.

"You're not going to give the book back, are you?" Topaz asked, her voice tight with worry. "I don't think we should. Not until we figure out what the hell is happening and what that book does."

A surge of protectiveness washed over Darby at the thought of giving up the grimoire. The idea of someone else taking it, of it being out of their hands, felt wrong on an instinctive level. She found herself stepping closer to Kara, drawn to the book.

"No," Darby said firmly, surprising herself with the intensity in her voice. "We can't give it back. Not yet."

Everyone nodded in agreement, and Darby felt a small relief that the others seemed to feel the same way.

"No, no," Kara assured them, clutching the grimoire a little tighter. "I was just going to take one more look. I agree – we need to research this book more. Something like this shouldn't be left lying about where just anyone could find it."

"So... what do we do now?" Darby asked.

"We should take it somewhere more private to discuss what to do," Kara said.

"Your place?" Topaz suggested.

They all agreed and headed out of the library into the evening air.

As they walked toward the apartment building, Darby couldn't get over how different she felt. The buzzing sensation in her veins had settled into something more constant, more subtle. When she walked down the street with the other women, she felt a connection to them – like invisible strings still tied them together – but she also felt a strange new connection to the outside world itself.

The feeling intensified when they walked past a small neighborhood park. Darby stopped, overwhelmed by the sensation. She could feel it all – the plants, the trees, every living green thing. Not just their presence, but their *being*. The slow stretch of growth, the quiet consumption of oxygen in the growing darkness, the quiet pull of nutrients traveling upward through roots and stems. The seeking, pushing, slow insistent creep of roots deeper into the earth. It was like hearing a thousand whispered conversations all at once, feeling a thousand tiny pulses of life. The grass beneath her feet – she'd always known it was alive, but knowing and *feeling* were entirely different things. She felt drawn to the plants, and impossibly, she felt them responding, a pull that answered her own.

"Do you guys feel that?" she asked.

"Feel what?" Kara asked.

"The park," Darby said, struggling to put it into words. "I can feel the life in the soil. In the plants. Like... like they're humming. Like I could reach out and touch that energy if I wanted to."

Ivette tilted her head, considering. "That's weird. I don't feel the park at all." She waved her hand around them. "I feel the power lines. Like I can sense the electricity running through them."

She turned to Jazmin. "What about you?"

Jazmin shrugged, looking uncomfortable. "I feel something, but I don't know what it is. It's not as specific as what you guys are describing."

"I feel... movement," Kara said slowly, her brow furrowed in concentration. "But not like physical movement. More like..." She gestured vaguely with her hands. "Like currents. Or maybe vibrations? Every time someone talks, I can almost feel the shape of their words in the air. And there's this constant awareness of... breathing? Not just mine, but everything around us. The breeze, car exhaust, the particles in the air." She shook her head, looking frustrated. "I don't know. It doesn't make sense."

"None of this makes sense," Topaz said, her voice tight with anxiety. "We really need to read through that book and figure out what the hell is going on."

A car horn blared at the intersection ahead, one driver leaning on their horn at another who'd been slow to move when the light turned green. The sudden sound made Darby jump like a spooked cat.

"Let's go," Ivette said firmly. "I'll feel better once we're inside and out of the public eye."

Darby was happy to follow those instructions and hurried her steps to keep pace with Ivette. When they passed a decorative fountain in front of an office building, Jazmin suddenly stopped.

"I feel the water," she said quietly. She walked over to the fountain and dipped her hand in. When she scooped some out, instead of flowing through her fingers like it should, the water stayed in her palm – a perfect sphere, defying gravity.

"Holy shit," Topaz breathed, reaching out to poke the ball of water. It wobbled but held its shape.

"What the—" Darby stuttered, staring at the impossible sight.

Jazmin let the water fall back into the fountain with a splash. For a long moment, they all just stared at the surface of the water, the implications of what they'd just witnessed settling over them like a heavy blanket.

Without another word, they hurried the rest of the way to the apartment building, none of them speaking as they rode the creaky elevator up to the sixth floor. Once they were safely inside Kara and Darby's apartment with the door closed and locked behind them, Kara pulled the grimoire out of her messenger bag.

"Alright," she said, setting it carefully on the coffee table. "Let's take a look at this thing."

CHAPTER 8

*K*ara set the grimoire on the coffee table, and for a long moment they all just stared at it, like they were worried it might bite them. Finally, Darby leaned forward and picked it up, the worn leather warm beneath her fingers.

Before she opened it, she looked around at the other women. Kara was perched on the arm of the couch, Ivette sat straight-backed in one of the chairs, Jazmin sat cross-legged on the floor, and Topaz leaned against the wall with her arms crossed.

"I don't know what's happening," Darby said quietly, "but I'm glad you're all here with me."

The others nodded, murmuring their agreement. Topaz pushed off the wall to sit beside Jazmin on the floor, and something in Darby's chest loosened at their unified presence.

She opened the book. The first page was the incantation that had started all of this – the words that had somehow bound them together. She turned to the next page and found it filled with cramped but elegant writing. Darby began to read aloud:

"*Witch magic is linked to the life force of the world itself, inherited from mother to daughter through bloodlines as ancient as humanity. All witches carry a spark that connects them to every living thing, a funda-*

mental bond with the pulse of life itself. Beyond this shared connection, each witch possesses an affinity – a particular elemental energy she can manipulate.

Each witch must find her affinity, the element that resonates most strongly with her soul. This connection is unique and cannot be forced or chosen, only discovered.

Guard your power well, for there are those who would seek to use what you possess for their own ends. History has shown that those without power will always fear and covet those who wield it."

Jazmin huffed. "History has definitely shown that to be true."

Darby kept reading:

"A coven is stronger than any solitary witch. When bound together in sisterhood, witches enhance each other's magic, their bond becoming both shield and strength. To create a coven, gather in a circle and speak the words of binding.

Ritual and structure enhance a witch's natural affinity. A coven – typically comprised of five witches – can use rituals, focuses, symbols, gestures, written sigils, and tools such as athames, wands, chalices, crystals, and herbs to aid in their spellcraft. These are the training tools of magic, the scaffolding upon which young witches build their power.

With practice and mastery, these aids become unnecessary. A witch who has perfected her craft can tap directly into the magic within herself, needing nothing but will and intent to shape the world around her."

When Darby finished reading, she looked up to find everyone staring at her with shell-shocked expressions.

"So," Ivette said slowly, "are we a coven of witches? We can create magic?"

Darby shrugged, feeling simultaneously terrified and exhilarated. "I guess there's only one way to find out."

She started flipping through the pages, reading spell titles aloud. "Healing minor wounds... scrying for lost objects... protection ward for the home... summoning wind... oh, here's one – conjuring fire." She squinted at the cramped writing. "This one gives a spell on how to light a candle. That seems simpler than those others, and it doesn't need a bunch of tools and herbs."

Everyone gathered close, peering over her shoulder at the page.

"We need a candle," Kara said. "I have one in my room. Let me go get it."

She disappeared down the hall and returned moments later with a jar candle – lavender-scented, from the smell of it – which she set on the far end of the coffee table. Then she moved back to join the others gathered around Darby.

Darby scanned the rest of the page. "It says we need to concentrate on the candle and focus on making the wick light while we say the spell words." She looked up at the others. "Our intent is as important as the spell itself."

They all stared at the candle for a moment, then at each other.

"So... we just... want it to light?" Topaz asked uncertainly.

"I guess so," Darby said. "Let's try it."

Together, they read the spell aloud, their voices overlapping and stumbling over the unfamiliar words:

"Flame awaken, fire bright,
Spark to life at my command.
Burn steady through the night,
Blaze bright now on my demand."

At the other end of the table, the candle burst into flame with a soft *whoosh*.

Everyone exclaimed at once, a chorus of shouts and gasps. Darby felt her heart hammering in her chest. They'd actually done it. They'd made magic.

But Topaz made a soft "ooh" sound and walked toward the candle as if drawn by an invisible thread. Her eyes had taken on a distant, almost trancelike quality.

"I can feel it," she murmured, reaching her hand toward the candle.

"Topaz, wait—" Ivette started to say.

The flame leaped from the wick into Topaz's palm.

Everyone screamed for a split second but then fell silent as they realized Topaz wasn't hurt. She stood there, holding her hand out flat, the flame hovering just above her palm like it was the most natural thing in the world. Her face was suffused with wonder.

"I can feel it," she said again, her voice clearer now. "It's warm, but it doesn't burn. It's like... like it's a part of me."

"Maybe fire is your affinity," Kara said, her voice filled with awe.

Topaz slowly closed her hand, and the flame winked out. She looked up at the others, her eyes bright with excitement and a hint of fear.

"What do we do now?" she asked.

Darby looked down at the grimoire still open in her hands, then back at her coven. Because that's what they were now, whether they'd meant to be or not.

"I don't know," she said honestly. "But I think we're going to figure it out together."

CHAPTER 9

a couple of hours later, the group seemed reluctant to leave, lingering in the doorway and exchanging uncertain glances as if separating might somehow break the spell – or worse, prove it had all been a shared delusion. But they all had lives that couldn't be put on hold, no matter how strange the day's revelations had been. But morning would come too soon for all of them, bringing work and school and all the ordinary demands of life that couldn't be ignored. One by one, they said their goodbyes and headed to their respective apartments, promising to meet up again soon to continue figuring out what all of this meant.

Back in her new bed in her new room, Darby eventually managed to fall into a restless sleep. She kept waking throughout the night, trying desperately to hold on to the wisps of dreams that dissolved the moment she opened her eyes.

When she woke for what felt like the dozenth time, she checked her phone. It was still a few hours before she needed to get up for work. The buzzing sensation in her veins had quieted, but hadn't disappeared entirely. It was muted now, a low hum beneath her skin that made falling back asleep feel impossible. Or maybe it wasn't muted so much as she was getting used to the sensation.

After another twenty minutes of staring at the ceiling with her mind spinning in circles, Darby finally gave up. She couldn't just lie awake in bed with her thoughts a tangled mess anymore.

She wandered out to the living room to get a drink of water and stopped short when she saw Kara sitting on the couch, the grimoire open on her lap, illuminated by the warm glow of a table lamp.

Darby filled a glass at the kitchen sink, then padded over to join her roommate on the couch. "You couldn't sleep either?"

Kara looked up and shook her head. "My mind won't stop spinning. Every time I close my eyes, I see us floating to the ceiling or that flame jumping into Topaz's hand." She gestured at the grimoire. "I keep thinking if I read through this enough times, it'll all start to make sense."

The group had agreed to leave the book with Kara, since she was a librarian and would have access to more research tools. It had made sense at the time, but Darby felt drawn to the grimoire even now, a magnetic pull she couldn't quite explain. She wondered if any of them would be able to stay away from it for long.

"Find anything interesting?" Darby asked, settling onto the couch beside her.

"Lots of sketches. Lots of spells. Some I can barely understand. The handwriting gets pretty cramped in places." Kara turned a page carefully. "I keep wondering how this book ended up in the basement of the library. It clearly doesn't belong there. No library stamp, no catalog number, nothing. And who would donate something like this? Something powerful and ancient."

"Do you think you'll be able to find the original owners?"

Kara shrugged. "Maybe."

"If you do find them, do you think you'll give it back?"

Another shrug. "I don't know. I honestly don't want to. I'm

drawn to it. I feel possessive of it." She ran her fingers over the worn leather cover. "Is that wrong?"

"I feel the same way," Darby admitted. "Do you think whoever left it in that office knows what it is?"

"I'm going to try to find out," Kara said. "But I don't want them to know I have it. I'll ask some careful questions of my coworkers. To see if anyone knows anything about old books being donated recently, or if anything unusual has been happening in the basement."

They sat together in comfortable silence, turning pages and reading passages aloud to each other. Some spells seemed straightforward: finding lost objects, purifying water, encouraging plant growth. That last one had Darby's immediate interest. Others were more complex and cryptic, requiring ingredients and preparations that neither of them fully understood. Darby was just glad not to see any ingredient lists with things like eye of newt or bat wings or anything else creepy. Thankfully, most spells seemed to require innocuous things like herbs, salt, and candles.

As they flipped toward the end of the book, Darby noticed a longer passage of handwritten text beneath what appeared to be a defensive spell. She leaned closer to read it.

"Wait, look at this," she said, pointing. "There's a note here. It's written underneath a spell for a defensive salt circle." She adjusted her glasses and read aloud: "Need to strengthen the boundary – add iron filings? Silver?" She paused, then continued. "Then there's a description of modifications to make the circle more effective."

Kara squinted at the cramped cursive. "This is different handwriting than the original spell. Looks like someone was adding their own notes, experimenting to make it more powerful."

"Look—" Darby pointed to the bottom of the passage. "Someone signed it. Alice Auclair."

Kara made a triumphant sound. "This gives us a place to start! A name we can actually research."

They exchanged a glance. "Do you think there are more notes from her?" Kara asked.

"Let's look." Darby started flipping back through the pages more carefully, scanning the margins and spaces between spells.

They worked methodically, turning pages slowly, looking for more examples of the same handwriting. It didn't take long to find them.

"Here," Kara said, pointing to a note beside a protection ward. "Same handwriting. She wrote: 'Needs moonstone to anchor properly.'"

"And here," Darby said, finding another one. "Beside this detection spell: 'Range is too limited. Try amplifying with copper wire.'"

They continued searching, finding more scattered throughout the grimoire. Some were simple notes like ingredient substitutions, timing adjustments for different moon phases, or observations about which herbs worked best. Others showed more experimentation.

"Look at this one," Kara said, her finger tracing a note beside a spell for warding a home. "'The old methods aren't working as well as they should. Need to layer multiple protections.'"

A thread of unease wound through Darby's chest, but she kept turning pages.

They were near the back of the grimoire when Kara paused. "Wait. There's something tucked in here."

She carefully extracted a piece of paper that had been folded and wedged between the last pages and the back cover. The paper was creased and brittle, covered in the same handwriting.

Kara unfolded it carefully and began to read aloud, her voice quiet in the stillness of the apartment:

"A group of men calling themselves the Torch Bearers have been harassing us. They seem to know when we're meeting and practicing. I'm worried they're watching and following us. Rumors have spread around town, calling us devil worshippers, saying we're corrupting the youth and supplying drugs to kids, which is insane. We need to be more careful about where and when we meet. Livie wants to stop practicing for a while, but I'm not sure that will help. I don't know what to do."

The note wasn't signed, but the handwriting was unmistakably the same as all the other additions throughout the grimoire.

Silence filled the room, broken only by the hum of the refrigerator and distant traffic sounds from the street below.

"Torch Bearers," Darby repeated slowly. The name sent a chill down her spine.

"Jesus. Torch Bearers," Kara breathed, still staring at the note. "That sounds ominous as hell."

"True, but all this information gives us a place to start," Darby said, trying to sound more confident than she felt. "Some names we can actually research."

She stood and retrieved her laptop from her room, returning quickly to settle back on the couch beside Kara. She opened it and typed "Alice Auclair" into the search bar.

The first result made her breath catch.

"Oh my god," she whispered.

Kara leaned over to look at the screen, and Darby clicked on the news article. The headline read: "Four Women Die in Tragic Fire at Local Garden Club."

Darby read aloud: "Alice Auclair, 49, her sister April Auclair, 46, along with Isabella Rousseau, 32, and Olivia Blackwood, 37, died in what authorities are calling a freak accident at the Willowbrook Garden Club in Briarton, Michigan. Brenda McAllister, 28, was the only member of the group to make it out of the building alive. The fire broke out during the club's monthly meeting and spread with unusual speed, trapping the four women inside. Fire investigators are still determining the cause of the blaze."

The article was dated just over five years ago. Darby scrolled down and found a photo – the burned-out shell of a building, its roof collapsed and walls blackened by soot. Several fire trucks surrounded the structure, hoses draped across the debris-strewn ground as firefighters stood in the foreground.

She kept scrolling and found individual photos of the victims. Alice Auclair had dark blonde hair streaked with gray and warm, crinkled eyes, smiling in what looked like a professional head-shot. Her sister April looked younger, with darker hair but the same warm open expression. April's photo looked like it had been cropped from a larger image – she wore a holiday sweater that made Darby imagine it had been pulled from a family Christmas card. The thought made her heart ache. Isabella Rousseau's photo showed a woman with black hair pulled back in a ponytail, caught mid-laugh at what appeared to be an outdoor event. Olivia Blackwood's picture was more formal, perhaps from a work ID or driver's license – she had short brown hair and wore a navy blazer, her expression serious and professional.

But there was no photo of Brenda McAllister, the survivor. Just her name mentioned in the text.

"Briarton," Kara said quietly. "That's in the southeast corner of Michigan, isn't it? Pretty rural area."

"Four women dead," Darby said, her eyes moving between the photos. "And one survivor. Alice wrote about something called the Torch Bearers harassing them." She looked at Kara, her stomach knotting with dread. "I mean..."

"And then they all die in a fire," Kara finished. "You could reasonably wonder if a group with that kind of name was setting fires."

They tried searching for information about the Torch Bearers online, but nothing concrete came up – just things like Olympic torch relays, hiking clubs, motivational speaker groups, outreach programs, and dozens of church organizations. Without knowing what kind of organization they were looking for, it was impossible to narrow it down.

They sat in silence for a long moment, the implications settling over them like a heavy blanket.

"We need to show the others," Darby said finally.

Kara nodded, but neither of them moved to close the laptop. They sat together on the couch, staring at the photos of four dead women who might have been just like them, until the sky outside began to lighten with the first hints of dawn.

The shrill beep of Darby's alarm jolted them both. She fumbled for her phone to silence it, blinking in disbelief at the time.

"I need to get ready for work," she said, her voice rough with exhaustion.

Kara rubbed her eyes. "Yeah, me too."

Darby stood and stretched, her joints protesting. "I have no idea how I'm going to function today. I haven't been at this job long enough to call in sick or give a bad performance." She walked to the small balcony off the living room and opened the sliding door, pouring her glass of water into the pot containing the mint plant. "I'm going to need some serious coffee to get through this. Water is not going to cut it."

"Tell me about it," Kara muttered, closing the grimoire carefully. She picked it up and held it against her chest. "I'm keeping this on me at all times. I don't want to let it out of my sight."

Darby nodded, understanding the impulse completely. She felt the same pull toward the book, that strange possessiveness they'd both admitted to feeling.

She headed toward her bedroom to get ready, already dreading the long day ahead. How was she supposed to focus on spreadsheets and tax returns when she now knew that magic was real, that she was apparently a witch, and that four women who might have been just like them had died in a suspicious fire?

She had a feeling it was going to be the longest workday of her life.

CHAPTER 10

arby knocked twice on Josh's door frame, even though the door stood open. Her boss looked up from his dual monitors, reading glasses perched on his nose with a second pair sitting on top of his head. Darby bit her lip to keep from grinning. In the little time she'd worked here, Josh had lost at least one pair of reading glasses per week. The team found them left forgotten all around the office: on the printer, by the water cooler, once balanced on top of the coffee maker. Darby had suggested putting a little basket on the lunchroom table to drop off found glasses as a joke, but within the week one had actually appeared, and now that's where everyone deposited Josh's lost reading glasses.

"Hey, Josh? I hate to do this, but I need to head out early today." The words came out more apologetic than she'd intended. "I've got a headache that's killing my concentration. I'm mostly on track with the Henderson project, but I'll come in early tomorrow to make sure I stay ahead of my deadline."

Josh waved her off before she'd even finished. "Go, go. Feel better, Darby. We've all been there."

"Thanks. I really appreciate it."

"Just take care of yourself," he said, already turning back to his screens.

Darby grabbed her bag and jacket, a small knot of guilt settling in her stomach as she walked past the rows of cubicles. She wasn't *really* sick. Well, she did have a headache – a dull throb that had started around lunch and hadn't let up – probably from her lack of sleep. But that wasn't why she needed to leave. The truth was, she hadn't been able to focus. Every time she tried to concentrate on spreadsheets or emails, her mind drifted back to the feeling of magic awakening in her veins like electricity, or the way the plants in the park had called out to her, or the sobering discovery that the Briarton coven had died. Real magic. And real danger.

Still, the lie sat uncomfortably. At least the headache was real enough to give it a foundation.

The elevator doors closed, and Darby let out a breath. Josh had been so understanding. No interrogation, no guilt trip, no performative concern that really meant *this better not become a pattern*. This company was actually... good. No awful office drama, no backstabbing politics – at least no more than the usual amount that happened when you put a diverse group of people inside a concrete box for forty hours a week. She'd worked places where calling in sick felt like confessing to a crime. She was lucky, and she knew it.

The subway was mercifully uncrowded for mid-afternoon. As the train rattled through the tunnel, Darby found herself smiling. She could stop by The Golden Apple, see how Topaz was doing. Maybe get a drink. The thought brightened her mood considerably.

* * *

THE LITTLE BELL above the door chimed as Darby stepped inside. The café smelled like coffee and cinnamon, afternoon sunlight streaming through the front windows in golden bars. Only a handful of tables were occupied. It was the post-lunch, pre-happy-hour lull.

Topaz spotted her immediately from behind the espresso machine, and her whole face lit up. She raised her hand in an enthusiastic wave, nearly spilling the milk she was frothing in the process.

Darby returned the grin and walked over, dodging a woman with a laptop and oversized headphones.

"Shouldn't you be at work?" Topaz asked, eyebrows raised as she glanced at the clock on the wall.

Darby shrugged. "Wasn't being productive anyway. My boss let me leave early."

"Oh my god, *same energy*." Topaz laughed, shaking her head. "I've screwed up so many drinks today, I thought people were gonna start a riot. I made several hot drinks when people ordered iced, put whipped cream on a drink that specifically said no whip, and completely forgot about a guy's cappuccino until he came up to ask where it was."

"Yikes."

"Right? Thankfully, we haven't been that busy today or it might've been worse," Topaz looked around the nearly empty café, then leaned in conspiratorially. "This place is a ghost town right now. Let me see if my boss will let me clock out a little early. We can hang out before we need to head to the library."

"You sure?"

"Totally. Just grab a table? I'll be right back."

Darby chose a spot by the window, settling into one of the mismatched chairs that gave the café its eclectic charm. She watched Topaz disappear into the back, heard muffled voices, and then Topaz reappeared, untying her apron with a triumphant grin.

A few minutes later, she emerged from around the corner holding a tray with two iced coffees and a plate with a couple of pastries: a chocolate croissant and something that looked like a berry Danish.

Darby's chest tightened with unexpected warmth. "You didn't have to do that."

Topaz set the tray down and slid into the chair across from her, giving what could only be described as a shy smile – unusual for the usually confident, boisterous woman. "Hey, we're, like, a coven now. That's family, right?"

The warmth in Darby's chest spread, filling spaces she hadn't realized were empty. "Hell yeah. To new families."

They clinked their plastic cups together, ice rattling, and both took long sips.

"You remembered my order," Darby said, surprised at how much that small gesture meant.

"Oat milk iced coffee, one sugar. I have a really good memory for repeat orders." Topaz tore off a piece of croissant. "I'm good with patterns. It's the following instructions part that trips me up."

"I'm the opposite," Darby said. "I'm good at following instructions."

Topaz grinned. "Oh, I bet you are. Such a good girl."

Darby felt her cheeks warm as she laughed. "Shut up."

They fell into conversation easily, the kind that meandered and deepened without either of them noticing the transition. Topaz asked about her recent move, and somehow Darby found herself talking about the town she'd lived in before – the suffocating sameness of it, how everyone knew everyone's business, the way it had felt like living in a fishbowl.

"It was one of those places where people ask how you're doing but they're really just fishing for gossip," Darby said, picking at her Danish. "And if you didn't fit the mold – married, kids, church on Sundays – you were either pitied or judged. Sometimes both."

"Sounds exhausting." Topaz took a long sip of her coffee. "No wonder you left. What about your family? Are they still there?"

"My dad and stepmom, yeah. They're still in town."

"What about your mom?"

Darby's expression shifted, something closing off. "No. Cancer took her just after I started college."

"Fuck cancer," Topaz said quietly.

Darby raised her coffee cup, and Topaz clinked hers against it in solemn agreement.

"Thanks." Darby took a breath. "Losing my mom made leaving easier, in a way. There wasn't much keeping me there."

"Except your ex?"

"Yeah. My ex-husband loved living in Granville. Said I was too particular about everything – that I couldn't just be happy with what we had. Like wanting more than a lifetime of casseroles and small talk was some kind of character flaw."

"Seriously… what an asshole."

Darby blinked, then laughed – a real laugh, the kind that loosened something in her ribs. "Yeah. Yeah, he kind of was."

"Sorry, I shouldn't—"

"No, you're right." Darby stirred her iced coffee absently. "He made me feel invisible in my own life. Like my opinions were just... inconveniences. And I stayed way longer than I should have because I kept thinking if I just tried harder, if I was less particular or less emotional or less *something*, it would work."

Topaz listened with an intensity that was almost unsettling. She gave the kind of attention Darby wasn't used to receiving. No interruptions, no attempts to fix it or minimize it. Just presence.

"That's bullshit," Topaz said finally. "You know that, right? That whole 'if you just change yourself, he'll be better' thing? That's Manipulation 101."

"I'm starting to see that now." Darby smiled, small but genuine. "Therapy helps. So does distance."

"Good. You deserve better than invisible." Topaz leaned back in her chair. "You deserve to take up space."

The words settled over Darby like a blanket. She didn't quite know what to say, so she changed the subject. "What about you? How'd you end up at The Golden Apple?"

Topaz groaned. "It's a job while I try to get my real career going. I'm working on getting my music out there, but it's taking way longer than I hoped."

"You're really talented," Darby said, remembering the way Topaz's voice had filled the space when she'd played. "I loved that one song about the ocean. Did you write that?"

"Thanks." Topaz grinned, a little sheepish. "Yeah, I write my own stuff too, not just covers."

"You're trying to get a record deal?"

"Busting my ass to try and get one. I need a record deal to really get my music out there. And I want to be famous, not gonna lie." Topaz laughed. "But in a few years, after a few records, I want to produce too. Help other artists find their sound, you know?"

"That's a solid plan. How's it going so far?"

Topaz's expression dimmed slightly. "I've been sending out demos of my originals, networking, all that fun stuff, but it's like throwing messages into a black hole. I know I need to utilize social media more, but a lot of what I've put out there hasn't gained traction yet. My plan is to try and build a following, but that takes time and money. Neither of which I have a lot of." She shrugged, trying to seem casual, but Darby could see the frustration underneath. "In the meantime, I make lattes for people who don't know the difference between a macchiato and a cappuccino."

"The glamorous life of a barista?"

"You don't even know... I'm so sick of customer service I could puke," Topaz said with a laugh. "I *hate* dealing with the public. You're lucky you don't have to deal with customers. You just sit at a desk and do your thing. I know office work would drive me crazy, but at least no one screams at you because you're out of almond milk."

"I don't know if I'd call myself lucky," Darby said, fighting a grin. "My coworker Jeff sends emails in all caps when he's upset. All caps, Topaz. And last week, someone left a passive-aggressive sticky note on the break room fridge about labeled food that started a three-day email chain."

"Oh, the horror." Topaz pressed a hand to her chest in mock sympathy. "How do you survive?"

Darby laughed. "Barely."

Topaz smirked wickedly. "Sometimes, when customers are real assholes, I switch them to decaf without telling them."

Darby laughed, but it came out a little dimmer. "That's... a little wrong, though."

"Oh, alright. I don't *actually* do it," Topaz said quickly, still grinning. "But I daydream about it. Extensively. Like, I have this whole mental list of people who deserve the secret decaf treatment."

"That's slightly better."

"Only slightly?"

"I'm still judging you a little."

"Noted."

They dissolved into laughter again, and Darby realized how easy this was – how she wasn't performing or editing herself. She was just... here. With someone who seemed to genuinely like her company.

The next hour and a half passed like a breeze, time slipping by in the way it only does during good conversations. Before Darby realized it, all that remained were crumbs, empty cups, and a full heart. The café had filled up slightly around them, the evening crowd trickling in, but their little corner by the window had felt like its own world.

Darby glanced at her phone and felt a small jolt. "Oh! It's almost time. We should head to the library to meet the others."

Topaz stretched, joints popping audibly. "Right. Back to magic school."

"Is that what we're calling it?"

"That's what *I'm* calling it. Kara will probably have a more official name like the Single Woman's Society of Witchcraft or something!" Topaz stood and gathered their trash onto the tray. "You ready for round two?"

Darby shouldered her bag, surprised to find that she was. "Yeah. I think I am."

They stepped out into the late afternoon sun, the city humming around them with its perpetual motion. Darby pulled out her phone to check for work emails but found herself smiling at nothing in particular instead.

"What?" Topaz asked, catching her expression.

"Nothing. Just... thanks for this. For hanging out."

Topaz bumped her shoulder companionably. "That's what coven sisters are for, right?"

"Right," Darby agreed, and meant it.

CHAPTER 11

The basement of the library felt different this time. Maybe it was knowing what to expect – the musty smell, the rows of storage shelves, the overhead lights that hummed just slightly off-key. Or maybe it was that they were no longer complete strangers fumbling through introductions, but something closer to... what? A team? A coven?

They sat in a loose circle around the table, the grimoire resting in the center like a silent witness. Darby bit her lip, eyeing the ancient book. To her imagination, the worn leather cover and yellowed pages carried a weight that had nothing to do with paper and binding.

Kara cleared her throat, her expression more serious than usual. "Before we begin, Darby and I need to share what we found out. We found a name written in the grimoire: Alice Auclair."

The room went quiet. Topaz leaned forward, elbows on her knees.

"Who?" Ivette asked.

Kara picked up the grimoire, handling it carefully as she opened it to a marked page. "We found notes Alice left throughout the grimoire. Mostly just additions or modifications to spells. She was experimenting, trying to make them more powerful." She paused, her expression darkening. "But we also found a note tucked in the back. Alice wrote about a group of men calling themselves the Torch Bearers who were harassing them – watching them, following them, spreading rumors around town."

"Torch Bearers?" Jazmin leaned in. "What the heck is that?"

"Well... When we looked Alice Auclair up online," Kara said, setting the grimoire back down, "we found an article. According to it, about five years ago, four women – including Alice – died in a fire at their garden club meeting in Briarton. Only a woman named Brenda McAllister survived."

"Do you think they were..." Ivette said slowly. "Like us?"

Darby nodded. "We think they might've been a coven, just like us."

"Jesus," Topaz breathed.

"I tried to find information online about Brenda McAllister," Kara continued, "but it's as if she's fallen off the face of the earth. Not that there was much about her to start with. All I could find was a group photo of the larger garden club in a news clipping, but the image is so small and blurry that it's pretty much useless."

"But she's gone? Do you think she went into hiding?" Ivette asked. "Because of these Torch Bearers?"

"Who knows? But I think it's possible," Kara said carefully.

Topaz crossed her arms. "Did you look into these 'Torch Bearer' people?"

"I did." Kara's mouth pressed into a thin line. "At first, all I found was stuff about the Olympics and a bunch of religious organizations. But as I dug deeper, I found some historical references to them being a faction during the Inquisition. I thought that might be relevant since the Inquisition was focused on hunting down and eliminating supposed witches."

A chill ran down Darby's spine.

Kara winced. "I also found a post on Reddit that mostly quoted scripture about witches. Things like 'Thou shalt not suffer a witch to live' and passages about stoning them to death." She paused. "It was signed 'Torch Bearers' underneath."

Ivette suddenly launched into rapid Spanish, her words tumbling over each other in a torrent of what was clearly profanity based on her tone.

"—ay dios mío, esto es una mierda, qué carajo estamos metidas en—"

Jazmin's eyes went wide as dinner plates.

The only word that Darby was familiar with was *mierda*.

Shit was right.

The silence that followed was heavy and oppressive. Darby could hear her own heartbeat in her ears.

"So," Jazmin said slowly, "if we get discovered, we could end up potentially being hunted by religious zealots who burn witches?"

"We don't know that for certain," Kara said, though her tone wasn't reassuring. "The Reddit post could be unrelated. Or it could be some fringe group using an old name. And we honestly have no way of knowing for sure that the Torch Bearers set the fire."

Jazmin snorted.

"Or," Ivette said quietly, "it could be the real deal, and we need to be careful. Either way, we need to keep what is happening under wraps. We do not tell a soul – not even people we trust. Not until we are sure that we're safe."

No one argued with that.

Topaz cleared her throat, giving each member of the coven a serious look. "Which is also why we need to understand our magic. Knowledge is our best defense."

Darby nodded, though her stomach had tied itself in knots.

"Right," Ivette said, straightening her shoulders. "So let's figure out what we can do."

"I think we should work on figuring out our affinities first," Kara said. "Before we try anything more... advanced."

"Seems pretty obvious that Topaz is fire and Jazmin is water," Ivette said, leaning back in her chair. "Based on what they were able to do."

Jazmin flexed her fingers, a small smile playing at her lips. Topaz just shrugged, but Darby caught the pleased glint in her eye.

"I think mine has something to do with technology," Ivette continued, her voice gaining confidence. "Or maybe... electricity?" She paused, then added with a rueful laugh, "One of the drivers I was scheduling got rude with me today, and I'm pretty sure I accidentally fried the computer at my station."

"Pretty sure?" Jazmin raised an eyebrow.

"Okay, I definitely did. My screen just... sparked and went black right when I was thinking about how much I wanted him to shut up." Ivette looked around the basement, her gaze trailing along the ceiling and walls. "Throughout the day, I've felt more and more aware of the electricity around me. The wiring in the walls, the lights, the hum of it all. It's like I can sense it moving."

"We'll test that then," Kara said with a nod. "See what we can figure out." She folded her hands on the table. "I think mine has something to do with wind or air. Or maybe just... spoken words."

"That makes sense," Jazmin said. "A librarian with word magic. Maybe your magical affinity has to do with existing skills or likes."

Kara tilted her head thoughtfully. "An interesting theory."

Jazmin turned to Darby. "What about you?"

Darby shifted in her seat, suddenly aware of everyone's eyes on her. "I'm not totally sure, but I don't think my affinity has anything to do with numbers or spreadsheets." She managed a weak smile. "But... I do feel... drawn to the earth. Like soil and plants."

"You mentioned you used to have a garden you loved at your old house," Topaz said, leaning forward.

"That's true, I did have a garden that I adored. And I *have* always loved gardening." The words came easier now, warming to the subject. "I would've majored in horticulture, but my parents and my ex-husband convinced me there was no future in that career."

Topaz murmured under her breath, just loud enough for Darby to hear: "See? Asshole."

Darby snorted and nodded, feeling a rush of affection for her new friend.

"I have an idea," Kara said, standing abruptly. "Wait here."

She disappeared into the stacks, and they could hear her footsteps echoing through the basement, followed by the sound of a door opening. A minute later, she returned carrying a sad-looking potted plant.

Darby recognized it immediately – a maranta plant, with red, yellow, and dark green leaves that should have been vibrant but were instead droopy and brown-edged. The poor thing looked like it had been forgotten on someone's desk, barely clinging to life.

The plant called to her.

Darby didn't even realize she was reaching toward it until her hand was hovering over one of its limp leaves. She hesitated, suddenly acutely aware of the weight of expectation in the room.

"What if it's not earth or plant magic?" she asked, her voice smaller than she'd intended.

"Then we'll figure out what it is," Topaz said firmly.

"What if I don't have magic?"

All of them shook their heads. Ivette spoke up, her tone gentle but certain, "Nah, I can feel you in our bond. There's magic there."

Darby blew out a breath, trying to steady herself. She pressed both hands to the dried-out soil at the base of the plant and closed her eyes. The way her hands cupped the stem, palms together around it, looked almost like she was praying. Marantas were called prayer plants, and right now, that felt appropriate.

Please, she thought. *Please let this work.*

She let her senses open, reaching outward – or was it inward? – toward the plant that seemed to be calling for her. At first, there was nothing. Just the feel of gritty, depleted soil under her palms and the faint warmth of her own skin.

Then—

There.

She could sense the roots, thin and desperate, digging down through the compacted soil. She could feel the veins running through the stems and leaves, the cellulose walls of individual cells crying out for nourishment. The plant needed water, minerals, and light. It needed to *live*. Darby wanted it to grow, to flourish, to be healthy. Lush and *whole*. The desire swelled in her chest, and without knowing how, she pushed that want into the plant.

A chorus of gasps and exclamations yanked her back.

Darby opened her eyes, and her vision was immediately filled with red, yellow, and green. The plant had exploded with growth, overflowing its small pot, now several feet tall with dozens of new leaves unfurling in vibrant patterns. The colors were so rich they almost looked unreal, and the leaves were perfect, not a brown edge or wilted tip in sight.

"Holy shit!" Jazmin breathed.

"Darby, that was incredible!" Kara was grinning like she'd won the lottery.

"Look at it!" Ivette stood to get a better view, her eyes wide.

Topaz simply smiled, serene and knowing. "Well done."

Darby rubbed her thumb over one of the leaves, enjoying the texture. The leaves were smooth, soft, alive. She could feel the plant's vitality thrumming through the leaf, a connection that filled her chest with warmth and wonder. This plant was hers now, in some inexplicable way. She could sense its contentment, its energy, its *life*.

GWEN DEMARCO

"I can feel it," she whispered. "I can feel it living."

"That's beautiful," Kara said softly.

Darby looked up at the other women, tears pricking at the corners of her eyes. She'd done it. The proof was right here in her hands, vibrant and alive, and the connection between them hummed like a perfect note. Like she'd finally found something that was wholly, completely hers.

"Now let's try you, Ivette," Kara said, already moving toward the stairs. "Let me get a lamp from one of the offices."

As Kara bustled off, Darby kept one hand on her plant – *her plant* – and felt the steady pulse of life beneath her fingertips. Around her, the others chatted excitedly, but she barely heard them.

She had magic.

Real *magic*.

CHAPTER 12

*T*hey'd worked on several spells once they'd finished confirming their affinities. The assignments felt right, like pieces of a puzzle clicking into place: Darby was earth and plants; Topaz was fire; Jazmin was water; Ivette was electricity; and Kara was air with an extra affinity for the power of words.

Given the possible threat of the Torch Bearers, they'd focused mostly on defensive magic for the last half of their meeting. Kara had led them through disorientation spells, and they'd taken turns trying to confuse each other about where things were in the room. It had been oddly fun watching Topaz reach for a chair that was actually three feet to her left, though the lingering dizziness afterward was less entertaining.

They'd also practiced drawing runes to create protective circles. According to the grimoire, magic circles had all sorts of uses depending on the runes you used – trapping, amplification, concealment, and more. For defense, they'd focused on barrier circles that nothing could cross, keeping out attackers. The problem was that they didn't have the right materials to draw a circle on the library's floor without damaging it. They'd need to buy chalk or charcoal for proper practice, so for now they'd settled for sketching the runes on paper to memorize the symbols.

Not wanting anyone to find evidence of their practice, they'd had Topaz turn the pieces of paper with their rune attempts to ash over a metal office trash can, while Jazmin stood ready to put out any flames with water conjured from thin air. Between the ash and water, they'd created a soggy black mess. Rather than leave it in the basement office where someone might notice, Kara had emptied the small bin into one of the library's main floor trash cans where it wouldn't stand out. They'd also worked on channeling magic through each other, discovering that when they held hands and focused, one person's power could flow through another, amplifying the effect.

After several hours of practice, the women headed up the stairs to the first floor of the library, laughing and talking excitedly. Darby's hands still tingled with residual energy that she'd expended, and she couldn't stop grinning.

"I'm just saying," Ivette was telling Kara, "You're incredibly thorough. Fire extinguisher for Topaz, even towels for Jazmin. You had backup plans for your backup plans."

"Better safe than sorry," Kara replied with a dismissive wave, but her eyes sparkled with pleasure. "Can't risk having this building burn down."

As they reached the main floor, Darby paused. "I want to go see if the library has anything on occult practices. Maybe a history about witches, just to see if I can find something relevant."

"Oh, I'm coming too," Kara said immediately.

Darby smirked. "If anyone could be a help searching, it would be you."

"Abuela, can we go look in the DVD rental section and pick out something?" Jazmin asked Ivette.

"Yes," Ivette said, then added, "and if everyone wants to come over to our place, I put Pollo Guisado in the crockpot before work. There's more than enough for everyone."

"Abuela always cooks like she's trying to feed an army," Jazmin said with obvious affection.

Ivette shrugged. "I can't help it. I'm Puerto Rican."

Jazmin laughed, and the sound echoed warmly through the library.

"A home-cooked meal sounds amazing," Darby said. "Then I don't have to settle for a Lean Cuisine eaten over the sink."

Ivette pressed a hand to her chest, looking genuinely horrified. "A Lean Cuisine? Over the *sink*? Darby, no. Absolutely not."

Ivette, Jazmin, and Topaz headed off to check out the DVD selection while Darby followed Kara toward the section of the library that might have something on witchcraft and the history of the occult. They wove through the stacks, the familiar smell of old books surrounding them like a comfort.

A book fell off a shelf and landed at Darby's feet.

The thwap of it hitting the ground startled the hell out of her, and she jumped back with a yelp.

"You okay?" Kara asked.

"Yeah, just—" Darby bent down and picked up the book, turning it over to see the cover. *Fire & Blood* by George R. R. Martin. A dragon curled across a burning banner. "Not my kind of book. I like fluffy romances and sexy vampires."

Kara laughed. "Same. Though don't tell anyone, librarians are expected to only love the classics."

They reached the occult section and began scanning the spines. Nothing promising jumped out. Certainly nothing about how to use their magic or anything that could shed light on who the Torch Bearers even were.

After a few minutes of searching, Kara sighed. "We should come back later in the week and look more thoroughly. I don't want to make the others wait."

"Agreed," Darby said, though disappointment settled in her chest.

They headed back toward the exit, meeting up with the others. Jazmin was clutching a DVD of an anime Darby wasn't familiar with, while Ivette had picked out a classic action film filled with lots of car chases. As they descended the library's front steps, the late autumn cold hit them immediately. The sky hung bruised and heavy overhead, darkened to dusky charcoal. It had been sprinkling while they'd been inside, and the stone steps were slick beneath their feet.

Darby was walking between Topaz and Kara, still talking about the spell they'd practiced earlier, when the squeal of tires cut through the evening air.

She looked up and saw a car losing control on the turn, spinning out on the wet pavement. There were a couple of people standing on the far street corner, and the car was heading right for them.

Without thought, Darby grabbed the hands of Topaz and Kara on either side of her. She could feel Kara instinctively pulling on her air magic. Darby did the only thing that made sense – she pushed her own magic through Kara to help, feeling it flow from her body into her friend like water through a hose. The small group of people on the corner got swept sideways by Kara's wind, thrown back from the curb.

But it wasn't enough. The car was still coming.

It happened in a heartbeat. Darby didn't think. She simply acted, reaching down into the earth beneath the concrete. She found a root, thick and strong, and commanded it to grow.

The root erupted through the asphalt like a spear, bursting up from the street directly in the car's path. Darby's magic fed it, swelling it to the thickness of a tree trunk in the space of a heartbeat. It rose just high enough to peak over the hood before the vehicle slammed into the massive growth with a deafening crunch, the hood crumpling on impact as it came to an immediate screeching halt.

"Oh my god," Darby exclaimed, the words tumbling out with the others' shocked voices as the realization of what they'd just done caught up to them.

"Holy shit," Kara whispered, exchanging a wide-eyed look with Darby.

People were already swarming toward the car and the knocked-over pedestrians who were now getting back to their feet, dazed but alive. Steam hissed from the ruined engine as the driver climbed out of the car, shaken but thankfully unharmed.

"We should go," Jazmin said urgently.

"Now," Ivette agreed.

Darby commanded the hardened root to slip back into the ground and out of sight, erasing the evidence of her interference. She bit her lip because there was nothing she could do about the hole in the road she'd just created. But at least it had all happened so fast that she doubted anyone could describe what they'd actually seen.

Making sure no one was looking in their direction, Darby followed the rest of the group as they hurried away toward the subway entrance. Her heart hammered in her chest, adrenaline making her hands shake.

They'd just saved those people.

With magic.

As they descended into the subway station, none of them spoke. But when Darby caught Topaz's eye, her friend reached over and squeezed her hand. The gesture said everything words couldn't.

They'd done something good tonight. Something that mattered.

Even if no one would ever know it was them.

* * *

THEY BURST through the door of Topaz's apartment in a chaos of voices and nervous energy. Darby felt oddly detached from it all, like she was watching the scene unfold from somewhere outside herself. Everyone else seemed to be vibrating with adrenaline, talking over each other, gesturing wildly. But she felt still. Calm. Like the quiet eye at the center of a hurricane.

Was this shock? Maybe. She wasn't sure.

"—could become vigilantes!" Jazmin was saying, pacing back and forth across the small living room, her eyes bright with excitement. "We could stop crimes! We could actually help people!"

"Hell no," Ivette sputtered, shaking her head emphatically. "Absolutely not. Do you know how dangerous that would be? We barely know what we're doing! And you are in high school. You're too young for this."

"I'm an adult. I'm eighteen," Jazmin argued.

"I want you safe, and I want you to focus on school. None of this vigilante crap."

"How 'bout if I promise to stop crime only *after* I finish my homework and chores," Jazmin sassed, and in spite of the tension, Darby snorted her amusement. Ivette gave Jazmin a flat look but didn't bother to comment any further.

Darby drifted toward the couch and sank into it, her legs suddenly feeling unsteady. The sounds of her friends' voices washed over her, but she couldn't quite seem to grab onto any single thread of conversation.

The couch dipped beside her, and she looked up to find Topaz settling in next to her, concern softening her features.

"You okay?" Topaz asked quietly, her voice cutting through the noise.

Darby took a breath and nodded. "Yeah. I think so." She paused, trying to find the right words. "I'm just amazed we were able to do that. It happened so quick, and I barely had time to think about it."

"Yeah," Topaz said, her face lighting up. "You were a badass, pulling a root right out of the ground in like a millisecond." She bumped her shoulder gently against Darby's. "How do you feel? Like, really feel?"

Darby took a moment to assess. She turned her attention inward and examined the state of her body and her magic. She expected to feel drained, maybe. Exhausted from the sudden burst of power. But that wasn't what she found.

"I feel... good. Better than good," she said slowly, surprised by the truth of it. "I feel amazing. Stronger. And the magic feels more accessible somehow. Like there's more of it inside me. Does that make sense?"

Topaz's grin widened, her eyes gleaming with excitement. "It's probably like a muscle – the more you exercise it, the stronger it gets." She leaned in closer, her voice dropping to an eager whisper. "Just imagine how we're gonna feel with more practice. I can't wait."

Despite everything – the near-accident, the risk they'd taken, the small amount of evidence they'd left behind – Darby found herself smiling back.

Neither could she.

Then reality crept back in. "What about the Torch Bearers?" Darby asked quietly.

Topaz's expression grew serious. "We're gonna figure something out," she said firmly. "But for now, we probably need to make sure we stay off their radar. Which means staying low-key and perhaps no more daring rescues..." She inclined her head toward Darby with a smile. "At least, for the time being."

CHAPTER 13

The subway car rattled through the tunnel, lights flickering overhead in that rhythmic, hypnotic way that always made Darby feel slightly disconnected from reality. She leaned against the window, watching the darkness blur past, occasionally punctuated by the harsh industrial lighting of the stations she passed through.

Her workday had been long but productive, which was a small miracle considering how little sleep she'd gotten the night before. Every time she'd closed her eyes to try to sleep, she'd relived that moment outside the library. Half her dreams replayed it exactly as it happened, her magic surging through her and into Kara, and the root erupting through the asphalt to stop the car. The other half were nightmares where her magic didn't work, where she reached for that power and found nothing, where she had to watch the car strike those people while she stood witness – helpless and useless. She'd woken up gasping more than once, her heart hammering and an aborted shout on her lips.

As the train slowed for her stop, Darby glanced at the tunnel wall and her breath caught. There it was, the graffiti she'd seen before. The spray-painted flame with words about blood beneath it.

Except now it was almost completely covered. New tags and street art layered over the old image, a riot of colors and designs that made the original message barely visible. Just a hint of orange peeking through and a fragment of text that she couldn't make out before the train pulled away.

Darby turned in her seat, staring at it until the train turned a corner, carrying the graffiti out of sight. She told herself it meant nothing. Street art was often provocative – crude tags like "Fuck the Police" or raunchy imagery meant to shock. That was just the nature of graffiti. She imagined a lot of it was created by bored teenagers trying to be edgy.

Still, something about it unsettled her. She wished she could remember what exactly had been written under the flame.

She emerged from the underground into the early evening air, pulling out her phone as she walked toward the apartment building. Her fingers moved automatically, opening the group chat.

Darby: *Hey! On my way home now. Still good to meet up?*

She'd barely made it to the street corner when her phone buzzed with a response. However, instead of Topaz's expected confirmation, a new message appeared in the group chat.

Topaz: *Change of plans! Found something you guys need to see. There's an occult shop in town called The Serpent's Garden. Been looking at their website, and they have EVERYTHING the grimoire lists for ingredients. Like, actual spell supplies.*

Darby's heart kicked up a notch. She stopped walking, reading the message twice.

Jazmin: *An actual occult shop?? In Medeon??*

Topaz: *Right? How did we not know about this? Their website has crystals, herbs, candles – all the stuff we'd need if we want to practice more complex spells. This place looks legit.*

Kara: *I figured we'd need to order stuff online, but a shop will be so much easier.*

Topaz: *My shift is almost over. Why don't we meet up and check it out instead of going to the library?*

Darby felt a surge of excitement. An actual occult shop! She just hoped it wasn't one of those novelty places that sold trick card decks and fake levitation kits, or worse – one of those weird gothy shops with animal skeletons and bugs under glass and black lace covering every surface. She wanted the real thing. Herbs and crystals and candles that actually meant something, supplies for witches who knew what they were doing. Topaz seemed confident about the place based on the shop's website. Still, there was only one way to find out for sure.

Jazmin: *YES. I want to see this place.*

Darby: *I'm on my way home, and actually just a couple of blocks from the café. Topaz, I can head your way, then we can walk to the apartment together?*

Kara: *I'm already at the apartment. Do you guys want to meet here?*

Ivette: *We'll head over as soon as Jazmin gets home.*

Topaz: *Perfect! See you at the cafe soon, Darby!*

Darby pocketed her phone and picked up her pace, heading toward The Golden Apple. She didn't know what one wore to an occult shop, but her work clothes didn't feel right. Something more... witchy? She almost laughed at herself.

* * *

Darby pushed through the door of the coffee shop to find Topaz behind the counter, wiping down the espresso machine. The café was mostly empty with only a couple of customers lingering over laptops in the corner.

Topaz's face lit up when she saw Darby. "Perfect timing! Let me just finish closing out my register. Then we can go."

Darby settled at a table near the counter, watching Topaz move through her closing routine with practiced efficiency. A few minutes later, Topaz emerged from the back, work apron gone and her messenger bag slung across her body.

"Ready?" she asked.

They stepped out into the early evening, the air cooler now that the sun was mostly hidden by the surrounding skyscrapers. Topaz pulled out her phone as they walked, scrolling through The Serpent's Garden website.

"Look at all this," she said excitedly, tilting the screen so Darby could see. "Mugwort for prophetic dreams, vervain for protection, dragon's blood resin for—"

"Dragon's blood?" Darby interrupted. "That can't be real. Sounds fake."

Topaz grinned and read from the screen: "Dragon's blood resin is a bright red sap from Dra-ca-*I-can't-pronounce-this* tree, used for power, protection, and banishing spells." She looked up. "See? Totally real."

Darby leaned in closer, pulling out her own phone to look at the same page. "Oh wow. Look at all the different types of salt they stock. I didn't even know there were different types of salt for magic."

"Black salt for banishing and protection, red salt for passion and courage, blue salt for healing," Topaz read, her voice bright with enthusiasm. "This is so cool. We could actually—"

Darby walked straight into someone.

She'd been so focused on her phone, on the exciting lists of magical supplies, that she hadn't seen the man in front of her. She collided with him, and the soda he'd been holding flew from his hand, the bottle tumbling through the air. It hit the pavement and exploded, sticky liquid spraying across the sidewalk and splashing onto his shoes and pants.

"Oh my god, I'm so sorry—" Darby started.

"Watch where the fuck you're walking, you stupid bitch!" The man's face contorted with rage, completely disproportionate to the minor accident. "You're lucky I'm nice!"

Darby stumbled backward, shocked by the sudden explosion of anger. "I'm sorry, I didn't mean—"

"You don't seem fucking nice to me!" Topaz was suddenly between them, her body language shifting into something dangerous. "Back the fuck off. It was an accident."

"Look at my fucking shoes! She just knocked my drink everywhere." He waved his phone in Topaz's face. "She's lucky she didn't ruin my phone too. Dumb, clumsy bitch."

"Who do you think you are? You don't get to talk to us like that." Topaz stepped closer, not backing down an inch. Her hands were clenched at her sides, and Darby could see the tension in her shoulders, the rage practically radiating off her. "It was a fucking accident, asshole!"

The man's face went red. "I'll talk to you any way I wan––"

His phone exploded into flames.

The man bellowed and dropped the burning device, shaking out his hand. He stared at the phone on the ground, flames licking up from the screen and casing with thick, stinky smoke beginning to pour off it.

"What the fuck? What the fuck?!" He stomped on the phone, trying to put it out.

Darby grabbed Topaz's arm. "We need to go. Now."

She practically dragged Topaz away from the scene, the man's shouts fading as they put distance between themselves and the burning phone. They didn't slow down until they'd turned two corners and were well out of sight.

Darby released Topaz's arm and spun to face her, her heart hammering. "Did you just... did you light his phone on fire?"

Topaz's chest was heaving, and her eyes were wild. "I didn't mean to. He was threatening you!"

"He was just being an asshole," Darby said, trying to keep her voice level. "Topaz, you can't just light people's property on fire because they're rude."

"He called you a bitch. He said next time he wouldn't be nice." Topaz's hands were shaking. "What was I supposed to do, just let him talk to you like that?"

"Yes! Or at least not literally set his phone on fire." Darby ran her hands through her hair. "Jesus, Topaz. What if someone saw? What if they connected it to us?"

"It happened too fast," Topaz said. "He'll think it was a battery malfunction or something. He'll probably think that damage from the soda caused it."

"If I didn't know better, I'd think you enjoyed that," Darby said quietly.

"Of course I did." Topaz lifted her chin. "Assholes like that shouldn't get away with being jerks without consequences."

Darby just looked at her, and something in her steady gaze made Topaz's defiance waver. She blew out a breath, her shoulders sagging. "But you're right," she said, the fight draining from her voice. "I just... I don't like seeing people treat you poorly."

"I know," Darby said, stepping closer, her voice gentler now. "And I appreciate you standing up for me. But we talked about staying low-key, remember? Not drawing attention to ourselves? We can't light everyone on fire who's rude to us. We'd leave a trail of burning carcasses across the entire city."

That got a weak smile from Topaz. "I guess that would be bad for staying under the radar."

"Just a little." Darby reached out and squeezed Topaz's hand. "Are you okay?"

"Yeah. I just—" Topaz pressed her palms to her eyes. "I didn't mean to do it. I was so angry, and I felt the heat building, and then it just happened. What if I'd hurt him? What if the fire had spread?"

"But it didn't," Darby said firmly.

Topaz lowered her hands, then straightened her shoulders and took a deep breath. "You're right. I need to be more careful. I shouldn't have let my temper get the better of me. Lighting some guy's phone on fire because he was rude is definitely not 'laying low.'"

"No, it's really not," Darby said, but she softened it with a smile. "Come on. Let's get to the apartment before anything else happens."

Topaz looked so dejected that Darby felt herself softening towards her friend. "I gotta admit that you were a total badass back there. Just... you know... let's not do that again."

Topaz snorted but nodded her agreement.

They took the shortcut through the cemetery, and the quiet serenity of the crumbling headstones and the ancient tree helped calm the last of Darby's nerves. They walked the rest of the way in silence, Topaz subdued now, and staying close to Darby. When the apartment building came into view, Darby felt a wave of relief.

"Can we not tell the others about this?" Topaz asked quietly as they approached the entrance. "At least not right away. I don't want them to think I can't control myself."

Darby hesitated, then nodded. "Okay. But Topaz? If something like this happens again, we need to talk about it. All of us. We're a coven. We need to help each other, not hide things."

"I know. And I will. I promise." Topaz managed a real smile. "Thanks for not freaking out on me."

"Oh, I was freaking out," Darby said as they entered the building. "I'm just really good at hiding it."

They rode the elevator up to the sixth floor, and as they stepped into the hallway, the lights pulsed. Just for a moment – a brief dimming and then back to full brightness.

A shiver ran down Darby's spine.

"The super really needs to fix the wiring in this building," Topaz muttered.

"Maybe I need to start taking the stairs," Darby said. "The

thought of being trapped in the elevator during a power outage is my nightmare."

They approached her apartment, and Darby unlocked the door to find Kara at the kitchen table with the grimoire open in front of her.

"Hey!" Kara looked up, adjusting her glasses. "Ivette just texted. She and Jazmin are headed this way."

As if on cue, there was a knock at the door. Darby opened it to find Ivette and Jazmin in the hallway, both looking excited.

"Ready to check out this shop?" Jazmin was practically vibrating with excitement.

They all gathered in the living room, and as they did, the lights flickered again.

"Did you see that?" Darby asked.

"Yeah." Kara frowned. "That's the second time today. Might be an issue with the building's electrical system."

The lights dimmed once more, and everyone looked up at the ceiling fixture.

"Okay, that's super weird," Jazmin said.

Kara turned to Ivette. "Is that you? Is your power acting up?"

Ivette frowned, looking genuinely uncertain. "I... I don't think so? I'm not thinking about electricity or trying to do anything with it. But maybe it's subconscious? I guess I still need more practice to have complete control."

"We all do," Topaz said, and she and Darby exchanged a quick, knowing look.

"Well," Kara said, gesturing to the open grimoire. "Before we go to the shop, we should figure out what we actually need. Let's pick a few spells we want to learn and make a list of ingredients."

They gathered around the table. For the next twenty minutes, they flipped through pages, debating which spells would be most useful.

"This one," Ivette said, pointing to a spell for creating a magic circle barrier. "We need protection. We just need chalk or charcoal. And salt."

"Agreed," Kara said, pulling out a notebook and starting to write. "What else?"

"Finding lost objects," Jazmin suggested. "That seems practical."

"Healing minor wounds," Topaz added. "Just in case."

"Scrying," Kara said, tapping a page. "Being able to see distant places or events could be useful for keeping watch."

"What about something to fight fire?" Darby asked. "The Torch Bearers have burned covens alive. We can't rely solely on Jazmin's water magic to protect us if they come after us."

The group went quiet for a moment. Jazmin looked down at her hands, her expression troubled.

"She's right," Kara said softly, flipping through pages. "Here – this is a spell for smothering flames. And another for fireproofing a space temporarily. We should add both to the list."

Kara quickly wrote down the ingredients needed to her growing list.

Darby slid the grimoire closer and scanned through the pages when something caught her eye. "Wait, look at this warding spell. It uses something called witch balls to encase the spell. Then you hang them in windows and doors to protect a space." She looked up. "What's a witch ball?"

Topaz grinned. "Let's find out."

Kara added it to the list, then copied out the ingredients each spell required, her handwriting neat and methodical. When she finished, she tucked the grimoire back into her messenger bag and folded the paper into her pocket. "Well," she said. "Should we head to the shop? I want to see this place."

They gathered their things and headed out. The subway ride took them to the edge of the trendy shopping district. An area filled with boutique clothing stores, artisanal coffee shops, and restaurants with exposed brick walls.

As they walked from the station, Darby felt her earlier excitement drain away, replaced by skepticism. This neighborhood screamed gentrification and overpriced everything. The Serpent's Garden was probably going to be one of those Instagram-worthy shops that sold seventy-dollar "sage bundles" and marketed crystals as home décor rather than actual magical tools.

They followed the directions on Topaz's phone until she stopped in front of a narrow storefront squeezed between a vintage clothing boutique and an organic smoothie bar.

"This is it," Topaz said, heading for the front entrance.

Darby followed, her heart beating faster than the situation probably warranted. It's just a shop, she told herself.

A door chime rang as they entered. Darby paused in the entrance, gaping at the interior. The smell hit her immediately: incense and dried herbs, sandalwood and the slightly musty scent of old books. She breathed deeper and caught something else underneath – something sweet and maddeningly familiar that slipped away before she could name it.

She muttered an apology when Jazmin bumped into her back.

"Holy shit," Jazmin gasped as she stepped around Darby, then glanced at her grandmother. "Sorry, Abuela. But seriously, holy shit."

"I'll allow it," Ivette said, looking around with obvious appreciation. "This is impressive."

The shop was smaller than Darby had imagined, but every available surface was crammed with merchandise. Shelves reached almost to the ceiling, and display cases created winding pathways through the space. Every corner revealed hidden nooks stuffed with treasures. Yet despite the overwhelming amount of inventory, everything appeared to have a place; organized in a way that made Darby want to explore, to linger and discover what might be tucked into each corner.

Candles covered one entire wall – every color, size, and shape imaginable on display. Darby realized that the smell she couldn't place was the creamy, honeyed scent of beeswax. Crystals of every size and color lined multiple shelves, some rough and natural, others polished to a shine. An entire section of the shop was dedicated to dried herbs stored in glass jars, each one labeled in neat handwriting with both common and Latin names. And books were everywhere – stacked on shelves, propped open on stands, tucked into corners.

And plants. Darby felt them before she saw them. Dozens of plants in terracotta pots, some trailing vines down the shelves and others reaching toward the light. She could feel their life force, their contentment in this space. Someone here knew how to care for them properly.

"Whoa," Topaz breathed, turning in a slow circle. "This place is incredible."

A woman emerged from behind a tall bookshelf, and Darby's first thought was striking. Long black hair fell past her shoulders in a sleek waterfall, and she wore layers of flowing fabric in deep jewel tones. Rings adorned every finger, and a pendant hung at her throat – some kind of serpent design that matched the shop's name.

She looked to be in her forties, though it was hard to tell. Her face was unlined and had a timeless quality, but the sharp intelligence in her eyes spoke of years of experience and knowledge.

"Good evening," she said, her voice warm and slightly husky. "Welcome to The Serpent's Garden. I'm Sage. How can I help you tonight?"

CHAPTER 14

*T*he five of them exchanged glances. Finally, Kara stepped forward.

"We're looking for some specific supplies," she said, pulling a folded piece of paper from her pocket. Darby noticed her other hand had moved protectively to her messenger bag where the grimoire was hidden. "I made a list from some... research we've been doing."

She handed the paper to Sage, who unfolded it and scanned the contents, her eyebrows rising slightly.

"This will take me a few minutes to gather." Sage's eyes moved over the five of them, and Darby had the distinct impression she was seeing more than just a group of women in her shop. "Feel free to touch anything. Everything here wants to be held, to be used. These aren't museum pieces."

She drifted back toward the counter, but Darby felt her awareness lingering on them like a warm hand on the shoulder.

"Okay," Jazmin whispered once Sage was out of earshot. "Is it just me, or did she seem like she knew?"

"Knew what?" Darby asked, though she had the same feeling.

"That we're... you know." Jazmin gestured vaguely at herself, at them. "Witches."

"Maybe she gets that a lot," Kara said, but she sounded uncertain. "People who are into the occult and looking for supplies. It's her customer base after all."

They spread out slightly, each drawn to different parts of the shop. Darby found herself in front of the plants, her fingers itching to touch them. She reached out and brushed the leaf of a potted rosemary plant, feeling its life force hum against her palm.

"Do you like plants?"

Darby jumped and spun to find Sage standing a few feet away, having moved with unsettling silence.

"Oh. Yes, I do." Darby pulled her hand back quickly. "They're nice."

"Mmm." Sage's gaze lingered on the rosemary for a moment, something unreadable in her expression, before she looked back at Darby. "We're having a sale on potted herbs this week, if you're interested. They need good homes." She reached out to adjust one of the pots on the shelf. "Fresh ingredients always produce better results than stale herbs, you know. For any spellwork."

"Thank you... I'll definitely get some herbs before I leave," Darby said.

"Anything else you're looking for today?"

"Actually... do you have witch balls?" The words tumbled out faster than Darby intended. "I read this article online about them, about how they were used historically for protection or... I don't know, I was just curious what they actually were. If they were real or just, like, a historical thing people made up—" Darby abruptly cut off her babbling, fighting the urge to duck her head at her overeagerness.

Sage's smile widened, amused but not unkind. "Oh, they're very real." She turned, gesturing for Darby to follow. "Come on. I've got a bunch of them in the back."

Darby fell into step behind her, leaving the plants behind. As she walked away, she realized that the rosemary looked greener than it had moments before.

Darby's steps stuttered for a moment, with her heart hammering. Had she just accidentally used magic? She hadn't meant to – she hadn't even tried. It had just happened naturally when she'd touched the plant.

She hurried to catch up with Sage, who was already weaving through displays of candles and crystal clusters toward the side of the shop. By the time Darby reached the counter, she'd convinced herself that no one was going to notice a slightly healthier-looking rosemary plant.

"Wait here," Sage said. "I'll grab some for you to look at."

She disappeared through a doorway behind the counter, leaving Darby alone at the display case.

Topaz appeared at her elbow, eyes wide. "The candles on that wall are arranged by magical purpose. Stuff like protection, love, prosperity, and banishing. See, I told you! This place is the real deal, Darby."

Before Darby could respond, Sage returned carrying a large wooden box. Its interior was divided into cushioned sections. Each compartment cradled a glass bauble of swirled, colorful glass – some roughly the size of grapefruits, others smaller, about the size of golf balls.

Sage lifted one of the larger ones carefully from its nest and showed it to Darby. The witch ball was made of swirling glass in shades of deep blue and silver that seemed to shift and move in the light. Delicate threads of white spiraled through the glass like smoky floss, and the surface had an almost iridescent quality, gleaming with hints of purple and green depending on the angle.

"Here," Sage said, offering it to Darby. When Topaz leaned forward with an eager look, Sage smiled and handed her a smaller one as well. Hers was swirled with amber and gold, compact enough to fit in her palm.

Darby turned the larger bauble over in her hands, feeling the cool, smooth glass against her palms. It was heavier than it looked, solid and well-made. Beautiful. She could picture them hanging in the windows of the apartment, catching the morning sun. If she could perfect the ward spell, she could do enough to ward all their doors and windows. Maybe even create enough for all the coven members. But if these were expensive...

"How much are they?" she asked, trying to keep her voice casual.

"The large ones are ten dollars; small ones are five."

Darby's gaze dropped back to the box, doing quick mental math. She gave the collection an assessing look, counting the sections. "If I bought the whole box... could I get a discount?"

Sage's smile was the expression of someone who knew they'd made a sale. "There are thirty in the box. Hmm... I could do the whole thing for one fifty." She tilted her head slightly. "That's a decent discount, and you'd have enough to ward every entry point in a mid-sized house."

Darby's eyes snapped up to meet Sage's. The shop owner's expression remained pleasant and professional, but there was a knowing glint in her eye that made Darby's stomach flip. She hadn't mentioned warding.

"That's... that's a good deal," Darby managed, her voice slightly strangled. "I'll take it."

"Excellent." Sage set the box aside and gestured toward the back counter, where an almost overflowing basket sat waiting. "I've grabbed everything else you asked for. It's all ready for inspection." The group gathered around as Sage moved to the basket and began pulling items out one by one, checking them off against the list Kara had given her.

"Six white candles, two black. Frankincense resin, myrrh. Sea salt, black salt – I ground that fresh this morning. Selenite wand, clear quartz points..." Sage continued laying items on the counter in neat rows. "Dried mugwort, dried yarrow, protection oil – that's my own blend. And the obsidian mirror you requested."

Darby's stomach tightened as the counter filled with supplies. Each item on its own probably wasn't too expensive, but together? She did quick mental math, watching Sage's hands move efficiently through the inventory. The witch balls alone were one hundred and fifty dollars. The candles, the herbs, the crystals. It was adding up fast. She had a little bit of money saved, but she hated dipping into her savings. That was supposed to be for emergencies – real emergencies, not spell supplies.

She caught Topaz's eye. Her friend looked delighted, already reaching for the obsidian mirror to examine it more closely. Of course Topaz wasn't worried about the cost, she never seemed to stress about money the way Darby did. Maybe it was the accountant in Darby who made her worry about every penny.

Darby swallowed hard and tried not to think about her bank account. She should try to learn to be more carefree like Topaz.

"This looks like everything," Ivette said, delight in her voice.

"Can I make a suggestion?" Sage asked, her tone carefully neutral as she surveyed the items spread across the counter.

Darby tensed slightly. "Sure."

"These are good choices – a solid foundation for practicing magic. But based on what you've selected, I'm guessing you're just starting out with formal spellwork?" Sage's gaze moved between them, not judging, just assessing. "You've got your candles, your herbs, your crystals. All the consumables. But you're missing some of the tools that make the work easier and more focused."

She moved to a display case behind the counter and pulled out a wooden box. "An athame, for instance. It's a ritual knife that you use to direct energy, cast circles, cut cords, and such." She opened the box to reveal several blades with black handles, their metal catching the light. "You don't use it to physically cut anything. It's purely an energy tool. But it makes a significant difference when you're trying to channel intention, especially for protection work and warding."

Darby stared at the knives, then at the growing pile of items on the counter. Her savings account flashed before her eyes like a countdown timer.

"How much..." she started, then cleared her throat. "How much would something like that cost?"

When Sage said the price, Darby let out a small breath of relief. It wasn't nearly as bad as she'd imagined.

Topaz leaned forward, studying the athames in the open box. "That one," she said, pointing to a blade with a smooth black handle wrapped in leather cord. "We'll take that one."

Sage lifted it carefully from the box. The blade was about six inches long, double-edged but unsharpened, made of dark steel that seemed to drink in the light rather than reflect it. The handle looked like it would fit comfortably in the palm, its leather wrapping worn smooth as if it had already seen use. A small moonstone was set into the pommel.

"Good eye," Sage said approvingly. She placed the athame in a separate wooden box lined with black velvet, then returned the others to storage behind the counter. "How long have you all been practicing?" Her tone was conversational as she worked, but her eyes moved across the group with that same assessing look she'd given Darby by the plants.

The five of them exchanged glances. Kara spoke carefully: "Not long. We're just starting. We're interested in learning about... herbal magic. Folk practices. Protections. That sort of thing."

"Ah." Sage's smile widened slightly. "First-time practitioners or continuing education?"

"Um," Darby said eloquently.

"It's okay." Sage's voice was gentle. "You're safe here. This is a sanctuary space. It has been for fifteen years. Whatever you're exploring, whatever path you're walking, I'm here to help, not to judge."

Something in her tone made Darby relax slightly. She looked at the others and saw her own relief reflected back. They'd been so focused on keeping their secret that walking into a shop that explicitly catered to magical practices felt like stepping into a spotlight.

"We're new to this," Kara said finally. "Very new. And we're trying to learn safely."

"Smart." Sage nodded approvingly. "Too many people jump into advanced work before they understand the basics. There are a couple of other items you might need. Let me pull them, and we can see what you'd like."

She began moving through the shop, pulling items from shelves and display cases with the ease of long familiarity. The five of them followed, watching as she assembled an additional collection on the counter.

"You'll want a proper mortar and pestle for grinding your herbs and powders," she said, setting down a heavy stone set. "And charcoal disks for burning loose incense and resins." She added a small tin to the pile, then moved to another shelf. "A few glass vials for storing oils and tinctures – amber glass is best. It keeps your potions from degrading in the light."

Sage returned to the counter and surveyed the growing collection. "And I'd recommend a good reference book. Do you have a grimoire, or are you working from online sources?"

The question was asked casually, but Darby felt everyone tense.

"We have... a resource," Kara said carefully.

"Good. Internet magic is hit or miss. Lots of misinformation." Sage pulled a book from under the counter. "This is my own compilation. Thirty years of practice distilled into one volume. Herb identification and correspondences, basic spells, safety protocols, and much more. Consider it a gift – first timers need all the help they can get."

She pushed the book across the counter toward them, and Darby saw the title: *The Practical Witch's Companion by Sage Thorne.*

"You wrote this?" Jazmin asked, picking it up and flipping through it.

"I did. Self-published, so it's nothing fancy, but it's saved more than a few novices from accidentally cursing themselves." Sage replied with a teasing grin as she began ringing up the other items.

Darby swallowed thickly at the total for everything, but it wasn't nearly as bad as she'd imagined it would be. She suspected that Sage was being extra generous with them.

They pulled out their phones, opening banking apps to send their portions to Kara. Jazmin started to reach for hers, but Ivette waved her off. "I've got you covered, mija."

Darby watched the notifications ping on Kara's phone one by one as everyone transferred their share. Once Kara had collected from everyone, she paid Sage, who packed everything into cloth bags.

"One more thing," Sage said, pulling out a shallow wooden box. Inside, small stone pendants on leather cords were laid out in neat rows, each stone different in color and shape. "Protection charms. Very basic, but they'll help shield you from unwanted attention and serve as a talisman to help you focus your magic. You wear them against your skin, preferably under clothing." She set the box on the counter. "Pick one that calls to you. That appeals to you."

"We didn't order these," Ivette said, though she was already leaning forward to study the stones.

"No charge." Sage gestured to the box. "Consider it an investment in your safety. The world isn't always kind to women with power."

Jazmin reached in first, selecting a deep blue lapis lazuli with flecks of gold running through it. Topaz's hand hovered over several before landing on a carnelian, its orange-red surface gleaming like banked coals. Ivette picked up a blue-grey labradorite that flashed with iridescent streaks of color when it caught the light. Kara chose a clear quartz, clear and light as the sky.

Darby's fingers drifted over the remaining stones until they stopped at a teardrop-shaped malachite pendant. The stone was a vibrant green with dark bands swirling through it like growth rings in ancient wood. It felt right in her palm.

"Good choices," Sage said quietly, watching them slip the necklaces over their heads.

"Thank you," Darby said quietly, as the stone settled against her chest, cold at first, but quickly warming against her skin.

CHAPTER 15

They gathered their purchases and headed for the door, but Sage's voice stopped them.

"One more thing." She looked at each of them in turn. "If you're practicing together – as a coven – you need to be careful. There are... individuals out there who don't take kindly to people practicing magic."

"Thank you," Ivette said. "We'll be cautious."

They left the shop with their supplies and their new knowledge, stepping back into the early evening. Despite Sage's warnings, the mood was buoyant. Kara kept peeking into the bags, admiring their haul, while Jazmin chattered excitedly, talking animatedly with her hands.

"That was amazing," Jasmin said, grinning. "Did you see everything they had? And Sage was so cool."

"I want to work on the witch balls as soon as we get back," Darby said, her mind already turning over the ward spell. "If I can get it right, we can hang them in everyone's windows and doors for protection."

"They're going to be so pretty when you're done," Ivette said warmly.

Darby found herself beaming, her hand drifting to the malachite pendant warm against her chest. They had real supplies now. Real tools. A second book about being a witch. And pendants that would help them focus their magic.

"We're actually doing this," Kara said, and there was wonder in her voice. "We're witches. We're a coven."

"And we're going to be good at it," Ivette said with quiet confidence.

"Hell yeah, we are," Topaz replied, squaring her shoulders with a defiant spark in her eyes.

The street seemed darker now and the shadows deeper, but somehow that felt right. They were women with power now, walking together. The darkness didn't feel threatening; it felt like it belonged to them.

"We should head back to the apartment," Kara said, pulling out her phone to check the time. "Look over what we got, maybe read through that book Sage gave us."

They rode the elevator up, energy humming between them as they talked over each other about herbs and crystals and the athame. When they reached the sixth floor and headed toward Kara and Darby's apartment, the hallway lights stuttered.

Just for a moment, it dimmed, then returned to full brightness.

"Ivette?" Kara asked, looking at the older woman.

"That definitely wasn't me," Ivette said quickly, noticing the others glance her way. She frowned up at the ceiling fixture. "I'll talk to the super about it. These old buildings..."

Now that Darby thought about it, she hadn't felt the tug of their bond when the lights wavered. When any of them used their powers, there was a slight pull, that awareness of magic moving through their connection. But just now, there had been nothing.

Except... no, that wasn't quite right. There had been something. She hadn't felt the warm pull of their coven bond, but something else. Something cold that had brushed against her awareness like static electricity, there and gone so quickly she'd almost missed it. A sensation that didn't feel like magic – or at least, not like *their* magic.

Darby rubbed her arms, suddenly chilled despite the warmth of the building.

But maybe she was just being paranoid. It had been a long, strange day.

Inside the apartment, Kara set her tote bag on the coffee table and began unpacking their purchases from the shop. The others added their cloth bags to the pile, and soon the table was covered with herbs and crystals. They passed Sage's book back and forth, examining the contents. Darby carefully lifted the lid off the box of witch balls, already thinking through how she'd approach the ward spell.

Outside the window, the city lights sparkled in the darkness. The world suddenly felt bigger than it had this morning. Darby imagined that somewhere out there, there were other witches practicing their craft, learning and growing just like them. Maybe some were alone, maybe some had covens of their own.

And yes, the Torch Bearers and other people who would hate them just for existing were out there too, though Darby tried not to think too hard about that part.

Darby looked around at her coven – her new family – and felt a warmth spread through her chest. Whatever was coming, they'd face it together.

"Alright," Kara said, opening the grimoire. "Let's see what we can do."

CHAPTER 16

A few days later, the apartment was quiet except for the soft hum of traffic filtering up from the street six floors below. Darby sat cross-legged on the living room floor, surrounded by a circle of supplies that made her feel both powerful and completely out of her depth.

Three broken witch balls lay in a cardboard box to her left. One was cracked cleanly in half, another shattered into a dozen pieces, and the third... well, that one had sort of melted into a misshapen blob of fused glass. She'd watched in horror as it had softened and collapsed in on itself like a deflating balloon. At least it hadn't burned the table surface she'd been working on. She'd grabbed it with a dish towel and dumped it in the box before it could do any real damage.

The grimoire lay open on the coffee table, its pages yellowed and covered in that old-fashioned handwriting that was sometimes hard to decipher. Sage's book sat beside it, bookmarked to a chapter on protective wards and containment spells.

Darby had set up a proper workspace on the living room floor. One of the white beeswax candles burned at each cardinal point around her, their flames steady and bright. The athame lay within easy reach, its dark blade gleaming in the candlelight. Small piles of dried herbs were arranged in front of her: rosemary for protection, mugwort for magical amplification, and a pinch of frankincense resin smoldering on a charcoal disk, filling the apartment with sweet, purifying smoke.

According to both books, traditional witch balls worked by trapping negative energy, spirits, or spells inside them. The hand-blown glass spheres were designed to be beautiful and eye-catching. Evil spirits would be drawn to the pretty, shiny objects, venture inside to investigate, and then become entangled in the delicate strands of glass inside, like a frozen spiderweb that would hold whatever entered. But these modern witch balls from The Serpent's Garden were smooth and empty inside. Which meant Darby had to create that containment structure herself. Magically.

According to the grimoire, she first had to find the metaphysical seam in the glass, an invisible doorway that existed outside normal space, and open it. Then she needed to weave a web of magical energy inside the glass, creating a snare that would hold the protective ward. Then she could seal the spell inside and close the seam. *Sure. Piece of cake.*

Darby picked up another witch ball from the box. This one was swirled with deep purples and blues that reminded her of a bruise. She turned it over in her hands, feeling the cool smoothness of the glass, trying to sense... what? A receptiveness? An openness to magic?

She had no idea what she was doing.

"Okay," she muttered to herself. "Let's try this again. Slowly."

She set the witch ball in the center of her workspace, equally distant from all four candles. Following the grimoire's instructions, she picked up the athame, feeling its weight settle comfortably in her palm. She was glad that the blade wasn't sharp. She probably would have sliced herself open hours ago because she kept glancing between the athame, the grimoire's instructions, and the witch ball, her attention scattered across too many things at once.

Darby held the athame over the witch ball and closed her eyes, reaching for that place inside herself where her magic lived. That warm, green space that smelled of earth and growing things. She felt it respond immediately, eager and ready to help.

Protection, she thought, shaping her intention carefully. *Safety. A barrier against harm.*

She opened her eyes and began to trace a pattern in the air above the witch ball with the athame's tip, moving clockwise. As the blade moved, she whispered the incantation: "I weave the threads that bind and hold..."

Green light followed the athame's path, leaving glowing lines in the air. She could see the threads of magic forming, delicate as spun sugar, weaving themselves into an intricate pattern. The light seemed to be drawn toward the witch ball, pulled by some invisible force.

"I weave the threads that bind and hold," she repeated, her voice stronger now, more confident.

The magical threads began to sink into the glass, slipping through the seam she'd opened, passing the glass's surface without breaking it. Darby watched in fascination as the green light disappeared into the purple-blue sphere. And for a moment, she could see the web forming inside the glass, strand by strand, creating a complex lattice structure that filled the interior.

The first three attempts had failed because she'd either forced the gateway too wide or pushed the threads too quickly into the ball. Each time the result was the same, the vessel couldn't handle the magical pressure and failed catastrophically.

This time, she would be gentle.

She kept the athame moving slowly, steadily, building the containment structure thread by thread. The candle flames strobed in response to the magic, and the frankincense smoke curled around the witch ball as if drawn to it.

When the web inside the glass looked complete, forming a beautiful, intricate snare of green magical light, Darby set down the athame and held her hands on either side of the sphere, not quite touching it.

Now came the hard part. She had to create the ward spell itself and compress it small enough to fit through the metaphysical seam and into the web she'd created.

Darby reached for the small ceramic bowl she'd grabbed earlier and began adding ingredients. A pinch of the dried rosemary for protection. Three small pieces of frankincense resin for purification and spiritual defense. A sprinkle of sea salt for barriers and boundaries. She added a few drops of the protection oil Sage had blended, watching as it coated the herbs and made them glisten in the candlelight.

Using her fingers, she mixed the ingredients together, focusing her intention with each circular motion. *Protection. Safety. A barrier against harm.* The mixture began to warm under her touch, responding to her magic.

She held her hands over the bowl and whispered,

"By earth and salt, by resin and leaf,
I build a shield, I call for relief.
Let no harm cross this sacred line,
Protection strong, this ward is mine."

A green light began to emanate from the mixture, soft at first, then growing brighter. The herbs seemed to dissolve into pure energy, transforming from physical matter into magical essence. Darby cupped her hands around the light, feeling it gather and condense between her palms.

She visualized a shimmering dome of energy, translucent and strong. A barrier that would repel harm and unwanted attention. The physical components had become the foundation, but now she had to shape them, compress them. Smaller and smaller. A sphere of protective magic no bigger than her fist, then smaller still, down to the size of a marble.

The compressed ward spell pulsed with power between her palms, eager to expand, to protect. She could feel it straining against her control, the herbs' protective properties amplified a hundredfold by her magic.

"I capture magic in this vessel," she whispered, invoking the second part of the spell.

She guided the ward toward the witch ball, pushing it through the metaphysical seam she'd opened. For a moment, there was resistance. The doorway wavered, threatening to close. But then she felt it stabilize, felt the magical web inside the sphere activate and pull the ward through.

The witch ball flared bright green from within, the light so intense Darby had to squint. The purple-blue glass seemed to pulse with energy, and she could see the ward spell caught in the web she'd created, held fast like a fly in a spider's snare. Faint traces of the herbs' essence swirled inside the magical structure – ghostly impressions of rosemary leaves, tiny sparks of frankincense, crystalline patterns of salt.

The witch ball grew warmer. Warmer. Then hot.

No, no, no—

Darby yanked her hands back just as a hairline crack appeared across the surface of the glass. The crack spread like lightning, branching across the sphere in a spiderweb pattern.

"Shit!" She scrambled backward as the witch ball made a sharp *ping* sound.

But it didn't explode. The crack stopped spreading, and the sphere sat there, intact but ruined, its beautiful swirls now interrupted by a maze of fractures. The green light inside faltered and died, the ward spell dissipating as the broken vessel failed to contain it. The herbal essence escaped through the cracks like steam, filling the air with the sharp scent of rosemary and frankincense.

Darby let out a shaky breath and flopped backward onto the rug. "Four," she said to the ceiling. "That's four broken ones."

She lay there for a moment, staring at the ceiling and trying not to calculate how much money she'd just wasted. All those witch balls reduced to broken glass, and she still didn't have a single working ward.

You're going to figure this out, she told herself firmly. *You just need to... what? Go slower? Push less energy? Find a different approach entirely?*

She sat up and reached for the grimoire, flipping back to the ward spell. The handwriting seemed to mock her with its elegant loops and flourishes. She checked Sage's book again, rereading the passage about containment spells and the need for a slow approach.

Darby rubbed her face. She was being gentle! Or at least, she was trying to be. Maybe she just didn't have the control yet. Maybe this was too advanced for someone who'd only been a witch for – what, a week? Less?

She picked up another witch ball, this one amber and gold like trapped sunlight. The largest one left in the box. If she broke this one, she'd have to decide whether to keep practicing with the smaller ones or admit defeat and try again another day.

"Fifth time's the charm," she muttered, setting the sphere in the center of her workspace.

She went through the process again, even more carefully this time. Athame raised, tracing the pattern in the air. "I weave the threads that bind and hold..."

The green light followed the blade's path, and she watched the magical web form inside the amber glass. This time, she paid closer attention to the metaphysical seam, feeling for its boundaries, understanding its limits. She'd pushed too much energy through too quickly before. The seam could only handle so much at once.

When it came time to create the ward spell, she prepared the herbs again – rosemary, frankincense, sea salt, protection oil –

but this time she used less. Half as much of each ingredient. She mixed them in the ceramic bowl, whispering the incantation:

"By earth and salt, by resin and leaf,
I build a shield, I call for relief.
Let no harm cross this sacred line,
Protection strong, this ward is mine."

The green light rose from the mixture, and she compressed it carefully. Smaller than before – barely larger than a pea. Less energy meant less strain on the glass.

"I capture magic in this vessel."

She guided the tiny, compressed spell through the seam, and it slipped inside easily, almost eagerly. The amber glass glowed softly, and she could see the ward spell caught in the magical web, pulsing gently with protective energy. The glowing spell settled into the glass like mist, creating delicate swirls of green light warmed by the amber color of the orb.

The witch ball grew warm in her hands, but not hot – just pleasantly warm, like a sun-heated stone. The metaphysical seam sealed itself, closing the passage and trapping the magic inside.

The light began to fade, settling and stabilizing.

Darby held her breath, waiting for the crack, for the sound of shattering, for the magic to reject the vessel or the vessel to reject the magic.

Nothing happened.

The witch ball sat between her palms, intact and whole, the faintest shimmer of green-gold light still visible deep inside if she looked carefully. The magical web had done its job. The ward was trapped inside, held securely, ready to activate when hung in a window or doorway.

"Holy shit," she breathed. "I did it."

She carefully set the witch ball in the box with the unbroken empty spheres and just stared at it for a moment, a grin spreading across her face. The candles around her seemed to burn a little brighter, and the frankincense smoke curled upward in a satisfied spiral.

One working ward. Finally.

But one wasn't enough. She needed dozens of these; enough to protect every window and door in everyone's apartments. But it was finally a step in the right direction.

Now she needed to confirm if the ward actually worked.

CHAPTER 17

*D*arby looked at the witch ball, then at the grimoire, and then at Sage's book. Neither book seemed to address how to *test* a protective ward. The grimoire had instructions for creating wards, but nothing about verifying that they functioned correctly.

She could hang it in the window and... what? Throw something at the window to see if the ward stopped it? That seemed both dangerous and stupid. Plus, it would probably just result in a broken window and an angry landlord.

Maybe there was a way to sense the ward's presence, to verify it was active without actually triggering it. Some kind of magical diagnostic test.

Darby reached for her laptop on the coffee table and flipped it open. The screen brightened, and she pulled up a browser. Surely someone on the internet had figured this out. There had to be forums or blogs or something about practical magic, about how to test your spellwork without destroying property or hurting yourself.

She typed "how to test protective ward spell" into the search bar and hit enter.

The results were about what she expected – a mix of fantasy fiction, role-playing game forums, and New Age websites that were long on aesthetic and short on actual information. She clicked through a few, skimming articles about "cleansing your energy" and "manifesting protection" that might have been useful if she'd wanted vague guidance instead of specific instructions.

After fifteen minutes of fruitless searching, Darby sat back and rubbed her eyes. This was frustrating. There had to be real witches online, people who actually practiced magic and shared practical knowledge. But how did you find them when ninety percent of search results were either fantasy or fluff?

She was about to try a different search term when her keyboard made a soft clicking sound.

Darby frowned. She hadn't touched anything. But as she watched, the cursor began moving across the screen on its own, gliding slowly toward the browser icon.

"What the..." She moved her hands away from the trackpad entirely and stared as the browser opened itself. A new tab appeared, loading a random website. Then another tab with a different site. Then another, windows multiplying across her screen.

The laptop wasn't old. She'd bought it a little over a year ago, but maybe it was having some kind of software malfunction. Malware, maybe? A virus? Though she was always careful about what she downloaded.

Darby pressed the power button, holding it down and waiting for the shutdown screen to appear. The laptop ignored her. More tabs kept opening, filling the browser window, the clicking sound of each new tab making her increasingly nervous.

"Okay, stop," she muttered, pressing on the power button even harder, as if that would make a difference.

The screen went black.

Darby let out a breath of relief. Whatever that had been – a stuck key, a weird software glitch, or maybe a pop-up ad stuck on loop – a reboot should fix it. She waited a moment, then pressed the power button again.

The laptop booted up faster than it should have, the screen brightening immediately without the usual startup logos or loading screens. The cursor moved across the screen on its own, opening a browser window.

"No," Darby said, her voice rising slightly. "No, what the hell is happening? This can't be real."

The cursor moved on its own, clicking the first tab. A page began loading – the Stenton Daily News. Darby sat frozen as the website appeared. She'd never heard of this news site, had never even been to Stenton.

The cursor scrolled down the page in fits and starts, moving in erratic jumps past headlines about local politics and high school sports, until it stopped on an article dated three years ago.

Deadly House Fire in Stenton Claims Five Lives

Darby's heart began to hammer. She leaned forward, reading despite every instinct telling her to slam the laptop closed and throw it across the room.

A devastating fire claimed the lives of five women in the town of Stenton on Tuesday evening. The explosion and subsequent blaze destroyed the home at 847 Maple Street, leaving little evidence for investigators to examine.

Initial reports suggest the women may have been involved in the production of methamphetamine, but members of the community have pushed back strongly against this characterization. "These were good people," said Patricia Hughs, a neighbor who knew the victims. "Emma was a schoolteacher. Rachel volunteered at the food bank. The idea that they were cooking drugs is insulting and wrong."

The victims have been identified as Emma Thornton, 34; Rachel Vasquez, 41; Mei Lin Chen, 28; Diana Foster, 52; and Brenda Wright, 26.

The fire department reports that the intensity of the blaze and struc-

tural damage made rescue attempts impossible. The cause of the explosion remains under investigation.

Darby's mouth went dry. Five women. Dead in a fire. The article didn't say they were witches, but she knew. She knew with the same certainty that she knew her own name.

Another browser window opened on its own, the cursor already moving to a new website. This article was from a different news site, the Michigan Daily Press, dated two years ago.

Tragic Fire Kills Four in Hillbrook Community

Four women. Another house fire. Another entire group dead.

Darby's hands were shaking now. That was two fires. Two separate groups of women, all of them killed. Both houses had burned completely, leaving nothing behind.

"Stop," Darby whispered, but the cursor kept moving, kept clicking, kept loading new pages.

She pressed her hands flat against the keyboard, trying to physically stop whatever was happening. "Who are you?" she demanded, her voice shaking. "What are you doing?"

The keys continued clicking beneath her palms, the laptop operating as if her hands weren't even there. Something touched the backs of her hands, a sensation like cold fingertips brushing across her skin. The touch was feather-light; there and gone in an instant.

Darby yanked her hands away, her heart hammering against her ribs. She rubbed at her skin, trying to erase the sensation, but the phantom touch lingered.

Two more windows opened in rapid succession, tabs multiplying across her screen. Her eyes darted from headline to headline:

Five Die in Suspicious House Fire

Lakemount. Five women. A little over six years ago.

House Fire Claims Three Lives in Birchdale

Four fires in total, spanning the past seven years. Seventeen women total. All killed in fires that investigators couldn't explain. All in buildings that burned so hot and fast that little evidence remained.

Darby stared at her laptop screen, her breath coming in short, sharp gasps. The cursor finally stopped moving. The browser windows stayed open, article after article displayed across her screen like accusations.

"What the fuck," she said out loud, her voice shaking. "What the actual fuck."

She stood up abruptly, backing away from the laptop as if it might explode. Her legs bumped against the couch, and she sat down hard, still staring at the screen.

This wasn't a malfunction. This wasn't a virus. Something had taken control of her computer to show her these articles. To make sure she saw them. To make sure she understood.

Women with power, Sage had said. *The world isn't always kind to women with power.*

Seventeen women dead in unexplained fires. Plus, the four women from Alice's coven. How many of them had been witches? How many had formed covens, learned magic, and tried to protect themselves?

All of them, Darby thought. All of them.

And someone had killed them for it.

The sound of a key in the front door made Darby jump so hard she nearly screamed. She spun around, her magic surging up instinctively. Her hand shot toward the mint plant on the windowsill, and the stems exploded outward, shooting across the floor toward her in a green wave. They surrounded her in seconds, rising up like snakes poised to strike before she recognized the familiar sound of Kara's footsteps in the entryway.

"Hey!" Kara called, her voice cheerful. "I grabbed us sandwiches from that place on— Darby? Are you okay?"

She appeared in the doorway to the living room, still in her work clothes, a paper bag in one hand. She stopped short, eyes widening at the mass of greenery writhing across the floor.

"Darby, what—" Her gaze snapped to Darby's face, and her expression shifted from shock to alarm. "What happened?"

With a wave of her hand, Darby sent the mint stems retreating across the floor, slithering back to the windowsill and coiling into the pot as if nothing had happened.

"I—" Darby's voice came out strangled. She gestured helplessly at the laptop. "Look. Look at the screen."

Kara set the bag down and crossed to the couch in quick steps, her eyes still darting between Darby and the now-innocent plant on the windowsill. She turned to look at the computer, her brow furrowing as she read the headlines visible across the multiple browser windows. Darby watched her expression change from confusion to horror as she moved closer, clicking through the articles one by one.

"These are all..." Kara trailed off, her hand covering her mouth. "All these women. All these fires."

"More than a dozen women in the last seven years," Darby said, her voice flat. "All here in Michigan. In each instance, the buildings were completely burned down. The investigations ended up being either inconclusive or blamed on meth labs or electrical fires or freak accidents. But look at the patterns, Kara. Look at who died."

Kara was quiet for a moment, still reading. Then she looked up, her face pale. "Groups of women. They were covens, weren't they?"

"I think so." Darby's hands were still shaking. She clasped them together to make them stop. "I think they were all covens. And someone killed them."

"How did you..." Kara looked from the screen to Darby. "How did you find these articles?"

Darby let out a laugh that sounded slightly unhinged even to her own ears. "I didn't. My laptop... it just—" She gestured at the computer. "The keys started pressing themselves. It opened these browser windows on its own and showed me these articles. I couldn't stop it. I tried to reboot, but it just... kept going."

Kara's eyes widened. "On its own? You mean like someone hacked it?"

"I don't know! Maybe? But it felt..." Darby struggled to find the words. "It felt like magic. Not like someone remotely accessing my computer. Like something else. As if something was trying to warn us."

"Warn us?" Kara's voice was barely a whisper.

"Yes." Darby looked at the screen again, at all those headlines, all those dead women. "Someone is hunting witches, Kara. Someone is finding covens and burning them alive. And something – some higher power or... or a ghost or I don't know what – just made sure I knew about it."

Kara sank down onto the couch beside Darby, her face ashen. For a long moment, neither of them spoke. The apartment was silent except for the distant hum of traffic and the quiet whir of the laptop's fan.

"The Torch Bearers," Kara finally said. "Sage warned us. She said there are people out there who hate anyone practicing magic. That we needed to be careful."

"I don't think she knew it was this bad." Darby's voice cracked slightly. "Four fires, Kara. Actually, five fires if you count the one we already found about the grimoire's previous owner. Five covens wiped out. And those are just the ones in these articles. How many more have there been that didn't make the news? How many witches have died?"

Kara reached out and took Darby's hand, squeezing it tightly. "We need to tell the others. Right now."

"I know." Darby looked at their joined hands, then at the witch ball faintly glowing in its box. One working ward. One small piece of protection against something that had killed all those women and left no evidence behind.

It didn't feel like nearly enough.

Kara was already pulling out her phone, her fingers moving quickly across the screen as she typed out a message to the group chat.

Darby turned back to the laptop, forcing herself to scan the articles more carefully. There had to be something here – some pattern, some clue about how these covens had been discovered. Had they been too public? Too careless? Was there a common thread that could help them avoid the same fate? She clicked through the tabs, searching for details about the victims, about who had known them, about what had made them targets.

Kara's phone buzzed with incoming responses, but she didn't look at it. She just stared at Darby, her eyes wide and frightened.

"I'm scared. How do we keep this from happening to us?" she whispered.

Darby didn't have an answer. She looked at the witch ball in its box, pressed her hand against her sternum, trapping her protective pendant against her chest, then swept her gaze across all their magical supplies spread across the living room floor. They'd been so excited about being witches, so full of hope and possibility.

Now all she could think about was fire.

CHAPTER 18

*T*opaz arrived first, barely five minutes after Kara's text. She must have dropped everything and run straight over. Her purple-streaked hair was still wet from the shower, and she was wearing sweatpants and an oversized t-shirt. Ivette and Jazmin showed up less than ten minutes later. Ivette was still wearing her work polo shirt with the freight company logo embroidered on the chest. Now they were all crammed into the living room, talking over each other, voices rising and falling in waves of panic that none of them were quite managing to suppress.

"Guys, stop!" Topaz's voice cut through the chaos like a knife. Everyone fell silent, turning to look at her. She was standing by the window, her arms crossed, her jaw set in a hard line. "One at a time. We need to think clearly."

Darby was sitting on the floor, cradling the one witch ball she'd managed to complete. The amber and gold sphere was warm in her hands, its protective magic humming softly inside the glass. The laptop was open on the coffee table, and Jazmin had been reading through the articles, her face getting paler with each one.

"Okay," Kara said, her voice shaking slightly. "Okay. So we believe that someone is attacking—"

"Not someone. The Torch Bearers," Darby interjected.

"We don't actually know that," Topaz said from her position by the window. "It could be anyone. Another group we don't even know exists yet."

"Does it matter?" Ivette's voice was quiet but firm. "Somebody killed all those women. Burned them alive in their homes."

Darby nodded slowly. "Whoever they are, we know they burn entire buildings to the ground. We know that at least five covens have been killed in the last seven years. Whether it's the Torch Bearers or someone else..." She looked around at all of them. "So, the question is: what do we do about it?"

The silence that followed was heavy and suffocating.

"Maybe..." Kara swallowed hard. "Maybe we should stop. Stop practicing, I mean. Stop meeting as a coven. Just... stop using magic entirely. To keep us safe."

Darby felt something twist in her chest at the suggestion. She opened her mouth to protest, but Ivette spoke first.

"I agree," Ivette said quietly. She was sitting on the couch next to her granddaughter, one hand resting on Jazmin's shoulder. "I will not risk Jazmin's life. Not for any amount of magic, not for any power. Not for *anything*. My granddaughter means more to me than any of this."

Jazmin looked up at her grandmother; her expression caught somewhere between gratitude and frustration. "Abuela—"

"No." Ivette's voice was gentle but firm. "You are eighteen years old, mija. You have your whole life ahead of you. I won't let you throw it away because some men—"

"Oh, for fuck's sake!" Topaz's voice was sharp enough to make everyone flinch. She whirled around from the window, her dark eyes blazing. "You think Jazmin isn't already in danger? You think any of us aren't? We're *already* witches! The magic is inside us!

Keeping her weak and uneducated isn't going to help her. It's going to get her killed!"

"But—" Jazmin started, her voice caught somewhere between agreement and protest. She looked at her grandmother, then back at Topaz, clearly torn.

"Topaz," Kara said carefully, "you're scaring them—"

"They should be scared!" Topaz's hands clenched into fists at her sides. "We should all be scared! But do you really think hiding is going to save us? You think pretending we're not witches is going to make the Torch Bearers ignore us? These fuckers are hunting women with power, and guess what? We have power! Shutting our eyes and hoping they don't notice us is a death sentence!"

"So what do you suggest?" Ivette's voice was cold. "That we paint targets on our backs?"

"I suggest we get stronger!" Topaz's voice rose. "I suggest we stop being victims and start being dangerous! For thousands of years, people have been killing women for any reason they could dream up. Too opinionated? Burn her. Too quiet? Burn her. Too pretty? Burn her. Too ugly? Burn her. A crop failed? Must be witches – burn them! A baby died? Witches! A man can't get it up? Fucking witches!" She was pacing now, her movements sharp and angry. "Think about the Salem witch trials. Do we even know if any of those people were actually witches? Probably none of them! They were just people who didn't fit. Women who were too independent, too outspoken, too weird. And even if they *were* witches, they didn't deserve to die screaming."

The room was silent except for Topaz's harsh breathing.

"She's right," Darby said, her voice dropping to something quieter but no less intense. "I'm sick of it. I'm sick of being afraid. I'm sick of people thinking they can hurt women and get away with it. I am sick of making myself smaller and weaker and quieter just to survive. And I will not – I will NOT – let these Torch Bearer assholes make me afraid to be what I am."

"But we need to be smart about this," Kara said carefully. "We need to be careful."

"You're right," Topaz said, turning to face her. "We do need to be smart. And the smart thing to do is to use the advantage we have."

"What advantage?" Darby asked.

"We know what we're up against." Topaz gestured at the laptop. "Alice and her coven knew the Torch Bearers were harassing them, but they had no idea how deadly they were. They thought they could just be more careful, meet in secret. But we know the pattern. We know these people don't just harass – they kill. We can prepare in ways Alice never got the chance to."

"Prepare how?" Jazmin asked.

"We get stronger. We practice. We learn defensive magic, offensive magic, protection spells – whatever we need to fight back." Topaz looked around at all of them. "We're already witches. I can't just turn off my power. Can any of you?"

Darby felt her magic respond to the question, that warm green energy humming under her skin. She tried to imagine pushing it away, suppressing it, forcing it back down into whatever place it had come from.

Nothing happened. The magic stayed right where it was, as much a part of her as her heartbeat.

"I can't," Topaz announced. "I tried earlier. I tried to pull it out of my body or push it back or... something. But it's just there. It's part of me now."

"Same," Darby said quietly. "When I try to imagine not having my power, it's like... like trying to imagine not having brown eyes. I can't just turn it off."

Kara shook her head. "Mine feels like it's woven into me. Like it's in my bones."

They all looked at Ivette. She was quiet for a long moment, her hand still resting on Jazmin's shoulder. Finally, she sighed.

"No," she said. "I can't turn it off either." She looked up at

Topaz, her expression conflicted. "But that doesn't mean practicing is the answer. It might make us more visible. More of a target."

"We're already targets!" Topaz's voice was almost pleading now. "Don't you get it? The magic is in us, whether we use it or not. Whether we practice or not. But if we don't practice, if we don't get stronger, then when they come for us – and we *have* to assume that they *will* come for us – we'll be helpless. Those other covens? They died. All of them. Maybe if they'd been stronger, if they'd known how to fight back, some of them would have survived."

"Or maybe they'd have died anyway," Ivette said softly.

"Maybe," Topaz acknowledged. "But at least they would have had a chance. At least they could have tried." She looked around at all of them, her gaze intense. "I'd rather die fighting than die afraid. And frankly, I'd rather not die at all."

Darby found herself nodding. Topaz was right – they couldn't just pretend the magic wasn't there. It was part of them now, for better or worse. And if the Torch Bearers, or whoever was behind this, were hunting witches, then they were already in danger. Hiding wouldn't save them.

"So what's your plan?" Jazmin asked, and there was something fierce in her voice now, something that matched the look in Topaz's eyes.

"We train," Topaz said simply. "We practice whatever magic spells that can keep us safe. We learn offensive spells too – things that can hurt someone if we need to fight back. We make ourselves strong enough that if the Torch Bearers come for us, they'll fucking regret it."

"That's right," Darby said, her voice gaining strength. Everyone turned to look at her. "We're not some gentle, nature-loving coven that meets in meadows and weaves flowers into our hair. We're not small-town witches who garden and make herbal tea. We're tough city women. We're made of grit and determination, with dirt under our fingernails and asphalt in our veins." She gestured at the window, at the city lights beyond. "We're not going to be easy to kill."

A slow smile spread across Topaz's face. "Damn right we're not."

"Hell yeah," Jazmin said, sitting up straighter. "A coven with asphalt in our veins."

Topaz laughed. "I fucking love that."

Kara looked at Ivette, and something passed between them – some wordless communication that Darby couldn't quite read. Finally, Ivette closed her eyes and sighed.

"If we're going to do this," she said, opening her eyes again, "then we do it smart. We prepare thoroughly. We don't take unnecessary risks. And we protect each other. Always."

"Deal," Topaz said immediately.

"Agreed," Kara added.

Jazmin nodded, and Darby found herself nodding too. They were really doing this. They were going to fight back.

"Okay," Kara said, and her voice sounded steadier now, more determined. "We need a place to practice. Somewhere private, somewhere we won't be seen or interrupted."

"I might be able to get us access to a space at a warehouse that I've used as a studio space before," Topaz offered. "There's an old storage room in the back that nobody uses anymore. I could probably—"

"No," Darby interrupted. "No buildings."

Everyone looked at her.

"Those other covens," she explained, gesturing at the laptop. "They all died in buildings. Houses, apartments, whatever. The Torch Bearers burn buildings down. They trap everyone inside and burn them alive." She shook her head. "I don't want to practice in a building. If they come for us, we can't be trapped."

"But we already all live in the same building," Kara pointed out, her voice tight with worry.

"Exactly," Darby said. "We *have* to live somewhere, and it can't exactly be in the woods. But if we keep our magic separate from our everyday lives, if we practice somewhere else entirely, then maybe the Torch Bearers won't be able to trace it back to our homes. We need to practice outside, somewhere we won't be trapped."

"Then where?" Jazmin asked.

Darby looked at Topaz. "The cemetery."

Topaz's eyes lit up. "That's a genius idea."

"Cemetery?" Kara asked, looking between them. "What cemetery?"

"It's one that Topaz showed me. We use it as a shortcut from the café. It's completely hidden between the old textile mill and the closed water treatment facility. It's surrounded by deserted factories. No one even knows it's there. It's abandoned, it's private, and most importantly, it's outside. If something happens, if someone attacks us, we're not trapped." Darby could see it in her mind – the overgrown paths, the crumbling headstones, the cracked pavement and weeds pushing through everywhere. "It's perfect."

Jazmin let out a laugh that sounded slightly incredulous. "A bunch of witches practicing magic in a cemetery? That's such a stereotype."

"I know," Darby said, grinning despite everything. "Isn't it great?"

"It's perfect," Jazmin corrected, and her grin matched Darby's. "Absolutely perfect."

"We should talk to Sage," Ivette suggested. "She might have advice about how to protect ourselves. She's been doing this longer than any of us. See if she knows anything about the Torch Bearers."

"I'll go," Topaz said immediately. "Tomorrow morning, first thing when The Serpent's Garden opens. I have the day off, and I don't want to wait any longer than necessary. The sooner we start preparing, the better."

"And I'll do research on the Torch Bearers at work," Kara added. "If anyone can dig up information on them, it's a librarian. There may be historical records, old news articles, or something we can use."

Darby carefully set the witch ball down on the coffee table, its amber surface catching the lamplight, then pulled the grimoire from Kara's hands, opening it to scan through the pages. "We need to figure out what we're up against and what we can actually do about it."

They spent the next hour huddled around the coffee table, all of them leaning over the grimoire, marking pages with Post-it notes. Some spells were clearly too advanced – complex rituals that required rare ingredients and took hours to perform. But others seemed manageable.

"Here's a cloaking spell," Kara said, her finger tracing down a page. "It hides magical signatures. Could keep the Torch Bearers from sensing us."

"Mark it," Topaz said, leaning over to read.

"This one creates shields," Topaz added, flipping to another page. "Barriers against physical and magical attacks."

"We need offensive spells too," Jazmin said firmly. When Ivette looked at her sharply, she met her gaze without flinching. "I'm serious. If they come for us, I want to be able to fight back. I don't want to just hide behind a shield and hope it's enough."

Ivette's jaw tightened, but after a moment, she nodded. "You're right. If it comes down to fighting, we need to be prepared. I'm not going to pull any punches, and neither should you, mija."

"Oh, here's one," Kara said. "It creates a concentrated funnel of wind – like a small tornado you can direct at a target. With my affinity for air, I bet I could do this one."

"That's useful," Darby said. "You could really mess someone up, give us time to run or fight back."

"We should all work on our affinities," Topaz stated. "Make them stronger and more controlled. I could learn to wield my fire – fight fire with fire, literally."

"I could use electricity as a weapon," Ivette said slowly, looking at her hands as if seeing them differently. "Learn how to channel it and direct it."

"And I have water," Jazmin added, her voice gaining confidence. "There are ways to use that offensively, right?"

"Hell yeah, there is," Topaz said with a grin.

Darby felt a sinking feeling in her stomach. "I don't know how plants could help us fight. I mean, what am I supposed to do, throw flowers at them?"

"Are you kidding?" Topaz looked at her incredulously. "Darby, you stopped a car with a root. You made it burst through concrete and made it hard enough to stop two tons of speeding metal. You saved those people's lives."

Darby blinked, remembering that moment – the way the root had responded to her call.

"Plants can be weapons," Kara said quietly. "Thorns. Vines that strangle. Roots that trip or trap. Poison."

"Exactly," Topaz said. "You're not weak, Darby. None of us are."

Darby was about to mark another page when she remembered something. "Wait. I need to show you something."

She reached over and picked up the witch ball from where she'd set it down. Carefully, she picked up the sphere and held it out in her cupped hand.

"I made this today," she said. The amber and gold glass caught the light, swirling with warm colors. But more importantly, she could feel the magic inside it – the protective ward she'd sealed within the glass, waiting to activate.

"I put a protection ward inside a witch ball." Darby explained how she'd made it, how she'd woven the magical web inside the glass and compressed the protective spell into it. "Traditional witch balls trap negative spirits and energy. This one should trap hostile magic and maybe even deflect physical threats. But I don't actually know if it works. I haven't tested it yet." She paused, turning the sphere in her hands. "And if I can put a ward inside the ball... maybe we could put other spells in them too. Like spell grenades. Something offensive we could throw."

"I say we test it at the cemetery," Ivette said. "If it works, we make more. We protect our apartments first, then the building if we can. And if we have enough, we also place them around the cemetery. Hell, maybe even our workspaces if we can."

"That's actually brilliant," Topaz said. "Multiple layers of protection. The witch balls as the outer layer, then whatever wards and shields we can cast ourselves as the inner layers."

They kept planning, their voices growing more animated and more determined. Darby could feel the fear that had filled the room earlier transforming into something else – something harder and sharper. They weren't going to hide. They weren't going to wait for the Torch Bearers to find them and burn them alive like all those other witches.

They were going to fight.

"When do we start?" Jazmin asked.

Topaz checked her phone. "I'll go to The Serpent's Garden first thing in the morning. Talk to Sage, get her advice, pick up any additional supplies we might need. Then we can meet at the cemetery tomorrow night."

"It has to be at night?" Kara asked nervously.

"Better for not being seen," Topaz pointed out. "And honestly? It's a cemetery. Practicing magic at midnight in a graveyard? I feel like it's on brand for a witch coven."

Darby laughed, and after a moment, the others joined in. It felt good to laugh, to feel something other than fear.

They stayed for another hour, going over their plans, discussing logistics, and marking more spells in the grimoire. By the time Topaz, Ivette, and Jazmin left, Darby felt exhausted but strangely energized at the same time. They had a plan.

Darby and Kara sat together on the couch, the apartment quiet around them. The witch ball sat on the coffee table, catching the lamplight, its protective magic humming softly inside the glass.

"Are we doing the right thing?" Kara asked quietly.

Darby thought about all those dead witches. All those women who'd been burned alive, who'd died screaming, who'd never had a chance to fight back.

"I don't know," she admitted. "But I know I'd rather try and fail than never try at all."

Kara nodded slowly, then reached out and took Darby's hand. They sat like that for a while, not speaking, just holding on to each other in the darkness.

CHAPTER 19

The night air bit cold against Darby's skin as the five of them made their way down the deserted street toward the cemetery. It was just past midnight, and the industrial district had gone quiet – nothing but distant highway traffic and the bass-heavy thump of music from Anchor around the corner, where Friday night was in full swing.

Jazmin walked beside her grandmother, both of them carrying canvas bags filled with candles, salt, herbs, and chalk for drawing circles. Darby had the witch ball carefully wrapped in a dish towel and tucked into her backpack, along with a flashlight and her own notes about the spells they'd marked.

"So," Topaz said, breaking the silence that had settled over them as they walked. "I went to The Serpent's Garden this morning like I said I would."

"And?" Ivette asked.

"Sage had never heard of the Torch Bearers." Topaz's voice was flat with disappointment. "I described everything we found: the fires, the pattern, the name from the grimoire, the other covens. She just looked at me like I was speaking another language. She knew about witch hunters in general, gave me the whole history lesson about the Inquisition and Salem and all that. But a specific group calling themselves the Torch Bearers? Nothing."

Darby felt her stomach sink. She'd been hoping Sage would have answers, some kind of wisdom or guidance about how to protect themselves from this specific threat.

"That's not entirely surprising," Kara said quietly. "I did some research at work today, and I didn't find much either."

"What do you mean?" Jazmin asked.

Kara adjusted her glasses, a nervous gesture Darby had come to recognize. "Well, first of all, searching for 'Torch Bearers' online is nearly impossible because of the Olympic torch-bearing ceremony. That completely dominated the search results. But once I filtered through all that, I did find several groups using that name or variations of it."

"How many?" Darby asked.

"At least a dozen different organizations across the country. Most of them are Christian-based. Most seem like they are just regular church organizations doing community outreach and calling themselves torch bearers because of the whole 'light in the darkness' metaphor. But others..." Kara paused, her expression troubled. "A couple had more concerning mission statements. A lot of talk about 'driving out corruption' and 'purifying communities' and 'spiritual warfare,' but they're vague about what they consider evil. I'm making a list of all of them to look into further."

They'd reached the gap in the chain-link fence that marked the entrance to the cemetery.

"The name itself is significant," Kara said, pausing before they went through. "A torchbearer is defined as someone at the forefront of a campaign or a crusade. Someone who carries the light, who leads others. It's a term that suggests righteousness and a sense of moral mission."

"Great," Jazmin muttered. "So covens are being hunted by zealots who think they're on the side of the angels."

"Are any of these organizations in Michigan?" Ivette asked, her voice tight.

"Three so far," Kara said. "One is a church group in Grand Rapids that seems relatively harmless – they do food drives and volunteer work. But the other two are more concerning. One is based in Lansing and describes itself as 'defending Christian values against modern corruption.' The other is in Ann Arbor, and their website talks a lot about 'cleansing corruption' and 'driving out darkness.'"

"Those three should get more scrutiny since they're nearby, especially those last two," Topaz said, and the others murmured agreement. She held the fence aside. "Come on. You need to see this."

They slipped through one by one into the overgrown space beyond.

Kara stopped so abruptly that Jazmin nearly walked into her back.

"Holy shit," Jazmin breathed.

They emerged into the hidden cemetery, the space transformed by darkness into something otherworldly. Moonlight filtered between the hulking shapes of abandoned factories, casting strange shadows across tilted headstones and toppled monuments. At the center, the towering elm tree rose like a dark guardian, its gnarled trunk silvered by moonlight. The crumbling monuments and tombstones seemed to glow faintly in the ethereal light, and the whole place felt suspended in time – ancient and forgotten, hidden in the heart of the industrial district like a secret the city had buried and lost

"This is..." Ivette trailed off, turning in a slow circle to take it all in. The derelict mills and plants towered above them, black outlines against the night sky, their cold and silent smokestacks like watching sentinels. "This is incredible. I had no idea this was here."

"Nobody does," Topaz said with obvious satisfaction. "That's what makes it perfect."

Darby felt a thrill seeing the cemetery at night for the first time. During the day, it had been a bit melancholy and forgotten; now it felt alive with possibility. Magical. The wind whispered through the brittle grass, making it rustle and hiss. The stone angel with the broken wing knelt in prayer. In the moonlight, it looked alive, as if it might stand at any moment.

They walked in awed silence along the cracked pathway between weathered headstones until they reached the center of the cemetery, a relatively flat area beneath the old elm and surrounded by taller monuments that formed a natural barrier from the secret entrance. The crumbling headstones created an amphitheater of sorts, with weathered angels and crosses watching over them like silent witnesses.

Darby set down her backpack and pulled out the flashlight, clicking it on and setting it on top of a low headstone where it could illuminate their workspace. The beam of light cut through the shadows, making the cemetery feel less eerie and more purposeful. The others began unpacking their supplies, moving with nervous energy.

"Okay," Topaz said, pulling out the grimoire and opening it to one of their marked pages. "Before we do anything else, we need to set up a containment circle. According to this, it will keep our magic hidden from outside detection."

"Smart," Ivette said, setting down her bag. "If the Torch Bearers can sense magic, we don't want to broadcast what we're doing here."

They found a relatively flat area near the elm tree, though "flat" was generous. The ground was uneven, with grass tufts, exposed roots, and cracked pavement making everything a challenge. Topaz pulled out chalk while Kara held the grimoire, angling it to catch the flashlight beam.

"We need to make the magic circle big enough for all five of us to work inside comfortably," Darby said, pacing out the diameter. "At least twelve feet across?"

"Fifteen would be better," Ivette said. "We need room to move without breaking the circle."

Topaz began marking the outer edge, moving carefully around the uneven terrain. The chalk caught on grass tufts and skipped over rough patches, leaving broken, uneven lines.

"The circle needs to be unbroken," Kara said, looking up from the grimoire. "If there are gaps, the containment won't work."

Topaz frowned at the interrupted line. "The grass is making it impossible to—"

"Wait." Darby knelt beside the circle's edge, pressing her palms flat against the ground. She closed her eyes and reached for that now-familiar pull of green magic inside her. The grass responded immediately, stems bending and roots contracting as the blades withdrew into the earth. She moved slowly around the circle's perimeter, smoothing the ground ahead of Topaz, leaving bare packed earth in her wake.

Topaz grinned. "Now that's useful."

With the path clear, Topaz continued marking the circle, the chalk line flowing smooth and unbroken across the earth.

"Now the runes," Kara said, squinting at the grimoire. "There are specific symbols that need to go at the cardinal points – north, south, east, west."

"Which way is north?" Ivette asked, looking around at the dark cemetery.

Jazmin pulled out her phone and opened a compass app. "That way," she said, pointing toward the old mausoleum.

They marked the four cardinal points, and then Topaz began carefully drawing the symbols at each position. She had to consult the grimoire constantly, making sure each one was correct.

"What do these even do?" Jazmin asked, watching Topaz work on an interlocking triangle at the eastern point.

"According to this, they power the spell," Kara said, angling the grimoire toward the flashlight. "This one binds, this one seals, this one conceals, and this one anchors." She pointed to each cardinal direction in turn.

"Movies don't show the part where you're drawing on grass and rocks in the dark," Topaz muttered, her voice strained with concentration as she added careful hash marks to the triangle's interior.

Between the four cardinal points, Kara directed them to add specific inscriptions along the circle's edge. The angular runes looked ancient, each one carefully copied from the grimoire. Darby took over for one section, her hand cramping as she tried to replicate the sharp lines and curves.

Finally, after nearly thirty minutes of work, the circle was complete. The chalk glowed faintly in the moonlight, the runes and inscriptions forming an intricate pattern around them.

"Should we add salt?" Ivette asked, already pulling out a container of sea salt from her bag. "Double protection couldn't hurt."

"Good idea," Kara said. "Pour it just outside the chalk circle. It'll create a secondary barrier."

Ivette moved slowly around the perimeter, pouring a steady stream of salt just beyond the chalk line. The white crystals stood out against the dark ground, creating a second ring of protection around them all.

When she finished, they all stood back and looked at their work. The double circle gleamed in the darkness – chalk on the inside with its careful runes and inscriptions, salt forming a protective barrier on the outside.

"Okay," Topaz said, carefully stepping over both lines into the center. The others followed one by one, moving cautiously to avoid disturbing their work. "Now let's try the cloaking spell. We need to make sure we can mask our magical signatures even when we're working outside the circle."

CHAPTER 20

*K*ara held the grimoire, her lips moving silently as she studied the words. "It requires visualization and sustained focus, plus some physical components. We need to anoint ourselves with protection oil. Just a drop on the forehead and wrists." She pulled a small vial from her bag. "And we should light candles at the cardinal points to anchor the spell."

Jazmin retrieved four white candles from her grandmother's bag and placed them at the north, south, east, and west markers, carefully lighting each one. The flames pulsed in the night breeze, casting dancing shadows.

"The spell says we can use an athame to direct the energy," Kara continued, pulling out their ritual knife. Its blade caught the candlelight. "We'll pass it around the circle as we cast."

Ivette opened the vial of protection oil, releasing the sharp scent of rosemary and lavender into the air. She anointed her forehead and wrists, then passed the vial to Jazmin. One by one they followed, the herbal scent lingering in the cold night air.

"Now," Kara said, holding the athame vertically in front of her. "We need to imagine our magic as something visible – light, energy, whatever resonates with us – and then picture it dimming, fading, and becoming invisible."

"Like turning down a dimmer switch," Jazmin said.

"Exactly." Kara looked around at all of them. "Should we try it together, or one at a time?"

"Together," Ivette said firmly.

They formed a loose circle within the protective boundaries, standing with their feet planted on the uneven ground. Darby closed her eyes and reached for her magic, feeling that familiar green energy humming beneath her skin. She pictured the green light she'd created when warding the witch ball – that brilliant, living glow that had felt like the very essence of her magic. Vibrant and alive, like new spring growth.

Now she needed to hide it. Not diminish it but conceal it.

She imagined the green light remaining just as bright, just as powerful, but drawing a veil around itself. Like a seed buried deep in the earth. Still alive, still growing, but hidden from view. The magic didn't fade; instead, it wrapped itself in shadows and darkness.

For a moment, nothing happened. Then Darby felt something shift – a subtle change in the way her magic moved through her body. It was still there, still humming with life, and if anything it felt stronger than before, as if the act of containing it had concentrated its power. But now it felt... hidden. Veiled. Like looking at a bright light through dark cloth. The light was just as strong, but you couldn't see it from the outside.

She could sense her magic growing with the effort, responding to her intent, learning this new shape. It was still hers, still powerful, just invisible now.

"I think I've got it," she said, opening her eyes.

"Me too," Jazmin said, sounding surprised. "My magic feels hidden now, like it's wrapped up and tucked away. But I can still feel all of you – our coven bond – from the inside. It's like we're all under a blanket together."

"I think mine worked, but I'm not totally sure," Kara admitted. "How can we tell?"

"We can't, not really," Topaz said. "Not unless we had a way to sense each other's magic in the first place." She paused, concentrating for a moment. "Wait. I can feel you all through our coven bond. But when I try to sense your magic the way a stranger would, without using the bond, I can't detect anything. It's just... gone."

"That's actually a good sign," Ivette said. "It means the spell might be working."

"Until we can find a better way to test its effectiveness," Topaz continued, "we may just have to go on faith."

They practiced the cloaking spell again and again until everyone could feel their magic wrap itself in concealment. By the fifth attempt, it started to feel natural, like the hidden state was simply another way their magic could exist. Darby found herself slipping into it more easily each time, the veil drawing closed around her power with barely a thought.

"I think we've got it," Kara said finally, a note of confidence in her voice that hadn't been there before.

"Good," Topaz said, flipping through the grimoire. "Now let's try something more visible. The binding spell. If we can immobilize an attacker, even for a few seconds, that could save our lives."

The binding spell was simpler in execution than the cloaking spell. They just needed a few specific words, a sweeping motion with both hands as if physically wrapping something around the target, and a clear visualization of restraints forming. "It says to use whatever trapping imagery feels natural to you," Topaz read aloud.

Vines, Darby thought immediately. Roots and vines wrapping tight.

"We need a test subject," Jazmin said, looking around.

"I'll do it," Ivette said, stepping forward. She positioned herself a few feet away from the group and planted her feet. "Jazmin, I want you to try it on me first."

"Abuela, are you sure?" Jazmin asked nervously.

"Completely sure. If this spell works, I need to know you can use it to protect yourself." Ivette's expression was firm. "Go ahead, mija."

Jazmin took a breath and raised her hands, making the sweeping motion they'd read about. She spoke the binding words carefully and thrust her hands forward, but nothing visible happened. Ivette stood there unrestrained.

"What were you picturing?" Topaz asked.

"A lasso," Jazmin said, frowning. "Like a rope wrapping around her."

"Try tapping into your affinity for water," Ivette suggested. "Use imagery that connects to your power."

"Okay." Jazmin nodded slowly. "I'll try to picture a bubble of water – like she's trapped inside it."

Jazmin took a moment before her second attempt, closing her eyes and biting her lip in concentration. When she opened her eyes and spoke the words, making that sweeping gesture with both hands, Darby saw something shift in the air around Ivette – a faint shimmer, like heat waves.

Ivette's eyes widened. She tried to jerk her arms away from her sides, but they only twitched and trembled, staying glued in place. She twisted her shoulders, her arms jerking uselessly but never moving more than an inch. "I can't move!" she said, delight breaking through her voice. "Jazmin, it's working. I actually can't move my arms!"

"Yes!" Topaz cheered.

"I'm going to try to break free with my magic," Ivette warned them. "Just to see if I can."

Darby watched as Ivette pulled against the bindings, her muscles straining. The invisible bonds held firm. Then purple-blue electricity began to spark around Ivette's body as she channeled her power against the restraints. The air shimmered more intensely where the binding met her magic, like two opposing forces grinding against each other.

It took almost a minute before Ivette finally broke through, her arms suddenly free as the spell shattered.

"Excellent work, Jazmin!" Ivette said, slightly breathless but smiling with pride. "That would definitely buy us time to run or fight back. One minute is longer than you'd think in a real confrontation."

"Let me try," Kara said, stepping forward. She looked at the others. "I need a volunteer."

"I'll do it," Darby said, moving to stand a few feet away from Kara.

Kara raised her hands and spoke the binding words, making the sweeping gesture. Darby felt something brush against her, the faintest sensation of pressure, like a breeze pushing against her, but it faded immediately.

"I felt something," Darby said encouragingly. "Just very light."

"What are you picturing?" Topaz asked.

"That's the problem," Kara said, frustrated. "Air is my affinity, but how do you trap someone with air? It just... flows around things. I can't picture how it would hold someone in place."

"Air has pressure," Ivette suggested. "Think about wind strong enough to pin someone down. Or maybe a vacuum that's sucking the air tight around them."

Kara nodded, biting her lip in concentration. She tried again, and this time Darby felt real pressure wrapping around her torso and arms, squeezing tight like invisible bands. Her arms pressed against her sides, immobilized.

"It's working!" Darby said, trying to pull her arms free. The pressure held firm, not painful but insistent, like being wrapped tightly in an invisible blanket. "But I can still move my legs. Try to picture binding my whole body."

Kara's brow furrowed deeper. "Okay, hold on."

She spoke the words again, her hands sweeping wider this time. The pressure around Darby's torso suddenly intensified and spread downward. Her legs locked together, immobilized from thigh to ankle.

Darby gasped and swayed, her balance thrown off by the sudden inability to move her legs. For a terrifying second, she thought she might fall, but then instinct took over. She reached out with her magic, calling to the elm tree behind her. A thick root broke through the ground and caught her back, holding her upright like a supportive hand.

Darby released the root once she had her balance, letting it sink back into the earth. "That was close. I almost went down."

"Nice save," Topaz said with a grin.

Darby tested the binding again, straining against the invisible pressure. Nothing budged. Her legs might as well have been stone. "Whoa," she breathed. "This is intense. I literally can't move anything below my neck."

She reached for her magic, calling to the plants around her. Vines and roots erupted from the ground and wrapped around her body, trying to pull off the binding. But there was nothing for them to grasp – the restraints were intangible magic. The vines just slid through empty space, unable to find anything physical to tear away.

"I can't break it," Darby said, impressed and slightly alarmed. "Even with my magic."

"Release," Kara said, speaking the word clearly.

The pressure vanished instantly, and Darby stumbled forward, catching herself. She rubbed her arms where the binding had been. "That's actually really powerful, Kara. If someone doesn't have magic to break it..."

She trailed off, the implication hanging in the air.

"It's good that we have a binding spell strong enough to hold someone," Ivette said carefully. "But we also need to make sure we can break out if it's used against us." She gestured between them. "I was able to use my electricity to break through Jazmin's spell, but Darby's plants couldn't touch yours, Kara. Different affinities might be more or less effective against different types of bindings. We should all practice escaping, make sure we're not helpless if someone uses this on us."

Everyone nodded in agreement.

"I'd like to try casting the binding spell now," Darby announced.

Topaz volunteered as her target, standing a few feet away with her arms relaxed at her sides.

Darby raised her hands and spoke the binding words, picturing vines wrapping around Topaz. But instead of invisible restraints, actual vines burst from the ground at Topaz's feet, snaking up and coiling around her ankles.

"Whoa, whoa!" Topaz jumped back as the vines continued growing, squealing as the vines slithered closer, reaching for her. "Darby, those are real!"

"Sorry!" Darby let go of the magic, and the vines retreated immediately, disappearing back into the ground. "I didn't mean to call actual vines. I was just using them to visualize the binding."

"It's okay," Kara said encouragingly. "Your connection to plants is strong. That's good. Just try to separate the visualization from the actual magic. Maybe try to picture the restraint as something invisible, like I did with air pressure."

Darby tried again, concentrating on the idea of restraint without picturing any particular shape. A faint green shimmer wrapped around Topaz's legs, and for a moment it seemed to work. Then roots broke through the earth, coiling upward.

"Darby!" Topaz laughed, dancing away from the creeping plants.

"I'm sorry! I'm trying!" Darby said, frustrated with herself.

On her fourth attempt, she finally managed it. No shimmer,

no vines, nothing visible at all, but Topaz's arms suddenly locked against her sides.

"It worked!" Topaz said, straining against the invisible restraints. "I can't move my arms at all."

"Yes!" Darby pumped her fist. "Finally!"

"Let me try to break out," Topaz said, and orange-red flames began to rise from her body. The fire grew more intense, wrapping around her torso and arms like a living thing. Where the flames touched the invisible binding, they revealed it in negative space, bending and shaping around bands of magic wrapped tight around her body. The fire began eating at them slowly, small pieces charring and flaking away like burning paper.

After almost a minute, Topaz let the flames die down, breathing hard. "I can't break through," she said, frustration clear in her voice. "Not yet, anyway. Can you let me outta this thing?"

"Release," Darby said, and the binding vanished instantly.

Topaz rolled her shoulders, as if working out stiffness. "I think it was weakening though. I could feel my fire affecting it. I need to work on strengthening my fire magic. If I could make it hotter and more intense, maybe I might be able to burn through bindings like this."

Topaz gave Darby an evil grin. "Okay, my turn. Prepare thyself, Darby!"

Snorting a laugh, Darby positioned herself a few feet away and waited. Topaz raised her hands and spoke the binding words. Orange-red energy flared around her palms, and Darby felt heat wrap around her body. It was pleasant at first, like standing in warm sunshine or near a campfire.

"I feel it," Darby said. "But it's getting hot—"

The heat intensified suddenly. Darby smelled smoke and looked down to see char marks spreading across her shirt in stripes – like whip marks where the invisible ropes of the binding had wrapped around her torso.

"Topaz!" Jazmin shouted.

Topaz released the spell immediately, and Jazmin rushed forward with a spray of water, dousing the smoking fabric before it could actually catch fire.

"Oh shit, Darby! I'm so sorry!" Topaz rushed over, her face stricken. "Did I burn you? Are you hurt?"

Darby looked down at her wet, charred shirt and checked her skin underneath. "Not a single burn. Just some scorch marks on my shirt." She pulled at the singed fabric with a grin. "And honestly? Roy gave me this shirt, so I'm not exactly sad to see it go."

Topaz let out a relieved laugh. "Jesus, you scared me. I thought I'd actually hurt you."

Kara laughed and raised her hands. "Hold still, Darby." A hot breeze swirled around Darby, gentle but persistent, the air moving in controlled spirals around her torso. Within seconds, the damp fabric began to dry, steam rising from the wet spots.

"That's handy," Darby said, feeling the warmth of the wind without any of the burning sensation from Topaz's fire.

"It's just directing warm air," Kara said with a grin. "I'm getting better at controlling the temperature."

They all stared at the charred spots on Darby's shirt.

"Okay," Topaz said, looking sheepish. "So I need more practice with the binding spell."

"Try it on one of the tombstones first," Ivette suggested. "Get control over your fire before trying it on a person again."

Topaz nodded and moved to face a squat granite headstone. She practiced the binding spell over and over, each time checking to see if the stone showed any scorch marks. After about ten attempts, she seemed satisfied.

"I think I've got it now," she said.

"I'll be your test subject again," Darby offered.

Topaz's eyes widened. "Are you sure? I almost set you on fire."

"You were nowhere near to setting me on fire," Darby assured her. "It was just some singed fabric. But let's have Jazmin ready with water, just in case."

Jazmin moved closer, hands ready. "Say the word and I'll douse you."

Topaz took a deep breath and raised her hands. She spoke the binding words, and this time when Darby felt the heat, it stayed warm but not burning. The invisible restraints wrapped around her arms and torso, holding her immobile, but no fire touched her.

"It worked!" Topaz released the spell and immediately pulled Darby into a hug. "Thank you. You're a total badass for being my test dummy. I can't believe you volunteered again after I literally burned your clothes."

Darby laughed, hugging her back. "That's what coven sisters are for, right?"

They continued practicing, proceeding with a little more caution as they tried each new spell. They tried the mirror ward next – a spell that was supposed to reflect hostile magic back at its source. None of them could make it work at all, though Kara thought she felt something shimmer in the air when she tried.

They tried the flash burst spell next, meant to create a blinding light that would give them time to escape. It went better than expected – perhaps too well. When Jazmin cast it, the flash was so bright it lit up the entire cemetery like a lightning strike, throwing stark shadows across the headstones and briefly illuminating the surrounding factory walls.

They all froze, looking around nervously to see if anyone had noticed, blinking away the spots in their vision.

"Maybe dial that back a bit," Darby said quietly. "We don't want to attract attention."

"Also," Kara added, rubbing her eyes, "we can't use it against an opponent if it blinds us too. We need to figure out how to shield ourselves from the effects while casting it."

"Good point," Jazmin said, wincing. "I'll work on controlling the intensity and maybe... closing my eyes before I cast it?"

"Or we could research a protective ward specifically for sensory attacks," Ivette suggested. "Something we can activate before using spells like this."

"We should practice fire suppression," Darby said. "We need to be able to fight back if the Torch Bearers try to use fire against us."

The mood sobered instantly.

Kara flipped through the grimoire until she found the page. "Here's the smothering spell. It's supposed to suffocate flames."

"I'll create the fire," Topaz said, stepping forward. She cupped her hands and conjured a flame about the size of a basketball and dropped it into an empty stone urn near one of the monuments. The fire crackled and danced inside the vessel, contained but eager. "Jazmin, you're our backup in case this goes wrong."

Jazmin nodded, raising her hands with water already swirling between her palms.

Kara went first. She spoke the incantation and made a pressing motion with both hands. The flame flickered and shrank but didn't die completely.

"Again," Ivette encouraged.

Kara tried once more, putting more force behind the gesture. This time, the flame collapsed in on itself and snuffed out completely.

"Yes!" Kara pumped her fist.

They each took turns practicing while Topaz patiently reignited the flame and Jazmin stood ready with water. After several attempts, most of them could extinguish the flame reliably.

"Bigger," Darby said after her third successful attempt.

Topaz raised an eyebrow but obliged, creating a bonfire-sized blaze that crackled and roared. It took more effort, but Darby managed to smother it, the flames dying with a satisfying whoosh.

"Good," Ivette said. "Now we have more options if they try to burn us out."

They worked on their elemental affinities next. Topaz practiced shaping her fire. First, she was able to compress it into the shape of a curved blade and then claws of flame that extended from her fingertips. Ivette learned to make electricity arc between her fingers in controlled bursts, then tried weaving the lightning into a crackling whip that snapped through the air. Jazmin experimented with shaping water into different forms – a sword with a razor-sharp edge, a shield that rippled and shifted. With concentration, she could also freeze the water solid, creating dense ice projectiles she could lob like cannonballs.

Kara tried the wind funnel spell from the grimoire. She stood with her hands raised, speaking the words carefully, and Darby watched as the air around her began to swirl. Leaves and debris lifted from the ground, spinning faster and faster, forming a small but definite tornado about three feet tall. It lasted for maybe ten seconds before Kara lost her concentration and it dissipated.

"That was amazing!" Jazmin said, her eyes wide.

"It was tiny," Kara said, but she was smiling. "But I did it. I actually did it."

Darby worked on her own affinity, focusing on control rather than simple growth. She selected a weathered tombstone and called to the ivy creeping nearby, coaxing the vines to wrap around the granite marker. At first, they moved sluggishly, but as she concentrated, they began to tighten like a boa constrictor, the stone groaning faintly under the pressure. She made the vines release, then tried again, working on the speed and strength of the constriction.

Thinking about protection, she turned her attention to the edges of the cemetery. She called to the vines growing along the chain-link fence, encouraging thorns to sprout along their lengths – small at first, then longer and sharper as she pushed harder. The thorns gleamed wickedly in the moonlight as she wove the vines together into a denser, more hostile barrier. Roots from nearby plants responded to her will, pushing up to create natural obstacles that would make the cemetery even more difficult to accidentally stumble upon. Her magic was slower than the others', less flashy, but there was something deeply satisfying about feeling life respond to her will. And knowing she was adding another layer of concealment and protection to their hidden practice space made her feel like she was pulling her weight.

*a*fter an hour of practice, they took a break, sitting on the steps of a crypt and passing around a water bottle Ivette had brought. The cemetery was peaceful around them; the city sounds distant and muted. Darby found herself glancing at the headstones, reading the names and dates carved into the weathered stone. How many of these people had lived and died in this city, their stories forgotten now except for these markers?

"Okay," she said, standing up and brushing off her jeans. "I want to test the witch ball."

The others gathered around as Darby carefully unwrapped the amber and gold sphere from her backpack. It caught the moonlight, gleaming softly, and she could feel the protective ward humming inside the glass.

"How do we do that?" Jazmin asked.

"I'm going to put it on the ground over there," Darby said, pointing to a flat area about ten feet away. "And then I'm going to try to hit it with one of our offensive spells."

"Which spell?" Topaz asked.

Darby had been thinking about this. Most of the magic they'd been practicing tonight was defensive in nature – bindings, wards, cloaking. She wanted something she could truly use to fight back against an opponent. There was one spell in the grimoire that seemed perfect: a hex that would hit the target with a bolt of concentrated magical force, like a punch made of magic.

"The striking hex," she said. "If the ward works, it should stop or deflect the attack. If it doesn't..." She shrugged. "Then I'll know I need to strengthen the ward before I make more."

"Are you sure you want to do this?" Kara asked nervously. "What if the spell is too strong and you break the witch ball?"

"Then I make another one," Darby said with more confidence than she felt.

She carried the witch ball to the flat area and set it carefully on a section of unbroken pavement. Then she walked back to where the others waited, putting about ten feet of distance between herself and the sphere.

"Everybody stand back," she said.

Darby took a breath and reached for her magic, feeling it rise up eagerly in response. But this time she didn't call to the plants. She focused on the witch ball, visualizing the striking hex – a sphere of pure magical force she could hurl at the target.

She spoke the words from the grimoire, feeling power rush through her and gather in her hand. The energy coalesced into a glowing greenish orb, crackling against her palm like static electricity. She drew her arm back and threw it.

The spell struck the witch ball and rebounded, shooting back at her before she could react. It was too fast to dodge.

Darby didn't have time to register what was happening before the deflected strike hit her square in the chest. The impact knocked her clean off her feet, sending her flying backward. She hit the ground hard, the breath driven from her lungs in a painful whoosh.

"Darby!" Kara rushed forward, but Darby was already laughing.

"It worked!" she gasped, staring up at the night sky with a

huge grin on her face. She coughed a couple of times, trying to get her breath back. "It actually worked! The ward deflected the spell back at me!"

Topaz helped her sit up while Ivette and Jazmin examined the witch ball, which sat exactly where Darby had placed it, completely undamaged.

Ivette picked up the sphere, holding it up to the moonlight. "I can see it – the threads inside the glass are glowing and pulsing faintly."

"Did it hurt?" Jazmin asked Darby.

"A little. I didn't make the strike hex as strong as I could have, so the spell just redirected at the same strength I used – not amplified." She rubbed her lower back, still grinning. "My ass hurts, but I managed to thicken the grass and moss right before I hit. Did it almost without thinking." Pride warmed her chest at that small victory. Her plant magic was becoming second nature. She struggled to her feet, wincing. "I need to make more witch balls. Like, a lot more."

"Slow down," Topaz said, but she was smiling too. "You're getting ahead of yourself. But yeah, this is huge. How many do you think you can make?"

"I don't know," Darby admitted. "Making them is a little bit time-consuming, and I'll need more orbs. Next, I want to create one and see if I can put a spell inside it."

They spent another thirty minutes practicing, their spirits lifted by the success of the witch ball. Darby's confidence grew with each spell they attempted, even the ones that didn't quite work. They were learning and getting stronger. Maybe not fast enough to face any enemies yet, but they were on their way.

Finally, as exhaustion began to set in, they packed up their supplies and headed back through the cemetery toward the gap in the fence.

CHAPTER 22

They were almost to the break in the fence – now even more well-hidden by the vines Darby had woven through the chain-link – when Topaz suddenly stopped walking.

"Hey," she said, turning to face Darby and Kara. "I've been wondering about something. How exactly did you two find all those other covens that were killed? How did you know to look for groups of women who had died?"

Darby and Kara exchanged a glance. They hadn't really discussed the details with the others. There had been too much else to worry about.

"It was strange," Darby said slowly. "I was trying to search for information about testing protective wards, and my laptop just... started acting on its own. The cursor moved without me touching the trackpad. Browser windows opened. It went directly to those news articles about the fires."

"Like someone hacked it?" Jazmin asked.

"That's what we thought at first," Darby said. "But it didn't feel like hacking. It felt..." She struggled to find the right words. "It felt like something was trying to communicate. Like someone wanted me to see those articles. Wanted me to know about the other covens."

"And it wasn't the first time," Kara added quietly. "Darby told me that she'd felt a presence before. Right, Darby?"

Darby nodded. "When the lights flicker in the apartment. It's been happening since I moved in, but it got more frequent after we started practicing magic. I thought it was just old wiring at first, but now..." She trailed off, thinking about that sensation of cold fingers brushing against her hands, and the keys pressing down on their own beneath her palms. "Now I think it might be something else."

"Like what?" Topaz asked.

"A ghost?" Ivette said slowly. She looked around at the cemetery surrounding them, her expression thoughtful. "When I was a kid, one of my cousins' houses was haunted. Lights would go haywire, and doors would slam shut on their own. Things would fly across rooms. My aunt swears the ghost tried to possess her once." She shivered at the memory. "Restless spirits that stay on the earthly plane? They're usually not good. There's a reason they haven't moved on."

"Did she ever figure out what it wanted?" Jazmin asked.

"No. But she eventually got her priest to cleanse the house." Ivette looked at Darby, her expression serious. "Does this presence feel angry? Evil? Has it been pushing at your consciousness, like it's trying to get in?" Her voice dropped. "It could be trying to possess you."

"No," Darby said firmly. "It feels cold, but not evil. And I've never gotten the sense that it wants to possess me. It only briefly brushed against my hands once; we were both trying to type on my computer at the same time." She paused, remembering that strange moment. "Those articles that it showed me – it gave us information we wouldn't have found on our own. It showed me that we might be in danger. I think it's trying to help."

"I have a Ouija board at home," Jazmin said suddenly. Everyone turned to look at her. "What? I bought it at a thrift store a couple of years ago. I thought it would be fun for parties, but I never actually used it because it felt too weird."

"You want to try to communicate with whatever's been helping Darby?" Kara asked.

"Why not?" Jazmin looked around at all of them. "We're literally witches standing in a cemetery at two in the morning. We just spent the last two hours casting spells and testing magical wards. A Ouija board is the least weird thing we've done all night."

Topaz let out a laugh. "She's got a point."

"When we get back to the apartment," Jazmin continued, "I could grab the board and we could see if it really is a ghost. Maybe it could tell us more about those other covens. Or at least tell us if it's trying to help or hurt us."

Darby felt a shiver run down her spine that had nothing to do with the cool night air. The idea of deliberately trying to contact whatever presence had been in her apartment, whatever had taken control of her laptop – it was both terrifying and compelling.

"I think we should do it," she said finally. "If there's something trying to communicate with us, we should at least try to understand what it wants."

Jazmin pulled out her phone as they walked, her thumb scrolling through search results. "Okay, so we already have the board... it says we need candles, and we should cleanse the space first. I have some sage bundles we can use." She squinted at the screen. "Ask for protection from negative entities, be respectful, don't taunt anything..." She continued murmuring instructions to herself, occasionally pausing to absorb the warnings and recommendations.

They walked the rest of the way back to the apartment building in tired silence, each of them lost in their own thoughts.

Darby's butt ached from being knocked down by her own spell, but she felt strangely energized. They'd practiced magic success-fully. They'd proven the witch ball worked.

And next... they might finally get answers about who, or what, was trying to help them.

CHAPTER 23

The walk back to their apartment building felt longer than usual, streetlights casting long shadows across the empty sidewalk. Darby kept glancing over her shoulder, half-expecting to see ghostly figures trailing behind them. But the street remained ordinary; even the bar around the corner seemed to be quieting down for the night, the usual raucous noise faded to a low murmur.

They took the elevator up, and Darby found herself watching the overhead lights, waiting for them to blink. But nothing happened. The elevator dinged cheerfully at their floor, and Jazmin and Ivette peeled off toward their apartment. "Give us a minute," Jazmin called over her shoulder. "I need to grab the board."

"We'll leave the door unlocked," Kara called after them, fishing out her keys.

Inside, Kara flipped on the lights as Darby and Topaz filed in. The apartment looked exactly as they'd left it that morning: breakfast bowls in the sink, Kara's crochet project draped over the armchair, a stack of library books teetering on the end table.

Normal and safe. The kind of space that shouldn't be hosting a séance.

"Living room or kitchen?" Topaz asked.

"Living room," Kara said, already heading that way. "More space. Let me make sure all the curtains are closed."

A moment later, Jazmin and Ivette let themselves in. Jazmin held up the Ouija board box triumphantly. Ivette made the sign of the cross.

"If my mother could see this, she'd roll over in her grave," Ivette muttered.

"Well, we could ask her opinion now," Jazmin said with a grin, gesturing to the Ouija board.

"Jazmin, don't start. My mother would've pulled out la chancla for that sass." But there was a hint of a smile tugging at Ivette's mouth.

"Okay, coffee table," Topaz announced, already moving the books to the floor. "Jazzy, can you get the candles?"

"Three white ones, like the internet said." Jazmin set the Ouija board box down and pulled out the candles, arranging them in a triangle on the cleared table. "We're supposed to light them before we start."

Ivette pulled out a bundle of sage from her bag, using one of the candles to light one end. "If we're doing this, we're doing it right." She wafted the fragrant smoke around the living room in deliberate sweeps, paying special attention to the corners and the space around the coffee table. "I release all negative energy from this space," she murmured, her voice steady and clear. "May peace and protection fill this home."

Darby watched as they set up, her stomach tight with nervousness. This was really happening. They were about to try to contact whatever presence had been messing with her computer. The sage smoke made the air hazy, giving everything a ritualistic weight.

"So how does this work?" Topaz asked, eyeing the board as

Jazmin pulled it from its box. The planchette, a heart-shaped pointer, gleamed in the candlelight.

"Two people put their fingers on the planchette," Jazmin explained, her voice taking on a professorial tone that made a grin pull at Darby's lips. "You ask questions, and the spirit moves it to spell out answers. Everyone else should sit nearby and observe but not touch the board or the people using it."

"Who wants to do it?" Darby asked, hoping some of the others would volunteer.

"I'll do it," Jazmin responded quickly, reaching for the planchette.

"Absolutely not." Ivette's voice cracked like a whip.

Jazmin's head whipped around. "Abuela—"

"My granddaughter is not opening herself up to some evil entity. No." Ivette crossed her arms, her expression brooking no argument.

"But I brought the board! I know how to—"

"Listen to your grandmother," Topaz said gently. She moved to sit cross-legged in front of the coffee table, gesturing for Jazmin to step back. "We don't know what we're actually dealing with here or what its true intentions are. We're not risking you."

"I don't believe it's an evil entity," Ivette said, her tone measured. "But we're being cautious." Her expression softened slightly as Jazmin reluctantly moved to sit on the couch beside her.

"I'll do it with you," Kara said, settling across from Topaz. She rolled her shoulders and stretched her neck side to side. "Worst case scenario, what? It spells out something creepy, and we throw holy water at it?"

"Do we have holy water?" Darby asked.

"No, but I'm sure we can improvise."

Jazmin pulled out her phone, her fingers flying across the screen. "Okay, I'm looking up what to do if things go wrong." She scrolled quickly, her eyes scanning. "If the planchette starts moving really fast – like counting down numbers or going through the alphabet – that's bad. It means something's trying to escape."

"Escape?" Darby's stomach dropped. "Escape where? Like, into our apartment?"

"Apparently." Jazmin kept reading. "Or if it makes a figure-eight pattern, or goes to all four corners of the board. Oh, and if anything identifies itself as 'Zozo,' we end it immediately."

Zozo? What the hell were they getting themselves into?

"What do we do if that happens?" Topaz asked, her voice steady despite the growing tension in the room.

"Say 'Goodbye' firmly, move the planchette to the goodbye spot on the board, then take it off and separate it from the board." Jazmin looked up, her expression serious. "We have to stay calm no matter what. This website says that panicking makes it worse."

"Got it," Kara said. "Anything else?"

Jazmin glanced back at her screen. "Just... be respectful, keep our questions clear, and don't ask about death or anything that could provoke it." She set her phone down beside her on the couch. "The second anything feels wrong, we shut it down. No hesitation."

Darby shook her head, moving toward the kitchen. "I'm making coffee. I'm not used to being up this late. I'm so glad it's the weekend." The normalcy of the task helped settle her nerves. The machine gurgled to life, filling the apartment with the rich smell of brewing coffee.

When she returned to the living room with her steaming mug, Kara and Topaz were already positioned at the coffee table. Candlelight cast dancing shadows across their faces.

"Everyone ready?" Topaz asked.

Darby settled onto the arm of the couch near Topaz, cradling her coffee mug in both hands. "As ready as we're going to be."

Kara and Topaz both placed their fingertips lightly on the planchette. It sat in the center of the board, surrounded by the alphabet arcing across the top half, numbers below, and *Yes* and *No* in the upper corners.

"Are we supposed to say something first?" Kara whispered.

"You're supposed to invite the spirit to communicate," Jazmin said. "Ask if anyone's there."

Topaz cleared her throat. "Is there a spirit present who wishes to communicate with us?"

For a long moment, nothing happened. The planchette sat motionless beneath their fingers. Darby took a sip of her coffee, the heat scalding her tongue.

Then the planchette began to move.

It glided smoothly across the board, both Topaz and Kara's eyes widening as it traveled to the upper left corner.

YES.

"Oh shit," Kara breathed. "Oh shit, it's real."

"Are you moving it?" Ivette leaned forward, suspicious.

"No!" Topaz's voice was tight. "I swear, I'm barely touching it."

Darby set her coffee mug on her knee, leaning in to watch more closely. The candlelight made it hard to see clearly, shadows obscuring the letters.

"Are you a ghost?" Topaz asked, her voice steadier now.

The planchette moved again, more quickly this time.

YES.

"Are we in danger?"

A pause, longer this time. Then the smooth glide across the board.

YES.

Jazmin made a small sound in her throat. Ivette put an arm around her shoulders.

"What is your name?" Kara asked.

The planchette began to move in a deliberate circuit around the board. B. E. L. L. A.

"Bella," Darby murmured. The name sent a chill down her spine, even though it should've sounded harmless. It was actually a pretty name. But hearing it made it all real somehow. It wasn't just a presence or an entity – it was an actual person.

The planchette was moving again, faster now, more urgently. It darted from letter to letter without waiting for another question.

B. E. W. A. R. E.

"Beware," Topaz read aloud. "Beware of what?"

The planchette kept moving, but faster, almost frantically now.

"I'm not moving this!" Kara said, her voice rising. "Topaz, are you—"

"No! I swear. It's moving on its own!"

T. O.

The planchette jerked toward the next letter. Darby leaned forward without thinking, and her coffee mug tilted in her grip. Hot liquid sloshed over the rim, burning her hand.

"Ah!" She jerked back, and more coffee spilled – this time arcing through the air to splash onto Topaz's shoulder and across the Ouija board.

"Ow!" Topaz yanked her hands away. The sudden movement sent the planchette skittering wildly across the board before it flew off the edge and clattered across the floor.

"Sorry! I'm so sorry!" Darby set her mug down quickly, grabbing tissues from the end table. "Oh my god, are you okay? Is it bad?"

"It's fine, just hot." Topaz pulled her shirt away from her shoulder, grimacing. "More startling than anything."

Kara was staring at the board, where coffee now pooled around the letters. "What was it trying to spell?"

Ivette appeared with a roll of paper towels, already tearing off sheets. She hesitated for a moment, eyeing the board with visible reluctance, then started carefully blotting the spill.

Jazmin leaned forward to study the board as Ivette wiped up the coffee. "What direction was it heading?"

"It was moving to the right," Kara said slowly. She traced the path with her finger, careful not to touch the wet board. "From O, moving right... I feel like it was headed to R next."

"Torch," Darby whispered. The word felt like ice in her mouth. "Beware Torch Bearers."

The candles wavered, though there was no breeze in the apartment. Everyone stared at the coffee-stained board, at the letters that spelled out their worst fears.

"Bella," Topaz said quietly. "You think that's her real name?"

"I don't know." Darby wrapped her arms around herself. The apartment suddenly felt too cold, too exposed. "But she's trying to warn us. Just like she did with the articles."

"Or scare us," Ivette said, but she didn't sound convinced.

Jazmin was typing furiously on her phone. "There has to be something online about this. About Bella, about the Torch Bearers—"

"Not tonight." Ivette stood, reaching for the candles. "I think we've done enough ghost hunting for one evening. Let's clean this up and try to get some sleep."

"Wait." Kara held up a hand. "We can't just leave it like this. She was in the middle of telling us something."

Ivette hesitated, looking reluctant.

"I don't know if it's a good idea," Topaz protested.

"One more try," Kara pressed. "Then we close it out the right way, like Jazmin said. We can't just walk away from an open session."

Jazmin nodded vigorously. "She's right. You're supposed to say goodbye. It's bad luck not to."

Ivette sighed, but she sat back down. "Fine. One more attempt. Then we're done."

Once the board was dry, Kara retrieved the planchette from where it had landed near the bookshelf. She and Topaz resumed their positions, fingertips resting lightly on the pointer.

"Bella?" Kara's voice was gentle. "Are you still there? We're sorry about the interruption. We want to hear what you have to say."

The planchette gave a faint, jerky twitch, then stilled.

They waited. The apartment was silent except for the distant hum of the refrigerator and the muffled sound of a car passing on the street below. Darby found herself holding her breath.

"Bella, if you can hear us, please respond," Kara tried. "We're listening."

The planchette shuddered, sliding half an inch before stopping, as if whatever was pushing it had run out of strength.

Topaz and Kara exchanged a glance. "Maybe she used up her energy," Kara said quietly. "Or maybe we scared her off when the board got disrupted."

"Or maybe she said what she needed to say," Topaz suggested.

They sat in silence for another minute, but the board remained still. Whatever presence had animated it before was gone – or at least, no longer willing to communicate.

Topaz took a breath. "Alright. Let's close this properly." She looked to Jazmin. "We just say goodbye and move it to the word?"

Jazmin nodded. "Say it out loud, move the planchette there together, then take your hands off."

"Thank you for speaking with us tonight, Bella," Kara said, her voice formal. "Goodbye."

"Goodbye," Topaz echoed.

Together, they guided the planchette down to the word printed at the bottom of the board. They lifted their hands. Kara immediately separated the planchette from the board, setting it aside.

"That's it?" Darby asked.

"That's it." Jazmin stood, stretching. "Session closed. Officially."

CHAPTER 24

 orning light filtered through the curtains, too bright and too early. Darby stumbled out of her bedroom in an old t-shirt and sleep shorts, her hair sticking up at odd angles. She'd managed maybe three hours of actual sleep, the rest spent staring at her ceiling, replaying the Ouija board session over and over.

She stopped short in the hallway. Kara was curled up on the couch in yesterday's clothes, her laptop balanced on her knees, surrounded by a nest of papers and open books. Dark circles shadowed her eyes, and her usually neat hair hung limp around her face. A single coffee mug sat on the table beside her, the inside stained with dark rings from repeated refills. Glancing toward the kitchen, Darby saw that the coffee pot was nearly empty.

"Did you sleep at all?" Darby asked.

Kara looked up, blinking like she'd forgotten other people existed. "A little." She rubbed her eyes. "I kept thinking about Bella. About who she might be."

Darby moved into the kitchen and grabbed the coffee pot. She poured the last of it into Kara's mug, reheating what was already there, then started a fresh pot brewing. She had a feeling they were going to need it.

She settled into the armchair. "And?"

"You remember the first coven we found? The one that died in the fire?"

"You mean Alice's coven from Briarton?"

"Yes." Kara turned her laptop around. On the screen was a newspaper article they'd found weeks ago, the image grainy and pixelated from being scanned. "The Willowbrook Garden Club fire. Alice Auclair, April Auclair, Olivia Blackwood, Brenda McAllister, and..." She tapped the screen. "Isabella Rousseau."

Darby nodded. "Bella."

"Maybe." Kara pulled the laptop back, scrolling through more articles. "I've been reading everything I can find about the fire. She was thirty-two. A nurse. She'd moved to Briarton about a year before the fire."

"Do you want to try the Ouija board again? See if we can talk to her?"

"No." Kara's response was immediate and firm. She shook her head. "I don't want to use that thing without everyone here. Just in case." She glanced toward the kitchen counter where they'd left the board, now safely back in its box. "I mean, I don't think Bella's dangerous. But we can't be sure. And both Topaz and Ivette have to work today."

"So what do you want to do now?"

Kara closed her laptop with a decisive snap. "Briarton's less than a two-hour drive from here. We could go there, take a look around, and maybe ask some questions. See if we can get a better sense of who these women were." She stood, gathering her scattered papers. "I've got my car. We could leave after breakfast?"

"A road trip to investigate a fire based on a ghost's warning." Darby laughed, but it came out shaky. "Sure. Why not? It's not like my life's weird enough."

An hour later, they were in Kara's little blue sedan, heading south out of Medeon. Darby watched the city roll past her window. The gray skyline of downtown gave way to older neighborhoods with brick houses and tree-lined streets. They passed the art museum with its distinctive glass facade, then the sprawling campus of the university, where students were already trudging to early Saturday morning classes.

The dense urban blocks slowly morphed into wider streets, the buildings growing shorter and farther apart. Strip malls appeared, their parking lots half-empty in the morning light. Fast food chains clustered together at intersections. The kind of suburban sprawl that could be anywhere in America.

Kara merged onto the highway, and the landscape opened up. Concrete and asphalt gave way to forest and fields. Some fields were planted with late-season crops, while others lay fallow and brown in the autumn chill. Farmhouses dotted the horizon, their red barns stitched into the gray landscape like bright patches on a drab quilt.

"It's pretty out here," Darby said, watching a flock of birds startle from a fence line and take flight.

"Mm." Kara kept her eyes on the road. "I grew up in a place like this. Before I moved to the city for college."

They drove in comfortable silence, the hum of the engine and the rush of wind through the slightly-open window the only sounds. The highway narrowed from four lanes to two. The farms grew smaller and more picturesque. White fences appeared – the kind that belonged in paintings.

"Ten more miles," Kara said, glancing at her phone in its holder on the dashboard.

Briarton announced itself with a faded green sign: *Welcome to Briarton. Population 1,437. Established 1887.*

The speed limit dropped to thirty-five, then to twenty-five as they entered what passed for the downtown area.

It was the kind of town that postcards were made of. The main street, which was literally named Main Street, was lined with two-story brick buildings housing small shops, a diner, a hardware store with dusty window displays, and a pharmacy that looked like it hadn't updated its facade since the 1950s. The sidewalks were clean, the flower boxes still held late-blooming flowers, and an American flag snapped in the breeze above the post office.

"Cute," Darby murmured.

"Very." Kara drove slowly through the town center, both of them craning their necks to look around. A few people walked the sidewalks – older folks mostly, moving with the unhurried pace of those who had nowhere to be.

They circled the small downtown square, where a white gazebo stood in the center of a neat park, then Kara turned down a side street. She followed the directions on her phone's GPS, winding through residential blocks lined with older stately homes. The houses grew sparser and the lots larger. They turned onto what was barely more than a gravel lane, passing a weathered church that stood like a pale ghost beside its overgrown cemetery.

"There." Darby pointed, slowing to a crawl.

Where the Willowbrook Garden Club building had once stood was now just an overgrown lot. Grass had taken over, tall and wild, punctuated by scraggly bushes and the occasional sapling. A lone wooden shed stood at the back of the property, its paint weathered to gray, but otherwise intact. No building. No monument. Nothing to mark what had happened here except for a general air of neglect. The place felt forgotten, set apart from the rest of town. Open fields lay to the right, while skeletal trees on the left revealed weathered headstones scattered across the cemetery grounds.

Kara pulled over to the curb and killed the engine.

"This is it?" Darby stared at the empty lot. From the newspaper photos, she'd imagined something bigger, more substantial. But the lot was modest; maybe sixty feet across. The foundation was still visible if you looked closely, concrete footings poking through the grass like old bones.

"Let's take a look."

They got out of the car. The air was colder here, away from the city's heat-absorbing concrete and wind-blocking skyscrapers. Darby pulled her jacket tighter as they stepped onto the lot. Their footsteps swished through the tall grass, and somewhere in the distance, a dog barked.

The foundation traced a rectangle about the size of a modest ranch house. The remnants of garden beds were scattered throughout the property, their shapes still visible beneath the years of wild growth. Paths wound between them, some paved with stones that poked through the grass, others barely discernible as slight depressions in the earth.

Darby picked her way across what was left of the building itself – nothing but crumbling foundation and a few scattered remnants. Twisted pieces of metal that might have been plumbing or fixtures, chunks of blackened wood that crumbled when she nudged them with her sneakers, shards of glass that caught the weak sunlight. It felt strange to walk through the space, stepping over the ghost of walls that no longer existed, standing where interior rooms had once been.

They moved slowly through the space, careful where they stepped. Kara crouched near what had probably been the center of the building, running her fingers over a section of floor tile that had survived.

The shed drew Darby's attention. It was small, maybe eight by ten feet, with a sloped roof and a single door that hung crooked on its hinges. Unlike everything else, it showed no signs of fire damage.

"Why didn't that burn?" she asked, pointing.

Kara looked up. "Far enough from the main building, I guess. Or maybe the wind was blowing the other direction."

A car engine approached, and Darby turned to see a police

cruiser pulling up behind Kara's sedan. An officer climbed out. The man was in his early sixties, Darby guessed, with a comfortable paunch straining against his uniform shirt and gray hair buzzed military-short. His hand rested casually on his belt as he approached, his expression more curious than hostile.

"Morning, ladies." His voice was friendly enough, but his eyes were taking inventory. "Can I ask what you're doing?"

Kara straightened immediately, her face sliding into a professional mask. "Good morning, Officer. We're insurance adjusters with Consolidated Heritage Mutual." The lie came out smooth as silk. "We're looking for Brenda McAllister."

The officer's eyes narrowed slightly. "This about the fire?"

"Yes, sir."

He let out a long breath, shaking his head. "What a shame that whole thing was. Truly devastated this community." He looked past them at the empty lot, his expression softening into something sad. "That fire claimed four good women. Alice Auclair taught my daughter piano. Olivia used to bring flowers from her garden to the church every Sunday."

"It must have been difficult," Kara said gently.

"Still is, for some folks." He turned his attention back to them. "But Brenda left town not long after the fire. Said she couldn't stay after everything that happened. Lost the people she cared about most in the world." He scratched his jaw. "Can't say I blamed her. Between the grief and everyone's pity – you know how small towns can be – she just couldn't seem to get past it. Last I heard, she went somewhere out west."

Kara pulled out her phone, tapping at the screen like she was checking a file. "Can you describe her? We have conflicting information in our records and want to make sure we're looking for the right individual."

The officer's eyes narrowed slightly. "Why are you looking for Ms. McAllister? What's an insurance company want with a survivor from a fire that happened years ago?"

Kara didn't miss a beat. "There's a settlement check we've been trying to deliver. It's been sitting in our system for years, and we need to either get it to her or officially mark it as unclaimed."

He studied them for a long moment. Darby forced herself to breathe normally, to look bored rather than nervous. Finally, he shrugged. "Dark hair. Medium build, maybe five-five, hundred and twenty pounds soaking wet. Pretty girl, mid-twenties if I had to guess. But that was a few years ago now."

"Any distinguishing features?" Kara asked. "Scars, tattoos, birthmarks?"

"Not that I recall." He hooked his thumbs in his belt. "She was just... normal looking, you know? She was pretty, but also the kind of person you'd pass on the street and not think twice about."

"Worth a try." Kara inclined her head. "Thank you for your time, Officer...?"

"Murphy. Sheriff Murphy, actually." He glanced back at the lot. "I should mention, even though there's nothing left here, this is still private property. The town owns it now. You need to move along."

"Of course. We were just taking a quick look. We'll get out of your way."

"Appreciate it." He nodded to them both, then headed back to his cruiser. But he didn't drive away immediately. He sat there, watching them through his windshield.

"Well, that was informative," Darby muttered, keeping her voice low as they walked back toward the lot.

"Brenda sounds like she could be anyone." Frustration crept into Kara's tone. "We'll probably never find her."

They had maybe a minute before Sheriff Murphy would probably force them to leave. Darby's eyes drifted back to the shed. "Let's check that out at least."

They walked around the perimeter of the foundation, angling

toward the shed. It looked even more weathered up close, the wood dry and splintered. The door hung open an inch with darkness visible through the gap.

Darby moved along the side of the shed, where the grass was thinner, worn down by rainwater runoff. Her shoes squelched in a muddy patch. She was about to suggest they just leave when something on the shed wall caught her eye.

She stopped short.

Spray-painted on the weathered wood, faded but still visible, was a crude drawing of a torch. The flame was rendered in orange paint, the handle in black. And beneath it, in messy letters that had faded to near invisibility, were words she couldn't quite make out.

"Kara." Her voice came out thin.

Kara hurried over. "What—" She saw the torch and went still.

They both leaned in, squinting at the graffiti. The spray paint had been worn by years of weather, the letters ghost-pale and incomplete.

"Can you read that?" Darby asked.

"Not... something." Kara traced the air above the faded letters. "Suffer, maybe? The rest is too worn."

Darby pulled out her phone, snapping photos from different angles, hoping the camera might pick up what her eyes couldn't. "It's a torch," she said quietly, her stomach dropping, thinking about Bella's warning.

"Sheriff Murphy!" Kara called out, her voice taking on that professional tone again.

The sheriff had been about to pull away, but he stopped, his window rolling down. "Yes?"

They walked back toward his cruiser, Kara gesturing to the shed. "We found some graffiti back there. A torch symbol with some text we can't quite make out. Do you know anything about it?"

Sheriff Murphy's brow furrowed. "The graffiti? That wasn't

discovered until a bit after the fire. A neighbor noticed it maybe...
a little after the fire? Hard to say if it was there before or showed
up after."

"You couldn't determine when it was painted?" Kara asked.

He shook his head. "By the time we found it, we couldn't be
sure. Could've been there a week, could've been there a month."
He drummed his fingers on the steering wheel. "We've got reason
to believe it was some local teens. You know how kids are – they
see a tragedy, think it's edgy to leave their mark."

"But you're not certain?"

"Not certain, no. But Alice and Olivia were particular about
keeping the place nice. If it had been there before and they'd seen
it, I'm certain one of them would've reported it." He paused.
"Course, the shed's around the back. Maybe they just hadn't
noticed it."

"There was text with the torch symbol," Darby said. "But it's
too faded to read now. Do you remember what it said?"

"Something about not suffering? I can't remember exactly
what it is now. I believe I put it in all the reports, so you should
have that information. If not, your company can reach out to me
through formal channels to get that report." He scratched his jaw,
thinking. "I mean... I figured it was meant as a memorial kind of
thing. You know, like they're at peace now, not suffering
anymore. Seemed like an odd way to put it, but people can be
strange when faced with tragedy..." He shrugged.

"Our reports state that the fire was ruled accidental," Kara said
carefully. "Faulty wiring, correct?"

"That's right. It was an old building with original wiring from
the twenties. Fire marshal was thorough." His tone was firm. "It
was a terrible tragedy, but it was an accident."

"Of course," Kara said smoothly. "We just need to be thorough
for our records. You understand. The graffiti gave us pause."

He nodded curtly. "You ladies should probably move along
now."

"Sheriff, wait! I apologize, but I don't have my business card on me. But here's my number if you need to reach me. And if anyone can help get me in touch with Brenda McAllister, I'd really appreciate it." She rattled off her cell number, watching him enter it into his phone.

"Thank you for your time, Sheriff."

They watched him drive away, then turned back to the shed.

"So, he doesn't know when the graffiti showed up," Darby said quietly. "Could've been before. Could've been after."

"If it was before..." Kara trailed off, staring at the faded torch symbol. "Then maybe it was a warning or something."

Darby pulled out her phone, swiping through the photos she'd already taken. The torch symbol looked even more ominous on the small screen, the faded letters beneath it still maddeningly illegible.

"So what do we do now?" she asked, pocketing her phone.

Kara looked back toward the main road, then at Darby with a knowing look. "If this town is anything like the one I grew up in, we need to head to the best place to get the local gossip."

Darby grinned back. She grew up in a small town, too. "The diner?"

"The diner."

CHAPTER 25

The diner wasn't hard to find. In a town this size, there was only one place that could fit the bill: Burgess Family Kitchen, occupying the corner spot on the main square. The two-story brick structure had been painted a warm tan, the color now faded but well-maintained, with a closed insurance office on one side and a side street running along the other. Angle-parked spaces along the curb held a scattered collection of pickup trucks and cars that had seen better days.

Darby pulled open the diner's front door, a little bell jingling overhead. The scent of coffee, bacon grease, and cinnamon-sweet apples filled the air. The diner was bigger than it looked from outside, with a long counter running down the left and a scattering of booths and tables filling the rest of the space. Every surface was laminated or vinyl, the kind of easy-to-clean material that spoke of function over form.

Every head turned their way.

The conversations didn't stop exactly, but they stuttered. Gazes followed them across the room; customers at the counter swiveled on their stools, diners in booths paused mid-bite, and old men froze with their coffee cups halfway to their mouths.

Darby felt the weight of those stares like a physical thing, assessing and curious. She kept her expression neutral, friendly but not too eager.

An older woman with gray-streaked hair, cut short and curled tight, made her way over. She wore khaki slacks and a blue apron with "BFK" embroidered in yellow thread. She moved with the efficient ease of someone who'd been doing this job for longer than Darby had been alive.

"Afternoon, ladies. You want a booth?" The woman's smile was polite but measured, warm enough to be welcoming without quite reaching friendly.

Darby scanned the room. Several of the booths were available, but there was a small table near the counter, positioned right where they could see – and be seen by – most of the diner. Darby pointed to that table. "Actually, could we sit there? If that's okay?"

"Course you can." The woman's expression warmed a fraction. "Follow me."

She led them to the table, grabbing two laminated menus as she passed the register and handing them to Darby and Kara once they'd taken their seats. The menus were sticky in that way diner menus always are, the plastic worn thin at the edges.

"Name's Pearl," she said as they opened their menus. "Can I get you ladies something to drink?"

"Just water for me, thanks," Darby said.

"Same," Kara added.

"Be right back with those."

Pearl moved off toward the kitchen, and Darby opened her menu, acutely aware of the attention still on them. Conversations started up again, but quieter now, punctuated by the click of silverware on plates and the tinny sound of a radio playing in the kitchen.

She glanced at Kara, who was studying the menu with a focus that seemed overly intense for a diner. "Nervous?" Darby asked quietly.

"A little," Kara admitted. "I forgot what this feels like. Being the outsider. Everyone's talking about us, but no one's talking to us."

"That won't last," Darby said. "Curiosity always wins."

Pearl returned with two glasses of water, ice clinking as she set them down. The conversations around them picked up in volume, people returning to their meals, but Darby could still feel the occasional glance thrown their way, that prickle of eyes on the back of her neck.

"You two need a minute with the menu?" Pearl asked, pulling a pad and pencil from her apron pocket.

Darby scanned the offerings. The menu was filled with the usual home-cooked comfort food. Glancing around, she spotted a list of daily specials written on a chalkboard near the entrance. "What do you recommend?"

Pearl's expression brightened. "Can't go wrong with the meatloaf. We make it fresh every day, and the mashed potatoes are real, none of that instant stuff."

Meatloaf. Darby had never particularly cared for meatloaf, but she smiled and nodded. "That sounds great. I'll have that."

"BLT and fries for me," Kara said, closing her menu.

Pearl scribbled down their orders, then paused, pencil hovering over her pad. "So what brings you ladies to Briarton? Don't get many visitors this time of year."

Here was their opening. Darby glanced at Kara, who set her menu aside and leaned forward slightly, her voice friendly but professional. "We're with the insurance company that covered the fire at the garden club a couple years back. We're actually looking for Brenda McAllister. She has some unclaimed assets from the settlement, and we're trying to track her down before the funds revert to the state."

Pearl's eyebrows rose. "Unclaimed assets? How much money are we talking?"

"I'm not at liberty to say exactly," Kara said apologetically. "But enough that we'd hate for her to lose it just because we couldn't find her."

"Well." Pearl tapped her pencil against her pad. "I knew Brenda. Everyone in this town knows everyone, really. But I haven't seen her since just after the fire."

"Do you know where she went?" Darby asked.

Pearl shook her head. "She just... left. Packed up her apartment and disappeared. I always figured the fire messed her up, you know? Losing all those friends at once. That kind of thing breaks a person."

"Did she say anything to you before she left? Any idea where she might've gone?"

"Not a word. That girl kept to herself mostly, even before everything happened." Pearl glanced over her shoulder toward the kitchen. "Let me put your orders in. Be right back."

She walked away, and Darby caught Kara's eye. "Well, that's something at least."

"It's not much," Kara murmured. "But it's a start."

A voice piped up from a table near the window – a middle-aged woman with reading glasses perched on her nose. "I heard from the church choir director that Brenda said something about heading to the west coast. Oregon, maybe? Or was it Washington?"

Darby turned toward her. "Did she seem... I don't know, upset? Acting strange before she left?"

The woman shrugged. "Hard to say. My sister said that she was a quiet woman – kept to herself mostly. They sang in the church choir together for a bit. Brenda had only moved here about a year before the fire. Hadn't quite found her place in the community yet, you know? And then losing all those friends..." She trailed off.

"She was always a little odd," a man at the counter added, not looking up from his coffee. "Hippy-dippy type."

"Oh, come on, Dan," another woman said from a booth. "You

think anyone's hippy-dippy if they don't hunt and go to church every Sunday." A few people chuckled. "But I'll say this... the whole garden club group got a little weird after she joined. Started keeping to themselves more."

Pearl returned a moment later and, having clearly overheard, pulled out the chair at the end of their table and sat down. "You know, now that I think about it, there was something strange around the time of the fire."

"Strange how?" Kara asked.

"The garden club ladies – Alice and April and the others – they were acting secretive. Real hush-hush about something." Pearl folded her arms. "But we all just figured it was about the float."

"Float?"

"For the town's anniversary celebration. Happens every September. All the local groups make floats for the parade. The Rotary, the church groups, the garden club, everyone. It's a whole thing." Pearl's expression softened with memory. "The garden club always went all out. Their floats were always gorgeous. They'd been working on it for weeks."

A man's voice called out from a nearby booth. "They weren't being secretive about a damn float, Pearl. Those women were smoking pot."

Darby turned to see an older man, maybe in his fifties, leaning back in his booth with his arms crossed. He wore a flannel shirt and a John Deere cap, and his expression was smug.

Pearl shot him a look. "Don't start, Eugene."

"I'm just saying what everyone was thinking," Eugene said. "They were acting paranoid. Jumpy. That's pot behavior if I ever saw it."

A woman at the counter spun around on her stool. She was younger than Eugene, maybe late-thirties, with short blonde hair and cat-eye glasses. "They burned incense, Eugene. That doesn't make them pot-smoking hippies. I burn incense too."

"I'm just saying—"

"You're just spreading vicious gossip," the woman said flatly.

Pearl sighed. "Carol's right. They weren't smoking anything. They were just... I don't know. I think it was the float or maybe they were stressed about something."

"Was there anyone strange in town around that time?" Darby asked. "Anyone new, or anyone acting unusual?"

Pearl let out a short laugh. "Honey, there were lots of strange people in town back then."

"How so?"

"That big box store, MegaMart, was sniffing around." Pearl's expression darkened. "Sending their corporate suits to look at properties, trying to buy up land. They wanted to put one of their stores here."

The mention of MegaMart sparked an immediate reaction. Eugene leaned forward in his booth. "That would've been the best thing to happen to this town! Jobs, for Christ's sake. My son could've worked there instead of having to move to the city."

"Jobs that pay minimum wage," Carol shot back. "And what about all the businesses we'd lose? The hardware store, the pharmacy—"

"Those places are hanging on by a thread anyway," Eugene said.

"Because people like you would rather save two dollars at some soulless corporation than support your neighbors!"

"I support my neighbors by not going bankrupt buying overpriced—"

"Okay, okay," Pearl said, holding up her hands. The diner had gone from curious to animated, all the other conversations stopping to listen to the argument. "Let's not rehash this again."

"What happened?" Kara asked. "Did MegaMart not come to town?"

Pearl's face lit up with triumph, satisfied in a way that made her look ten years younger. "We pushed those corporate vultures right out. Town council voted it down, thank God."

"It wasn't just the council," Carol added. "The whole town rallied. There were protests, petitions. We weren't going to let them destroy what we'd built here."

"Look what happened to Greenfield," Pearl said, and several people in the diner murmured in agreement. "MegaMart moved in barely three years ago, and now? Their hardware store's gone. The fabric place closed last year. Hell, I heard that even their grocery store is struggling."

"Place is a ghost town now," Carol said. "Everything shuttered up except for the MegaMart and the gas stations."

"That's what happens," Pearl continued. "These big stores come in, promise the world, and then suck the life out of a place. We weren't going to let that happen here."

Darby absorbed this, her mind working. "So MegaMart wanted to build here, but the town said no. When was this exactly?"

"Started maybe six months before the fire?" Pearl looked around for confirmation, and a few people nodded. "They were here through the summer, trying to sweet-talk property owners. But by fall, we'd made it clear they weren't welcome."

"They gave up that easily?" Kara asked.

Pearl shrugged. "I guess they moved on to Greenfield. Easier pickings there, apparently."

Eugene muttered something that sounded like "Greenfield's smarter than us," but Carol threw a wadded-up napkin at him, and he shut up.

"Do you think the garden club ladies were stressed and acting strange because of MegaMart?" Darby asked carefully. "The pressure of fighting it?"

Pearl considered this. "Maybe. Alice was one of the biggest opponents. She spoke at the town council meeting, organized a petition. That kind of thing takes a toll."

"Could've been the church thing too," an older man at a nearby table added. He had a weathered face and work-worn hands wrapped around his coffee mug. "That organization that was thinking about moving into the abandoned church."

"What church?" Kara asked.

"The old Methodist church, right next door to the garden club," Carol said. "Been abandoned for years. That Beacon of Light group was interested in buying it and fixing it up."

"Why would that stress them out?" Darby asked.

The older man leaned back in his seat. "Well, there was some concern about the cemetery. It butts right up against the garden club's property line. Questions about whether the new church group would want to expand it, or if there'd be issues with the graves and the garden beds being so close together."

"The garden club ladies took care of that cemetery," Pearl added. "Kept the grass mowed, the headstones clean. They were protective of it."

"What happened with the church? We drove past it, and it looked abandoned." Kara asked. "Did the organization not end up buying it?"

Pearl shook her head. "Deal fell through after the fire. Building's still sitting there empty."

The bell above the door jingled, and a family walked in – a mom, dad, and two kids. Pearl stood up from the table. "I should get back to work. Your food'll be up in a few minutes."

"Thank you," Kara said. "You've been really helpful. We'll put in our report to search the west coast for Brenda."

"Pearl, wait—" Darby reached out. "Do you have a piece of paper? I'd like to leave my number with you, just in case anyone can think of a way to get a hold of Brenda."

Pearl pulled out her order pad, tore off a sheet, and handed it to Darby along with her pen.

Darby scribbled down her name and cell number. "I really appreciate all your help."

Pearl smiled, the first genuinely warm expression she'd given them. "Hope you find her. She was a sweet girl. I'd hate for her to miss out on money that's rightfully hers."

As Pearl moved off to greet the new arrivals, Darby leaned toward Kara and lowered her voice. "I can't imagine that Mega-Mart had anything to do with the fire. But... Beacon of Light? A torch is kind of a beacon, right?"

Kara nodded and pulled out her phone. "I completely agree. When we get back home, I'll start doing some research and see what I can dig up on these Beacon of Light guys."

"And we should go check out that church. And the cemetery."

Kara nodded slowly, glancing toward the window in the direction of where they'd come from. "After we eat?"

"After we eat." Darby sat back in her chair. The abandoned church wasn't going anywhere, and the meatloaf – however unappealing – would give them an excuse to linger a little longer and see if anyone else had information to share.

CHAPTER 26

The church had been a bust.

Darby had offered to drive back to Medeon so Kara could research Beacon of Light. Now she gripped the steering wheel, eyes on the highway as farmland rolled past in a blur of brown fields and skeletal trees. Beside her, Kara scrolled through her phone, thumbs moving quickly across the screen.

"Anything?" Darby asked.

"Not much – and that's what worries me." Kara's voice was tight with frustration. "Their website is basically a shell. Generic mission statement, no physical address, no staff directory. But local news sites mention them making donations to youth programs, sponsoring community events across the state." She turned her phone toward Darby. "And there are references to affiliate chapters in at least six cities across three states. This isn't some small local church group."

"Any names? Contact information?"

"Nothing. Completely anonymous. No staff, no board of directors." Kara hesitated. "They have a contact form. I'm tempted to fill it out with fake info just to see if anyone responds, but I want to talk to everyone first."

Darby considered this. The boarded-up church had offered nothing. There were no signs of recent activity, no clues hidden in the overgrown cemetery. They'd managed to peer through a few dusty windows on the side of the building, cupping their hands against the grimy glass. Inside, the sanctuary was completely stripped bare: no pews, no altar, no prayer books. Just empty wooden floors, water-stained walls, and the ghost of a cross on the back wall where paint had faded around where it once hung. Neither of them had been willing to pry the boards off any of the doors and break in during broad daylight. Instead, they'd walked the entire property, checked every headstone, and peered into every overgrown corner. There was nothing to indicate anyone had even set foot on this property in years.

"Let's talk to the others first," Darby said. "Let's see what they think."

Kara nodded and tapped her phone. A moment later, the dial tone filled the car through the Bluetooth speakers.

It rang three times before Topaz answered. "Hey! Where are you guys? I just got off work and stopped by your apartment. No one answered."

"We took a little road trip," Kara said. "Hold on. Let me conference everyone in. We have some news."

The line clicked and beeped as Kara added Ivette and Jazmin. Their voices overlapped immediately with Ivette asking, "Is everyone okay?" while Jazmin demanded, "What's going on?"

"Hey guys, we just left Briarton," Darby said. "We went to check out the town where the garden club fire happened."

There was a beat of surprised silence.

"You drove all the way out there?" Topaz asked. "When?"

"This morning," Kara said. "We should've told you, but we weren't sure if we'd find anything worth reporting."

"You should've let us know what you were doing," Ivette said, her voice tight. "Just in case something went wrong."

"She's right," Topaz added. "We're supposed to be in this together. What if those Torch Bearer people had been there?"

"You're both right. I'm sorry," Darby said, feeling a pang of guilt. "We weren't thinking."

"So, did you find anything?" Topaz asked, her tone softening slightly.

Darby glanced at Kara, who gestured for her to start. "Sort of. We didn't find much, but what we discovered is... interesting."

She filled them in on the trip: the diner conversations, the mentions of Brenda McAllister heading west, the tension around MegaMart's attempted invasion, and most importantly, the Beacon of Light Ministry's failed attempt to purchase the old Methodist church next to the garden club. She told them about the torch graffiti they'd found. "I left my cell number with the sheriff and with Pearl at the diner," Darby added. "In case anyone remembers anything else about Brenda."

"A torch is basically a beacon," Topaz said. "But it could just be a coincidence."

Jazmin's scoff said what she thought about that.

"Yeah, it doesn't feel likely," Kara agreed. "But the church property didn't give us anything useful. It's been abandoned for years. Completely boarded up."

"And the website for the Beacon of Light is useless," Darby added. "Just vague religious language. No way to track them down."

"What about filling out the contact form on their website?" Kara asked. "I could use a generic email address, nothing tied to my current one. See if anyone responds?"

There was a pause.

"Let's save that as a last resort," Ivette said. "If we can't find anything through other channels first."

"I agree," Topaz said. "Even with a fake email, it still puts us on their radar in some way. Better to exhaust other options first."

"Makes sense," Kara said. "I'll use the library resources to dig deeper. See if I can pull any property records, tax filings, anything that might connect the Beacon of Light to a physical location or real people. If that doesn't turn up anything, then we can consider reaching out."

"And in the meantime, we keep preparing," Ivette added firmly. "We don't stop just because we hit a dead end."

"I agree. We should keep strengthening our magic and working on the offensive and defensive spells," Topaz said. "I'm going to try and practice every day."

"I'll make more witch balls," Darby offered. The glass spheres had proven effective. "I'd like to pick up some supplies to make enough that we can place them around the apartment, around the building, anywhere we think we might need protection."

"Good," Ivette said. "We stay vigilant. We stay together."

"Since we need more supplies anyway, we should also go back to The Serpent's Garden," Kara added. "Talk to Sage again. She knows more about the magical community than we do. Maybe she's heard of the Torch Bearers or the Beacon of Light Ministry."

"When?" Jazmin asked.

Darby checked the dashboard clock. They'd been driving for over an hour. "We're about half an hour out. How about we meet at the apartment and go together?"

"Perfect," Topaz said. "Text when you're close."

They said their goodbyes, and the line went dead. Kara let out a long breath and leaned her head back against the seat. "I feel like we're chasing shadows."

"We are," Darby said. "But at least we know more now than we did yesterday."

The rest of the drive passed in silence, both of them lost in their own thoughts. The landscape shifted from rural farmland to suburban sprawl, then finally to the familiar streets of Medeon. Darby felt some of the tension ease from her shoulders as they entered their neighborhood.

She pulled into the apartment building's lot and texted the group chat: *We're here.*

By the time they'd grabbed their bags and locked the car, Topaz was already waiting by the entrance, hands shoved in the pockets of an oversized jacket. A minute later, Ivette and Jazmin emerged from the stairwell.

"We should take my car," Kara said, pulling her own jacket tighter. "It's too cold to walk."

"Yeah, we'll all fit," Topaz said, though Darby caught the note of doubt in her voice.

They piled back into Kara's sedan – Topaz in the front passenger seat, Darby squeezed into the back between Ivette and Jazmin. It was tight, shoulders pressed together, with Jazmin's elbow digging into Darby's ribs.

"Sorry," Jazmin muttered.

"It's fine," Darby said, though she was acutely aware of how warm the car had become with all five of them crammed inside.

Kara drove the few blocks to The Serpent's Garden, but the street parking was full. She circled around to the next block and found a spot. They walked back together, moving as a unit down the sidewalk.

The shop's hand-painted sign swayed slightly in the breeze, a serpent coiling around a flower bouquet. Kara pushed open the door, the bell chiming overhead.

The scene inside stopped them cold.

Three men stood near the counter, their voices raised. Sage stood behind the register, her arms crossed, her expression tight and controlled. One of the men jabbed his finger toward her. He was tall, possibly in his early thirties, wearing a crisp button-down shirt and designer jeans with boots that probably cost more than Darby's monthly rent.

"You're poisoning this community!" he shouted. "Spreading the influence of Satan with your witchcraft and evil!"

"I think you need to leave," Sage said, her voice level but strained.

"We'll leave when we're done delivering God's message," another man said. He was shorter, stockier, with a neatly trimmed beard and a black baseball cap. "People like you are the reason this world is falling apart. You reject the light and embrace darkness!"

The third man stood slightly behind the others, younger and skinnier, nodding along but not speaking.

Darby's hands curled into fists. She stepped forward, Kara at her side, the rest of the coven close behind. "Hey. She asked you to leave."

The men turned, surprise flashed across their faces. Up close, Darby could see how young they were. Their anger seemed almost performative, like they were playing roles they'd rehearsed. But there was something in their bearing, a confidence that came from never having faced real consequences.

As the tall one gestured, Darby's eyes caught on his wrist. He was wearing a leather cuff bracelet with a small torch charm. The flame portion looked like tiger eye, the polished stone catching the afternoon light streaming through the shop window. It shimmered with an amber glow, the striations in the stone seeming to catch the light like real fire. Her breath caught. The symbol was nearly identical to the torch graffiti.

"This doesn't concern you," the tall one said, his voice carrying the entitled edge of someone used to getting his way. "We have every right to—"

"Leave her alone!" Jazmin's voice rang out, sharp and fierce.

The man in the black cap sneered at her. "What are you, her little devil-worshiping who—"

Ivette moved in a flash, pulling Jazmin behind her and stepping directly up to the man. She was shorter than him, but somehow she seemed to fill the space, her presence commanding. "Say that to *my* face."

The man's sneer faltered. He took a step back.

The rest of the coven moved forward as one, forming a wall between Jazmin and Sage, and the men. They stood shoulder to shoulder, silent and unmovable.

The tall man in the button-down glanced at his friends, then back at the coven. His bravado crumbled. "This isn't over," he muttered, but he was already backing toward the door.

"You're all going to hell!" the one in the ball cap added, his voice weaker now, almost petulant.

"Yeah, well, you're all a bunch of weak-ass losers!" Jazmin shouted as they stumbled out the door. "Go home to your mommies!"

"Jazmin," Ivette said, but she was trying not to laugh. The bell chimed as the door swung shut, cutting off the men's retreating insults.

For a moment, the shop was silent except for the muffled sounds of traffic outside the window. Then Ivette shook her head, rolling her eyes. "Rich kids playing at being holy warriors."

Sage let out a shaky breath, her shoulders dropping. "Thank you. Really. I— thank you."

"Are you okay?" Kara asked, moving closer.

"Yeah. I'm fine." Sage ran a hand through her dark hair. "It's not the first time some religious wackos have given me trouble. Comes with the territory, I guess."

"Have you ever heard of the Torch Bearers?" Darby asked. "Or the Beacon of Light Ministry?"

Sage frowned, thinking. "Beacon of Light Ministry... I don't think so. But honestly, I don't usually pay attention to their names. They all blur together after a while."

Darby pulled out her phone and scrolled to the photo she'd taken of the torch graffiti on the garden club's wall. She held it up. "Have you ever seen this image?"

Sage leaned in, studying the screen. Her frown deepened.

"Actually... yeah. I think one of the guys who was just here might've had that tattooed on his arm. The one in the hat."

The coven exchanged glances. Darby's pulse quickened. "Are you sure?"

"Pretty sure. I noticed it when he was pointing at me." Sage's expression shifted, growing more serious. "Why? What's this about?"

"The tall thin one was wearing a leather cuff bracelet with the same symbol," Darby said. "Did you notice it?"

Sage's eyes widened slightly. "No, I didn't catch that." She looked back at the photo on Darby's phone. "So both of them had this torch thing? What does it mean?"

Kara hesitated, then seemed to make a decision. "There have been attacks. On witches. Covens, like ours. Over the past few years, multiple groups have been killed. Burned alive in their homes."

Sage's face went pale. "What? I—I can't believe I haven't heard anything about this."

"The authorities don't know the women were witches," Topaz said quietly. "It's been spread out over several years, all over the state. No one's connected the dots. All of the fires were deemed accidents."

"Jesus," Sage whispered. She gripped the edge of the counter. "Have they... has anyone been bothering you?"

"No," Darby said. "We've been keeping a very low profile. No one knows we exist."

"That's wise." Sage looked at each of them in turn, her expression grim. "Keep it that way. If these Beacon assholes are targeting witches..." She trailed off, shaking her head.

"We're being careful," Ivette said. "We're preparing."

"Good. Good." Sage took a breath, steadying herself. "Okay. Let me help. What do you need?"

"Two dozen more witch balls," Darby said immediately. "And the supplies to turn them into wards."

"I can do that," Sage said with a nod.

"Do you sell any books on ghosts, poltergeists, and possession?" Darby asked.

Sage raised an eyebrow. "That's a shift in topic. But yeah, I've got a decent collection on supernatural entities. Looking for anything specific?"

"Just thinking we should cover all our bases," Darby said. "Knowledge is power, right?"

"Smart thinking," Ivette said with approval when Sage left to grab the book. "We need to figure out what we're dealing with when it comes to 'Bella'."

They spent the next twenty minutes gathering supplies – more black salt, protective herbs, candles, crystals, and the glass spheres Darby requested. Sage moved through the shop, pulling items from shelves and bins. When Kara handed her a credit card at the register, Sage rang everything up and applied a hefty discount.

"Consider it hazard pay for dealing with those idiots," Sage said firmly.

As they loaded everything into canvas bags, Sage walked over to the door and flipped the sign to "Closed."

"It's only four o'clock," Topaz said.

"I know." Sage pulled out her phone. "I'm locking up early. I need to make some calls. There are other practitioners I know, other shop owners. If the Beacon of Light guys are hurting witches, everyone needs to be warned."

She looked at each of them. "Can I get your numbers? I want to make sure we can reach each other if anything comes up."

They rattled them off one by one, Sage typing quickly into her phone. When they finished, she sent a quick text to the group. "That's me. Save it. And please, if anything happens – anything at all – call me right away, okay?"

They said their goodbyes and filed out onto the sidewalk.

Behind them, Sage turned the deadbolt on her door with a decisive click.

The sun was lower now, casting long shadows between the buildings. Darby pulled her jacket tighter, suddenly aware of how exposed they were on the empty street.

"Come on," Kara said, her voice quiet. "Let's go home."

They walked back to the car in silence, each of them scanning the street, the alleys, the windows of nearby buildings. Darby couldn't shake the image of the torch spray-painted on the garden club's shed.

As they drove home, crammed once again into Kara's sedan, Darby stared out the window and tried to ignore the knot of worry tightening in her chest.

CHAPTER 27

*D*arby pushed through the apartment door a week later, immediately enveloped by the warmth inside. She dropped her work bag and wrestled out of her jacket while juggling the book on spirits and possession she'd been carrying. She'd been devouring it during every spare minute since they'd gotten it from The Serpent's Garden, reading through her lunch breaks at work, highlighting passages, and dog-earing pages.

"Kara?" she called out, toeing off her shoes. "You home?"

A moment later, Kara emerged from her bedroom, hair pulled back in a messy bun, wearing sweatpants and a threadbare Lyceum Public Library t-shirt. "Hey. What's up?"

Darby held up the book. "I have good news."

Kara's eyebrows rose. "Oh?"

"Ivette doesn't need to worry anymore." Darby flipped through the pages until she found the section she'd marked with a sticky note. "According to this, a ghost *can't* possess someone unless they invite them in. Like, explicitly. It's all about consent and will. A spirit can influence the physical world, like slamming doors and moving objects – that kind of thing. But actual possession? The living person has to allow it."

"That's..." Kara moved closer, reading over Darby's shoulder. "That's actually really good news. Both Ivette and Topaz have been really worried about Bella trying to possess one of us."

"I know. Ivette keeps texting me about exorcisms. However..." Darby turned a few more pages, then paused. She pointed to another passage, glancing up at Kara, and pressing her finger to her lips in a silent gesture to stay quiet. She kept her expression carefully neutral.

Kara leaned in, scanning the text about binding spells and spirit containment. She looked back at Darby, her eyebrows raised. "You're thinking about trying this with Bella?"

"Yeah." Darby closed the book and looked around the apartment. "Bella? If you're here, could you let us know? Maybe give us a sign?"

They waited in silence. The lights remained steady. No cold spots materialized. No doors creaking open. The apartment was utterly still. Just like it had been since the Ouija board séance. Bella had gone quiet.

"That doesn't mean she's not here," Darby said quietly. "According to the book, spirits that try to contact the physical world exhaust themselves and need time to recover. She might just be... I don't know... asleep or dormant. Or she might not want to reveal herself."

Kara nodded slowly. "So what are you thinking?"

Darby set the book down on the coffee table, keeping it open to the page, and walked over to the shelf where they stored the supplies from The Serpent's Garden. She pulled out one of the smaller witch balls they'd purchased. The glass orb was about the size of a golf ball, a deep plum color that seemed to shift in the lamplight and held it up.

According to everything she'd read, a witch ball could trap and contain a spirit the same way it trapped a spell. Bella was magical energy too, just a different form of it.

Kara looked at the witch ball, then back at Darby, understanding clear in her eyes. "I think it's a good idea. Let's do it now, just in case."

Darby's heart kicked up a notch. "Now?"

"Why wait? If this situation is dangerous, every minute we delay is a risk." Kara crossed her arms. "And if she's not, well... we'll figure out what to do with Bella later."

It was sound logic, even if Darby's stomach clenched at the thought. She picked up the book again, holding it open in one hand while cradling the plum-colored witch ball in her other palm. The glass was cool and smooth in her hand, and surprisingly heavy for its size.

"Okay," Darby said, taking a breath. "Here goes nothing."

She centered herself, the way they'd been practicing. Darby drew on the well of power that lived somewhere beneath her ribs, that connection to something older and deeper than herself. The apartment seemed to hold its breath.

"Isabella Rousseau," Darby said, her voice clear and steady. "I call forth your spirit."

For a heartbeat, nothing happened.

Then the air pressure dropped, like the moment before a thunderstorm breaks. Darby's ears popped, and the temperature plummeted, her breath misting in front of her face.

She started reading the binding spell, the words feeling strange and sandy in her mouth.

The cabinet doors slammed open with explosive force. Dishes rattled. A glass fell from the counter and shattered on the kitchen floor. An impossible wind whipped through the apartment, sending papers flying off the kitchen table in a cyclone.

A howling sound echoed through the space, rising and falling like a siren. It came from everywhere and nowhere, reverberating in Darby's bones.

"Darby—" Kara's voice was tight with alarm.

"I've got it!" Darby had to grip the book with both hands now, the witch ball pressed between her palm and the leather cover.

The pages tried to flip closed, fighting against her hold. Wind whipped her hair across her face. The howling grew louder and more desperate.

She raised her voice, nearly shouting over the chaos.

"By earth and fire, by water and air—"

The cabinet doors slammed shut, then flew open again. The rhythm matched the pounding of Darby's heart. Picture frames rattled on the walls. The light overhead flickered.

"—I bind your spirit to this vessel—"

A book flew off the shelf and hit the wall with a bang. The couch cushions lifted and dropped. The kitchen faucet turned on full blast, and water sprayed everywhere.

"—to hold and contain until released by my will!"

The howling reached a crescendo, almost human in its anguish. Then Darby saw a wisp of white materializing near the ceiling, gossamer thin and translucent. It writhed in the air, coalescing into something more solid.

The wisp twisted and fought, but it was being pulled, inexorably, toward the witch ball in Darby's palm. It stretched into a stream, a ribbon of glowing white light that began spiraling down.

Darby could almost hear words in the howling now. Fragmented and desperate. "—stop... please... tried to—"

She gritted her teeth and kept the ball steady, even as the power flowing through her made her arm shake. The stream of white light funneled faster, spinning as it was sucked into the small glass sphere.

The final wisp disappeared into the ball with a sound like a gasp cut short.

Silence crashed down.

The cabinet doors hung open, now motionless, as papers drifted slowly to the floor. The faucet still ran, water hitting a forgotten bowl and spraying across the counter. Darby's ears rang in the sudden absence of noise.

She and Kara stared at each other, breathing hard. Darby's hands trembled as she lowered the book. The witch ball in her palm glowed faintly, a soft white light pulsing from within like a trapped heartbeat.

"Holy shit," Kara whispered.

The apartment door exploded inward with a crack that made them both jump. Darby nearly dropped the ball, her fingers fumbling before she caught it and held tight. Ivette rushed through the threshold with lightning already crackling between her raised hands, blue-white electricity arcing from her fingertips. The air filled with the sharp smell of ozone.

Jazmin burst in right behind her, palms up and with glassy balls of water encasing her hands, her eyes scanning the room for threats.

Darby's hair lifted with the static electricity saturating the air, standing on end. Her skin prickled.

"What happened?!" Ivette demanded, lightning dancing across her knuckles. "We felt something from across the hall. The dishes in our cabinets even rattled—"

"Are you hurt?" Jazmin moved further into the room, surveying the destruction.

"We're fine!" Kara held up both hands in a calming gesture. "We're okay. Stand down."

The lightning didn't fade immediately. Ivette kept her hands raised, eyes still wild with adrenaline. Slowly, gradually, the crackling began to dissipate. However, the smell of ozone lingered.

"What in the world?" Ivette looked around the trashed apartment, bewildered.

Darby held up the witch ball. The white glow within it swirled and pulsed. "We trapped Bella."

Both Ivette and Jazmin stared.

"You what?" Jazmin lowered her hands, though mist still shimmered in the air around her palms.

"The book I got about ghosts said a spirit can't possess someone without explicit permission," Darby explained quickly. "But it also had a binding spell. We thought… we wanted to make sure Bella wasn't a threat, but keep her contained. Just in case we need to ask her any questions."

Ivette moved closer, studying the glowing ball. "Is that her? In there?"

"Yeah," Kara said. She crossed to the kitchen and turned off the still-running faucet. Grabbing a dish towel, she began mopping up all the water spray. "Bella lost it. I think she realized what we were trying to do. Cabinets flying open, papers everywhere, that howling sound—"

"We heard it through the walls," Jazmin said. She ran a hand through her hair, looking shaken. "It sounded like someone was dying."

Darby's stomach twisted. The words she'd almost heard in that final moment – stop, please – what had Bella been trying to say?

"So… what do we do with it?" Ivette asked. She reached out as if to touch the ball, then thought better of it. "Do we want to… I don't know. Get rid of it somehow?"

"We could bury it somewhere," Jazmin offered.

"No." The word came out more sharply than Darby intended. She pulled the ball closer to her chest, feeling weirdly protective. Bella hadn't actually done anything wrong, other than just existing. It's not like she could do anything about being dead. "She helped us once, so I feel like we owe her respect, even if we don't fully trust her. I'll put the witch ball somewhere safe. Just in case we need to talk to her again. She might know something useful."

Ivette and Jazmin exchanged a look.

"You sure that's a good idea?" Ivette asked carefully. "I think she might be dangerous. Topaz agrees—"

"Then she's contained," Darby replied. "But we don't know for sure that she was actually a threat. I never felt a threat from her, and I also never got the sense that she was trying to possess anyone."

"Or maybe she was playing you," Ivette said, but her voice was gentler now. "Either way, you're right. We should keep her accessible, just in case."

The door, still hanging open from Ivette's dramatic entrance, suddenly filled with another figure. Topaz burst through, breathing hard, her eyes wide and excited. "I have the best news!" she shouted, then stopped short, taking in the scene.

Four pairs of eyes turned to stare at her.

Topaz's excitement drained away, replaced by confusion. "What happened here?"

Darby let out a slightly hysterical laugh. Kara pressed a hand to her mouth, shoulders shaking. Even Ivette cracked a smile.

"Long story," Darby said with a snort. "But first... What's your news?"

Topaz glanced around one more time, clearly torn between demanding answers and sharing her excitement. Excitement won. "I got a gig! I'm going to be the opening act for The Velvet Ruins next month. Like, a real venue with a real stage, the whole thing."

"Topaz!" Kara dropped the towel and rushed over to hug her. "That's amazing!"

"The Velvet Ruins?" Jazmin's eyebrows shot up. "They're huge right now. How did you manage that? Do you think you'll get to meet Scarlet Ruin? I love her lyrics."

"They needed an opener, someone with a similar sound, and their manager heard my set from the café the other day. I impressed them!" Topaz was practically vibrating with energy. "It's at the Crossroads on Saturday night. You guys will come, right?"

"Obviously," Jazmin said.

"Wouldn't miss it," Darby added.

Topaz beamed, then looked around again. "Seriously though,

what the hell happened? It looks like a tornado went through here."

"We trapped Bella," Kara said simply.

Topaz blinked. "You— what?"

"Bella, the ghost," Darby explained, holding up the witch ball so the white glow was visible. "We did a binding spell. She's in here now."

"In the ball." Topaz's voice was flat.

"In the ball," Ivette confirmed.

Topaz slowly nodded, processing. "Okay. Sure. Ghost in a ball. Why not?" She shook her head. "I swear, my life has gotten so weird since I met you all."

"Says the woman who can shoot fire from her hands," Jazmin pointed out.

"Fair point."

They stood there for a moment, the five of them taking in the disaster zone of the apartment, the glowing ball in Darby's hands, the weight of everything that had happened in the last few days.

"I guess we should clean up," Kara finally said.

"I'll help," Ivette said. "But first, Darby, put that thing somewhere we won't accidentally break it open."

Darby looked down at the witch ball. The light within pulsed steadily, like a tiny, captured star. Somewhere inside that sphere was Isabella Rousseau – or whatever was left of her. Friend or foe, helpful spirit or malevolent entity, they still didn't know for sure.

But at least now she was contained.

"I'll put her in my room," Darby said. "Top shelf of my closet. She should be safe there."

She carried the ball carefully to her bedroom, acutely aware of the weight of it, the warmth beginning to emanate from the glass. Behind her, she could hear the others starting to clean up – the scrape of glass being swept, cabinet doors closing, and papers being gathered.

In her room, Darby stood on her desk chair and placed the witch ball on the highest shelf of her closet, tucked behind a stack of sweaters. The glow was dimmer now, barely visible unless you were looking for it.

"I'm sorry if you were really trying to help," she whispered. "But we had to be sure."

The light pulsed once, brighter, then settled back to its steady rhythm.

CHAPTER 28

$\mathcal{A}$lmost a week later, Darby was lacing up her boots in the apartment when her phone buzzed. The screen showed an unfamiliar number. She glanced at Kara, who was braiding her hair for their practice session at the cemetery.

"You getting that?" Kara asked.

Darby hesitated, then swiped to answer. "Hello?"

"Is this—" The voice was female, soft and uncertain. "Is this the woman looking for Brenda McAllister?"

Darby's heart jumped. She straightened, motioning urgently to Kara. "Yes. Yes, this is. Who is this?"

A pause. "This is Brenda."

The apartment door opened and Ivette walked in with Jazmin. Darby frantically waved them over, pressing a finger to her lips.

"One of my friends from Briarton said you and another woman were in the diner asking about me," Brenda continued. Her voice had a tremor to it, like she was fighting to keep it steady. "She said you mentioned missing insurance money. We both know that's not real. So why were you asking about me?"

Darby took a breath. "This is going to sound strange, but... I believe you and the rest of your garden club were targeted because there were people who thought you were witches."

The line went silent. Darby could hear breathing on the other end, but nothing else.

"Are you still there?" Darby asked.

"What..." Brenda's voice cracked. "What do you know about this? What do you know about witches?"

"I know that the same group that targeted and killed your friends is now in Medeon. And they're still hunting witches."

Another long silence. Then, barely a whisper: "How do you know this?"

"Have you heard of the Torch Bearers?" Darby asked carefully. "Or the Beacon of Light?"

The sound that came through the phone was half gasp, half sob.

"I'm so sorry to bring up something so painful," Darby said quickly. "But we need to know everything you can tell us. They're here, and we think that they're targeting people."

"Why?" Brenda's voice was raw. "Why do you want to know this?"

Darby looked at the others gathered around her. Through the open door, she saw Topaz coming up the stairs. "Can I put you on speaker? I have my friends with me. We're... we're a coven."

A sharp intake of breath. "You are?"

"Yes."

Darby switched to speaker and held the phone out.

"Hi," Kara said gently.

"Hello," Ivette added.

Topaz slipped in and closed the door behind her, eyes wide with questions. Jazmin waved her over.

"I'm Darby. With me are Lily, Morgan, Beth, and..." Darby said, deciding on the fly not to give the rest of the coven's real names, wishing she'd thought to give a fake name when they were in Briarton. She looked at Topaz.

"Phoenix," Topaz supplied, catching on immediately.

"Can you tell us what happened?" Darby asked.

For a moment, she thought Brenda had hung up. Then the woman began to speak, her voice thick with emotion.

"When I moved to Briarton all those years ago, I didn't know anyone. The town was... standoffish. Small town, you know? Suspicious of outsiders. But the garden club welcomed me. Alice, April, Olivia, and Isabella. They were so kind." She paused, gathering herself. "A couple of months after I joined, Alice told me she could sense something in me. Magic, she called it. I thought she was crazy at first, but then she showed me. Real magic. And I could do it too."

"We practiced in the garden club after hours," Brenda continued. "Just simple things at first. Growing plants, moving small objects. It felt... it felt like coming home to something I didn't know I'd been missing. We got stronger together. Braver."

Darby heard her take a shaky breath.

"That's when the Beacon of Light showed up. Five or six men, claiming they wanted to start a congregation at the church next door. At first, we were thrilled. The building had been empty for years, falling into ruin. We thought having active neighbors would be good for the community. But these men... they didn't care about God. They cared about us. They watched the garden club. Followed us home. Made comments about ungodly women – about being unholy. They'd show up at our club when we were there, find excuses to interrupt our meetings."

"I wanted us to stop. I felt like they somehow knew we were witches," Brenda said, her voice breaking. "I begged Alice and April. I told them it wasn't safe. But Alice said we had every right to practice our craft, and April..." She made a choked sound. "April said she wouldn't let bullies drive her away from the only real community she'd ever had."

The coven stood in silence, listening.

"The night of the fire, we were having our weekly practice.

Tuesday evening, like always. I'd been uneasy all day. Couldn't shake this feeling of dread. Around eight o'clock, I smelled smoke." Brenda's breathing grew faster. "By the time we realized what was happening, the exits were blocked. They'd barricaded the doors from outside. I could hear them out there, chanting. Praying for our souls while they burned us alive."

"Jesus," Ivette whispered.

"Alice and April tried everything – water spells, cold air, even a smothering charm. Nothing worked on the fire. It was like the flames were protected somehow. April tried to blast the door open, but her magic just fizzled against it. Olivia passed out. Isabella was trying to get to the windows, but they wouldn't budge. She even tried smashing one with a chair, but it was like hitting concrete. They'd sealed them somehow – with magic or something else, we couldn't tell. I was coughing so hard I could barely see." Brenda paused. "That's when I noticed one of them – one of the men, standing looking in through the small window in the back door. He was watching us. Making sure we couldn't escape."

"I was closest to the door. I remember thinking – this is it. I'm going to die here. Alice had this old grimoire she'd inherited from her grandmother. We'd been studying it for months. I don't know why but I thought of this one that was called 'The Unraveling' – it was supposed to undo knots and tangles in thread or rope."

Brenda's voice grew quieter. "I was so desperate, so angry. These men were killing us for no reason except fear and hate. I looked at that Beacon man through the smoke, and I thought – what if his protection is like a knot? What if I can unravel it? So I spoke the words from the grimoire, not really believing it would work. It was just thread magic. Sewing circle magic."

"What happened?" Darby asked softly.

"He screamed." Brenda's voice shook. "It was like... like something invisible was being ripped away from him. He stumbled backward and clutched at his chest. And then I hit him with everything I had left – just raw force, pure rage. My magic is air-based. He flew backward. I heard him hit something hard."

"Why do you think the unraveling spell worked when nothing else did?" Ivette asked.

"I don't really know. I've thought about it a lot – practically every day since. Their protection, whatever they use, I'm not sure if it's amulets or charms or prayers, but I think their magic works on the principle of opposition. It recognizes hostile intent and deflects it. Fire against fire, force against force. The Unraveling is different. It's sympathetic magic, built on the idea of gentleness, of carefully teasing apart tangled threads without breaking them. There's no aggression in it; no violence. Their magic, or whatever it was they used against us, didn't recognize it as a threat until it was too late."

Brenda's voice grew stronger. "I used the spell on the door itself. I could feel the wards they'd placed on it unraveling like pulling a thread from a sweater. Then I blasted it with force. The wood splintered. I started crawling through the smoke to the opening, screaming for the others to follow me. But no one answered. The smoke—" Her voice cracked. "By the time I made it outside, I couldn't hear them anymore. No coughing, no movement. Just the roar of the fire. I turned to go back in, but the roof collapsed. The whole thing just came down. They were already gone. There was nothing I could do."

"I crawled away, out into the garden. There were three of the Beacon men there, probably watching to make sure no one escaped. When they saw me, they started toward me. I was so weak, covered in soot, coughing so hard I could barely stand. But I'd just used the Unraveling on the door, and on that other man. I spoke the words again. I could barely get them out between coughs. But then I felt their protection dissolve, and saw the shock on their faces when they realized they were exposed. Then I pushed with everything I had left."

"Two of them went down hard. The third scrambled backward. That's when I heard the sirens of fire trucks and the police. Someone must have called it in. All three of them panicked and ran for the fence, climbing over it and disappearing into the cemetery next door. I collapsed right there in the garden. The next thing I remember is waking up in the hospital with smoke inhalation and second-degree burns on my hands and arms."

"I was so terrified. Every time someone walked past my hospital room, I thought it was them coming to finish the job. The nurses kept asking what happened. The police came to interview me. I told them the fire spread so fast, I had no idea how it started. That I'd barely made it out. I didn't tell them about the barricaded doors or the men watching through the windows or any of it. I was so scared they'd come back to finish what they started."

"The fire had completely consumed the building. Nothing was left but the foundation and ash. All of my friends were dead. The Beacon of Light guys told everyone they'd arrived to find the church already burning. They were treated like heroes." Her voice turned bitter. "And I was the lucky one who survived. As soon as I could leave the hospital, I disappeared. I left my number with only one person in town I trusted to let me know if the Beacons came back looking for me. I changed my name and moved several times since leaving. I couldn't risk them finding me again."

"I'm so sorry," Darby said. "I'm so sorry you went through that. And I'm sorry about your friends."

"They were more than friends," Brenda whispered. "They were my sisters."

The apartment was utterly silent except for the sound of Brenda crying softly on the other end of the line.

Darby's throat tightened. She looked at her own coven gathered around her and understood exactly what Brenda meant.

"You need to know this," Brenda said, her voice urgent now.

"The Beacon of Light or whatever you said they're now called – they're protected somehow. A direct attack will not phase them. You need to find the spell called the Unraveling. They are deadly and will not hesitate to kill you. They don't care about anything but their supposed 'calling.'"

"We have a grimoire," Darby told Brenda, leaving off the fact that it used to belong to her friend Alice. "So, we'll work on learning that spell."

"Is there anything else?" Ivette asked. "Any way to identify these guys?"

"They mark themselves," Brenda said. "As far as I can tell, they all have the same tattoo. A torch, usually on the inside of their right wrist or forearm. They often keep them hidden by their sleeves, but I saw it on a few of the men."

"Brenda," Kara spoke up. "How did they find your coven in the first place? Do they have a way to track witches? To detect magic?"

There was a pause. "I don't know," Brenda admitted, her voice frustrated. "I've asked myself that question a thousand times. We were so careful. We only practiced after hours in the garden club with the doors locked. We never talked about it in public. But somehow they found us. They showed up not long after we started getting stronger with our magic. I don't know if they can sense it somehow, or if someone told them, or..." She trailed off. "I just don't know."

"Thank you," Darby said. "Thank you for telling us this. I know it couldn't have been easy."

"Just..." Brenda's voice was fierce despite the tears. "Promise me you'll be careful. And promise me that if you can stop them – if you can prevent what happened to my sisters from happening to anyone else – promise me you will."

"We promise," Darby said.

"All of us," Kara added firmly.

Darby thanked her for sharing something that was clearly

difficult to talk about, and Brenda made her promise to be careful. They said their goodbyes and hung up.

For a long moment, the five of them stood in the apartment, processing everything they'd just heard.

"So offensive magic doesn't work on them," Jazmin finally said. "That's why none of the other witches were able to fight them off. Their protection blocks direct attacks."

"But," Ivette said slowly. "If we unravel their protection first, then we can hit them."

"Don't forget the tattoos," Topaz said. "We need to start looking for those. Anyone who corners us, anyone who seems too interested in us – we check their wrists."

"We need to be smarter about this," Kara said. She moved quickly to where they kept the grimoire and pulled it out, already flipping through the pages. "We need to find that Unraveling spell immediately. I think I remember seeing something about unraveling... or untangling... it was early in the book, I think."

Darby's gaze drifted to the box of witch balls she'd been working on, nearly two dozen of them now, each one carefully filled with ward magic.

"The witch balls," she said suddenly. "Once we learn the Unraveling spell, what if we could add it to the wards? We were already going to place the witch balls around our homes and the cemetery. If we charge them with both protection *and* unraveling magic, anyone who attacks us would lose their defenses the moment they cross the threshold. The Torch Bearers would be vulnerable before they even realized what hit them."

"They'd walk right into their own trap," Ivette finished, understanding lighting her eyes. "The second they get close, their protection fails."

"And then we hit them where it hurts. I love it," Jazmin said.

"Do we still go to the cemetery tonight?" Kara asked, looking up from the grimoire.

"Yes," Darby decided. "We practice the Unraveling spell until we can do it in our sleep. And then I'll start adding it to the witch balls. We're not going to be sitting ducks anymore."

"Finally," Topaz said with grim satisfaction.

They gathered their things – jackets, bags, grimoire, and all the supplies they'd need. As they headed out into the cold night, Darby felt the weight of Brenda's story pressing on her shoulders.

Somewhere out there, the Torch Bearers were hunting. And until they figured out how these men found their targets, the coven had to assume they could be next.

But now the coven knew their weakness.

And they would be ready.

CHAPTER 29

The greenery had taken over.

Darby stood on her balcony in the pale morning light, running her fingers along the leaves of honeysuckle that had grown thick as rope in just a few weeks. Sweet fragrance drifted from the vine as it climbed the brick walls of the balcony; lush and green despite winter's chill, shielded from neighbors' view by the privacy screen she'd installed weeks ago under the guise of blocking wind. Inside, more plants crowded every surface – spider plants cascading from shelves, herbs flourishing in the kitchen windowsill, a fiddle leaf fig that had tripled in size and now brushed the ceiling.

It wasn't just growth. It was communion.

She could feel them, the way she felt her own heartbeat. The slight lean of a stem toward sunlight. The pull of roots seeking water. When she touched a wilting leaf, she didn't just see what it needed; she knew it, felt it like a word on the tip of her tongue that finally came loose.

"You're doing it again," Kara said from the kitchen, smiling. She held two mugs of coffee.

Darby blinked and realized she'd been standing completely

still, one hand pressed against the honeysuckle plant, eyes half-closed. The vine had wrapped itself gently around her wrist.

"Sorry." She carefully unwound the tendril and accepted the coffee. "I was just checking on them."

"They look like they're checking on you, too."

It was true. The apartment felt alive, watchful in a way that was comforting rather than eerie. Jazmin had started calling it the jungle, but even she admitted she liked it. The air felt cleaner, softer even.

The cemetery had also been transformed. What had been a somber landscape of weathered headstones, scraggly grass, and bare earth was now lush with unexpected growth. Moss crept thick over the old stones, wildflowers bloomed between graves despite the chill, and ivy wound up the iron fence in dense, vibrant curtains. Darby hadn't meant to do it – not consciously, anyway. But every night they practiced there, her magic seemed to seep into the ground, coaxing life from the cold soil. The other coven members had noticed, but no one complained. If anything, the greenery made the space feel protected and claimed. When they practiced their magic there, surrounded by all of the green life, everything felt like it came easier.

These last few weeks of nightly practice had transformed them all.

Jazmin could pull water from the air easily and shape it into complex forms – shields, barriers, even temporary weapons that held their form as long as she wanted them to. Ivette's lightning no longer felt wild and unpredictable; she could thread it through her fingers like yarn, release it in controlled bursts or devastating strikes. Kara had mastered air in ways that seemed almost impossible – she could weave words into the wind itself, sending whispered messages across the cemetery, shape the air into solid barriers that held firm as stone, or pull every bit of oxygen from a space, creating a suffocating vacuum. And Topaz burned brighter than ever, her fire magic so controlled she could light a candle unseen from another room with just a thought.

And the Unraveling spell. They'd practiced it until the words felt like second nature, until they could feel the spell taking shape even before they spoke it aloud. That gentle, insidious magic that didn't attack – it simply undid.

The witch balls were done. All of them.

Darby had spent hours on each one, first inserting the protective ward, then carefully and methodically weaving the Unraveling spell into the glass itself. They glowed softly when she held them, thrumming with layered magic. She'd placed them at every entrance to their apartments and hung them from the eaves of every window. She'd also created a perimeter around the cemetery. Each of them had taken one for their workspace, too. Jazmin had tucked hers inside her school locker, hidden behind textbooks where no one would think to look.

The balls were connected to the coven as well. It had been Kara's idea to link each one to every member. If someone with ill intent triggered a ball, all five of them would feel a sharp mental ping and know immediately which location had been breached.

"We're as ready as we're going to be," Ivette had said two nights ago, standing in the cemetery surrounded by a ring of glowing witch balls.

Darby hoped she was right.

"Hey," Kara said, setting down her coffee mug with a quiet clink. "I think I finally got something on the Torch Bearers."

Darby's attention snapped from the vine to Kara's face. "What? Really?"

"I checked the email this morning." Kara's smile was small but satisfied. "They got back to us."

They'd created the fake email address three days ago. They created a man named George Randolph, complete with a generic Gmail account, and filled out the contact form on the Beacon of Light Ministry's website with a carefully crafted message.

'George' was a recent transplant to Medeon and was looking for a new congregation. The message was simple and innocuous. The kind of inquiry any church would expect.

"And what did the Beacons say?" Darby prompted.

"They invited George to a worship service. This evening at seven." Kara pulled out her phone, scrolling to the email. "Said they'd love to have him join them. Sent me the address where they're holding their service."

"We should look it up," Darby said. "See what we're dealing with."

"Already looked into it," Kara said. "The address is an old movie theater on Mason Street. Went out of business a few years back, but it looks like the church moved in about a year and a half ago."

"We should tell the others." Darby was already reaching for her own phone. "See if everyone wants to check it out."

Kara quickly typed out a message to the group informing them about George's invitation.

Darby: *I just looked up the location. There's a coffee shop across the street with a view of the entrance. Anyone up for some recon?*

Jazmin: *I have a study group but I can skip*

Topaz: *Working tonight. I can call out tho.*

Ivette: *Don't. Neither of you should do that. We shouldn't all go together anyway. If the Beacons notice us, we don't want them connecting all five of us. I'll go. We can keep you two in the loop if anything happens.*

Topaz: *We still don't know how they detect witches*

Darby: *Good point*

Topaz: *What about that glamour spell we've been practicing? Change our looks just to be safe?*

Kara: *Smart. That way even if someone sees us, they won't be able to recognize us later.*

Jazmin: *Be careful*

Topaz: *Report back everything. And I mean EVERYTHING.*

* * *

THE COLD HIT Darby like a slap when she emerged from the subway. Winter in Medeon had teeth. It felt like the wind weaseled its way into every gap in her coat and burrowed in. She stuffed her hands deep in her pockets, hunching her shoulders against the chill.

Her right hand closed around something smooth and warm. The purple witch ball, small enough to fit in her palm. Bella's prison.

Darby had started carrying it everywhere. She told herself it was practical – there was no telling when she might need to consult with the witch's spirit. But the truth settled uncomfortably in her chest every time she thought about it: she felt guilty stuffing the ghost into the back of her dark closet.

She saw Ivette and Kara approaching from the opposite direction, their breath forming small clouds in the frigid air. Darby waved them over, grateful to push away thoughts of Bella.

"Over here," she said quietly, gesturing toward a narrow alley between buildings.

They ducked behind a dumpster, the smell of rotting garbage almost preferable to the icy wind. Kara pulled out a small ziplock bag filled with what looked like crushed charcoal mixed with herbs and something that shimmered faintly.

"Ready?" she asked.

They each dipped their thumb into the mixture. The powder felt gritty and oddly warm against Darby's skin.

She pressed her thumb to her forehead and whispered the words they'd practiced.

"Stranger's face upon my own,
Let me walk from here unknown."

The spell washed over her like cool water, a prickling sensation that started where her thumb met skin and rippled outward across her face, then down her neck. It didn't hurt, but it felt like wearing a mask she couldn't touch. Like wearing a second skin that hummed with magic. She could feel it settling into place, a gentle pressure that said the glamour had taken hold.

It was strange watching the glamour transform her friends. Kara's features shifted subtly. Her nose appeared slightly longer, her jaw more angular, her eyes changing to green. Ivette's face seemed to narrow, her cheekbones sharpening, her hair growing longer and straighter under the illusion.

"Let's go," Ivette said, her voice unchanged but coming from an unfamiliar face.

They left the alley and started toward Mason Street. The cold made conversation difficult, but Ivette managed it anyway.

"You heading back home for Thanksgiving?" she asked Darby.

"Yeah. My parents are expecting me." Darby grimaced. "Not exactly looking forward to it."

"Skip it," Ivette said without hesitation. "Come to our place instead. The rest of the coven's coming over."

Darby glanced at her, surprised.

"All of us without much family left need to stick together," Ivette continued. She met Darby's eyes, and despite the unfamiliar face, her expression was warm. "You're family now. All of you are."

Something loosened in Darby's chest. "That sounds way better than dry turkey with a side of guilt gravy."

"Then it's settled."

"There," Kara said, pointing ahead. "That's the place."

The Beacon of Light Ministry occupied what had clearly been an old movie theater. The boxy marquee still jutted out over the sidewalk, its plastic panels yellowed with age, but instead of movie titles, black plastic letters spelled out "Beacon of Light Ministry" in bold. "All Are Welcome" was arranged beneath it in smaller letters. The brick facade had been painted over in clean white. Large windows that had once displayed movie posters were now covered with thick curtains, hiding the inside from prying eyes.

"I used to go here to watch movies," Ivette said quietly. "Before the new multiplex opened across town. Covid was probably the final nail in its coffin."

The church service didn't start for another hour, which meant they could watch who came and went.

They pushed into the coffee shop across the street, warmth washing over them in a welcome wave. Darby ordered an oat milk latte and a croissant, suddenly ravenous. They found a table by the window with a clear view of the theater's entrance.

Darby caught her reflection in the window and startled. An unfamiliar face stared back; one with rounder cheeks, wider eyes, and darker hair. She'd almost forgotten about the glamour.

For the next hour, they watched.

People trickled toward the theater in ones and twos. Families with small children. Elderly couples holding hands. A group of college-aged kids laughing together. They all looked painfully, boringly normal.

Darby photographed each person as discreetly as she could, angling her phone like she was scrolling social media.

"They look like they could be going anywhere," Kara murmured. "PTA meeting. Book club."

"That's the point, I imagine," Darby said quietly. "Can't exactly wear your 'Witch Murderers-R-Us' t-shirts around town."

Kara made a strangled noise. Her hand shot out, gripping Darby's wrist. "Look," she hissed, nodding subtly toward the theater entrance. "Isn't that one of the guys who was harassing Sage?"

Darby squinted through the window. A tall, thin man was climbing the theater steps. Once again, he was dressed in neat blue slacks and a white button-up with a thin blue tie, all of it mostly hidden beneath a huge puffy jacket. His brown hair was tucked under a knit beanie.

But it was him. The same sharp features. The same way he moved, all coiled tension.

"Yeah," Darby breathed. "That's him."

They watched him disappear through the theater doors. Darby's hand found the witch ball in her pocket again, squeezing it like a stress ball.

The last few stragglers hurried inside just before seven. The street fell quiet.

"The email said services usually run about an hour and a half," Kara said. "So we wait."

Darby settled back in her chair, her coffee going cold in her hands, and watched the theater doors like they might reveal all their secrets if she stared hard enough.

CHAPTER 30

Twenty minutes crawled by. Darby drummed her fingers against her coffee cup, watching the theater's entrance with an intensity that was starting to make her eyes water.

"I want to check the back," she said suddenly.

Kara looked up from her phone. "The back?"

"Yeah. Old movie theater like that? It has to have a back entrance. A loading dock, or an employee entrance, or something." Darby was already pushing her chair back. "The service isn't supposed to end for another hour. We could get a better sense of the layout."

Ivette nodded slowly. "Not a bad idea. But we shouldn't all go. I'll stay here, keep an eye on the front. Watch out for cameras. Even though we have disguises, we should avoid being filmed."

"For sure. Text us if anything changes or you see anyone heading our way," Kara said, already standing.

They left Ivette at the window and stepped back into the biting cold. The wind had picked up, carrying the smell of exhaust and something greasy from a nearby restaurant. Darby pulled her coat tighter and headed down the block.

The side alley was narrow, barely wide enough for a car. Graffiti was scrawled across the brick walls in layers; tags on top of tags, some fresh, others faded to ghostly outlines. Darby scanned, but none of the graffiti looked like a torch. A chain-link fence separated the alley from a small parking lot behind what appeared to be an auto parts store. The asphalt was cracked and uneven, puddles of dirty water frozen into slick patches.

They picked their way carefully past overflowing dumpsters and scattered trash.

"Glamorous work, this witch business," Kara muttered, making Darby chuckle.

The back of the theater opened onto a small service area hemmed in by the neighboring buildings. A rusted fire escape clung to one wall. Empty pallets were stacked haphazardly, leaning against each other. A back door of dented metal, painted industrial gray, sat beneath a small security light that cast a weak yellow glow.

Darby pulled out her phone and snapped a few photos, sending them to the group chat.

Darby: *Back entrance. Nothing exciting.*

Topaz: *Be careful*

Jazmin: *Any windows you can see through?*

Darby walked along the back wall, checking. All the windows were either bricked over or covered with the same thick curtains they'd seen from the front.

Darby: *Nope. Everything's blocked off. Heading back now.*

She was sliding her phone back into her pocket when the back door banged open with a metallic shriek.

Darby's heart lurched into her throat. She grabbed Kara's arm and yanked her sideways, dragging her behind the nearest dumpster. They dropped into a crouch, the smell of rot thick as they made themselves small in the shadows.

In the doorway stood the thin man, his silhouette backlit by the lights inside. He'd turned back toward the interior, saying something to someone Darby couldn't see.

"—just need some air," he was saying. "I got a headache coming on."

Another figure joined him in the doorway. The man had a stockier build and was shorter. Even in silhouette, Darby recognized him. He was the second man from the Serpent's Garden, the one who'd been wearing the baseball cap.

Darby's pulse hammered in her ears. She pressed herself tighter against the dumpster, felt Kara doing the same beside her. She fumbled for her phone with shaking hands.

Darby: *HIDING. Two men from Serpent's Garden just came out the back door.*

The reply from Ivette came almost immediately: *Stay hidden. Don't move.*

Darby was suddenly glad that she'd silenced her notifications. No need to alert the witch hunters to their presence.

"Headache, huh?" the shorter one said, his voice rough. He pulled out a pack of cigarettes, shook one loose for himself, then offered the pack.

The thin man took one. A lighter flared briefly, illuminating gaunt features before darkness swallowed them again.

Darby strained to hear, but their voices had dropped to murmurs, too low to make out from behind the dumpster. They stood near the back door, cigarettes glowing as they talked.

They started walking, heading across the back lot toward the alley. Their path would take them past the dumpster. Darby's breath caught in her throat. She went completely still, and felt Kara do the same beside her.

The men passed by, heading toward the alleyway. Darby's pulse hammered as they drew closer, but they kept to the theater wall, never veering in the direction of the dumpster. She exhaled slowly, relieved. Their voices grew clearer as they walked passed.

"I'm serious, Rick," the stocky man said. "And the congregation keeps getting smaller. Did you see how many empty seats there were tonight?"

"Don't forget our mission. How many people show up to service doesn't change what we're here to do."

Their voices faded as they rounded the corner. Darby waited until she couldn't hear them anymore before risking a glance around the dumpster. She released a relieved breath to find the backlot empty.

Darby: *They're heading toward the front.*

She and Kara crept forward, staying low, moving to the back corner of the building. From there, they could see down the alley to where it spilled out onto the road in front of the theater. Darby eased her head around the edge just enough to see.

The two men were halfway down the alley, one flicking away his cigarette as they hunched into their jackets. They looked like they were heading straight toward the coffee shop.

Darby and Kara stayed pressed against the corner of the building, mostly hidden in the shadows of the back lot, watching the men's progress. Darby pulled out her phone with shaking hands.

Darby: *Ivette they're headed in your direction.*

Through the coffee shop window, Darby could see Ivette's glamoured profile. She was looking down at her phone, reading the message. Even from this distance, Darby saw her tense.

Ivette stood, gathering her things. She was trying to look casual, but she was moving quickly. She pushed through the coffee shop door and turned down the sidewalk and directly into the path of the two approaching men.

"Shit. No," Darby whispered.

Ivette realized her mistake a second too late. She tried to backtrack, to turn around, but the thin man, Rick, was already raising his arm.

The torch on his cuff bracelet blazed to life with a sickly orange glow that cut through the gathering dusk.

Rick stopped dead. He grabbed his companion's arm and pointed directly at Ivette.

They started walking faster, their casual pace shifting into something deliberate and predatory, closing the distance to Ivette like hunting dogs that had caught a scent.

Darby didn't think. She just moved.

She rounded the corner at a run, already sensing something building around the two men – a prickling heat, threads of unfamiliar magic coiling tight. Rick's hand dove into his pocket, fingers closing around something she couldn't see.

Without hesitation, the words of the Unraveling spell spilled from Darby's lips. Her voice rose, steady and clear, each phrase precise despite her pounding heart.

The spell shot from her like an arrow, invisible but potent. She felt it leave her in a rush and reach the two men just as they closed the distance to Ivette. Her magic tore through whatever they'd been building, unweaving it before it could finish forming.

They jerked in place as if they'd hit an invisible wall. Rick's hand went to his throat, his face twisting in confusion. The stocky man stumbled at his side.

The magic was working. The Unraveling spell was doing exactly what they'd practiced – methodically dismantling whatever they'd tried to build.

But it wouldn't last long.

Darby reached for her plant magic – that green pulse she could feel even in winter's cold grip. She immediately sensed a weed forcing its way through a crack in the sidewalk, stubborn and vital. She grabbed hold of that life and pulled.

The weed exploded upward with violent speed, growing six feet in the span of a heartbeat. Its thick stem whipped sideways and caught both men across the chest with a meaty thwack.

Both men flew backward and hit the pavement hard, landing in a heap of flailing limbs.

Darby felt Kara's magic stir the air beside her, a sudden gust of wind whipping Darby's hair around her face. There was fury in it, sharp and hot, so different from Kara's usually calm and peaceful magic. The wind caught the fallen men and lifted them like they weighed nothing, tossing them roughly back down the street, away from Ivette and the coffee shop. Pedestrians stopped dead, watching in confusion and shock.

"Get the bracelet," Kara hissed.

Darby reached for another vine, this one thinner but just as strong as the last. Darby sent it snaking across the pavement toward Rick's wrist. It wrapped around the bracelet with the precision of a pickpocket, gave one sharp yank, and the cuff came free.

The vine delivered it to Darby's outstretched hand. The charm was still glowing faintly, warm against her palm.

"Go!" Ivette was already moving, grabbing both of them and pulling them forward into the crowd that was forming around the fallen men.

"Oh my god, are you okay?" A woman in a business suit was bending over Rick.

"Someone call 911!"

"Did you see what happened?"

The three of them melted into the confusion, moving fast but not running. Darby shoved the bracelet deep into her pocket next to the witch ball. Her heart was hammering so loudly in her ears that it was drowning out everything else.

They made it around one corner, then another. The sounds of concern behind them faded.

Once they were out of sight, they ran.

Their footsteps echoed off the buildings. They cut through another alley, emerged on a street Darby didn't recognize, but they kept going. The cold air felt like knives in her burning lungs.

After several more blocks, they finally turned into a small plaza wedged between buildings, empty except for a few winter-dead trees and benches missing slats.

Darby doubled over, hands on her knees, gasping. Beside her, Kara leaned against a tree trunk, her breath coming in white clouds.

"Glamours," Ivette panted. "Off. Now."

They each pressed their thumbs to their foreheads. *"Let my true face be shown."*

The magic released like a held breath, and Darby felt her own features settle back into place. The pressure vanished, leaving behind a faint tingling sensation.

Kara and Ivette's faces shimmered and settled back into place, familiar and real again.

"Did that actually just happen?" Kara's voice was shaking. "Did we just—"

"Attack two Torch Bearers in public?" Ivette finished. She started laughing, a slightly hysterical edge to it. "Yeah. Yeah, we did."

Darby straightened up, still breathing hard. Her hand closed around the stolen bracelet in her pocket. It was vibrating gently, a low buzz against her palm that made her skin crawl.

"Wait," she said. "I have an idea."

She pulled out the bracelet and placed it carefully on one of the benches. The torch charm glowed with that sickly orange light, pulsing faintly. She could hear the faint buzz of its vibration against the wooden bench.

"Back up," Darby said. "Slowly. Let's see what happens."

They moved away from the bench, step by step. They moved five feet away, then ten. The charm kept glowing, kept buzzing.

At about twenty feet, the light pulsed once and then died. The vibration stopped.

The bracelet sat dark and lifeless on the bench.

"Now let's get closer," Darby said.

They moved forward together.

After just a few steps, the torch charm sparked back to life, its orange glow faint in the dusky light. The vibration resumed.

"Son of a bitch," Ivette breathed. "That's how they detect us."

Darby's stomach dropped. Twenty feet. If the men had passed any nearer to the dumpster where she and Kara had been hiding, the charm would have gone off. They would've been trapped there, with nowhere to run.

Darby snatched the bracelet off the bench, the vibration pulsing a steady beat against her palm. She shoved it back in her pocket.

"We need to get out of here," she said.

They merged back into the evening foot traffic, walking quickly but not running, just three more women heading home in the cold. Darby kept her hand in her pocket, feeling the bracelet's constant buzz against her palm.

CHAPTER 31

*D*arby had been sitting on the floor at the coffee table for hours. Long enough that her back ached, her eyes burned, and the words in the grimoire had started to blur together. Papers surrounded her – crumpled failures littering the floor, loose sheets covered in frantic handwriting pinned under her coffee mug and spell supplies. Candle stubs sat melted around the edges of the table. A plate holding a half-eaten piece of toast sat forgotten on the arm of the couch.

She barely registered the sound of the front door opening.

"Jesus," Kara's voice cut through her concentration. "What happened in here?"

Darby's head snapped up. Kara stood in the doorway, purse in one hand and a bag of groceries in the other, taking in the disaster zone that had once been their living room.

"I'm trying to figure out how to beat the bracelet," Darby replied, exhaustion and defeat bleeding through the words.

Kara set down the groceries and sank onto the floor beside Darby, folding her legs beneath her. "Okay. What have you tried so far?"

"Everything." Darby gestured at the chaos surrounding her.

"At first, I was focusing on a spell to use against the bracelets themselves. You know, something to disable them or scramble the detection. But then I realized that doesn't actually help us." She rubbed her eyes, feeling the grit of exhaustion. "We'd have to know who's wearing them to target them, and by then it's too late. They've already detected us."

"So unless we can figure out a way to detect every Torch Bearer or find all the bracelets, it won't work," Kara said slowly.

"Exactly." Darby flipped another page in the grimoire. "The key is making ourselves invisible to the bracelets in the first place. If they can't detect our magic, they can't find us."

"What about the containment circle?" Kara asked. "It keeps magic from leaking out. Could we adapt it somehow? Use it to mask our signatures?"

Darby shook her head. "I thought about that. But the circle's anchored to cardinal points – it's tied to the ground. There's no way to attach it to our bodies and still be able to move around. We'd be stuck standing in one place."

"What about adapting the invisibility spell?"

"That was my first thought." Darby's laugh was bitter. "I've been trying variations on it all morning. But every time I cast it, I just make myself completely invisible instead of just hiding my magical signature. I've vanished three times already. Once, everything below my hips disappeared. That was a super weird sensation. Another time, the only thing visible was my hands."

She caught the hint of a grin tugging at Kara's lips.

"Just your hands?" Kara asked. "You could go as Thing from the Addams Family for Halloween."

"Kara."

"Sorry." But she didn't look particularly sorry. Still, her expression shifted to something more serious. "Okay. Let's take a step back. Maybe we're approaching this wrong."

Darby slumped back, defeated. "I'm open to suggestions."

"First, let's order some Chinese food. Then we'll look through the grimoire together. Fresh eyes, you know?"

For a moment, Darby just stared at her. Then something in her chest loosened, just a little. "You're a really good friend. And coven member."

"Right back at you."

"I should get Topaz a flower arrangement or something," Darby said, feeling a hint of her usual humor creeping back. "For bringing us together. It's been such a stroke of amazing good luck."

"She'd probably prefer a bottle of tequila."

"Even better."

Kara pulled out her phone and started scrolling through delivery options. Darby returned to the grimoire with a heavy sigh, flipping pages mechanically. The sound of turning pages filled the apartment, punctuated by Kara's occasional hum as she debated between restaurants.

"Lotus Garden okay?" Kara asked. "They have those soup dumplings you like."

"Perfect." At least something was going right today.

Before Kara could place the order, there was a knock at the door. Both of them looked up, exchanging glances. They weren't expecting anyone.

Darby pushed herself up from the floor, her legs protesting after hours of sitting. When she opened the door, Topaz stood there in her ripped jeans and a flannel shirt over a black tank top, hair pulled back in a messy bun. Darby swallowed her spark of envy that Topaz could make any outfit look like cool rocker chic.

"Hey," Topaz said. "I was thinking maybe movie night? I was just at the venue working out some sound stuff for the show and —" She stopped, taking in Darby's appearance and what she could see of the apartment behind her. "What happened? You look like hell."

"Thanks," Darby said dryly, but stepped aside to let her in. "Come see for yourself."

Topaz walked into the living room and stopped, surveying the chaos. "Okay, what am I looking at here?"

"Darby's been trying to figure out how to beat the bracelets," Kara explained. "All day, apparently."

Topaz's expression shifted immediately, the tiredness giving way to sharp focus. "And?"

"And I've made myself invisible several times, given myself a killer headache, and wasted about seventeen pieces of paper," Darby said, dropping back down to the floor beside the coffee table. "We were just about to order Chinese food and keep trying."

"Movie night can wait," Topaz said without hesitation. "Let's get to work."

"Before we dive in," Darby said, "how's the show prep going? Is it all coming together?"

"Yeah, actually. It's good. Really good." She paused, and her face brightened. "Looks like there's a solid shot that some important industry people might show up. There's a rumor going around that a couple of label reps are coming, maybe even someone from Vibe Records."

"That's great," Kara said, looking up from her phone.

"Yeah." Topaz's smile faded at the edges. "I really need this to go well." Her voice dropped, losing some of its usual confident edge. "Like, really need it to. This feels like it might be my last shot at making it big, you know?"

Darby scoffed. "Are you serious? You're not even thirty yet, and you're insanely talented."

Kara nodded. "You've got plenty of time. You just need to be patient."

A flash of ire filled Topaz's eyes. "I *have* been patient." Her voice came out sharper than usual, edged with something raw.

"So patient. But it's my time now, and I'm going to make it happen."

The intensity in her words hung in the air for a moment. Darby and Kara exchanged a glance.

"You're right," Darby said firmly. "You absolutely deserve this break."

"More than deserve it," Kara added, her voice softer now. "You've earned it."

Topaz's shoulders relaxed slightly, the fire in her eyes banking but not disappearing entirely. "Thanks. I just... I need you guys to understand how important this is."

"We do," Kara said. "We really do. I promise."

"Then we'll make sure nothing interferes with it," Darby said firmly. "That's why we're doing all this, right? So you can focus on your music and not worry about Torch Bearers crashing your show. Your show is going to be amazing. Everyone is going to get to see how talented you are."

Topaz's expression softened. "Thanks. Both of you." She straightened her shoulders, visibly pulling herself together. "Okay. Let's figure out how to beat these bastards."

Kara snorted but turned back to her phone. "I'm going to order us some dinner. What do you want?"

"Not Lotus Garden," Topaz announced with a grimace.

"How did you know we were going to order from there?"

"Because you always do!" Topaz replied with a huff. "Can we please get Golden Dragon for once? I really want their orange chicken."

"I don't mind," Darby said. "Their dumplings are just as good."

They weren't really, but Topaz was right – they did always order from Lotus Garden. It would be good to expand their palates.

While Kara placed the order, getting enough food for six people, not three, Darby watched her friends with something like relief. She hadn't realized how much she'd needed another person here, another set of eyes working on this problem.

Topaz tossed herself on the couch with a groan that said she'd had a long day as well.

"It'll get here in thirty minutes," Kara said. "Want to start looking now?"

Darby waved a hand at the grimoire. "Be my guest. I've been staring at the same pages for so long the words are starting to swim."

Kara came to sit beside her on the floor, tucking her legs underneath her. The grimoire lay open, its pages filled with elegant handwriting and the occasional margin note in different ink. Darby watched Kara start at the beginning of the section she'd been working through, reading more carefully than Darby had the patience for at this point.

Time passed and Darby lost track of how long they sat there. Her mind kept drifting, exhaustion making it hard to focus on anything. The buzzer startled her badly enough that she jumped.

Kara pushed herself up from the floor. "That's the food. Be right back."

While Kara was gone, Darby and Topaz pulled out their phones and sent their portion of the bill via a cash app. When Kara returned with the bags of fragrant takeout, the smell wafting from them made Darby's stomach roar.

"Oh my god, yes. I could eat a horse," Topaz announced.

They spread the containers across the coffee table, pushing aside papers and spell supplies to make room. Steam rose from the lo mein, the scent of garlic and ginger temporarily overpowering the waxy smell of burnt-down candles.

Darby reached for the soup dumplings. Topaz claimed the orange chicken and settled cross-legged on the floor, while Kara went for the lo mein.

CHAPTER 32

They ate and looked through the spells, passing the grimoire back and forth, reading passages aloud, and debating the mechanics of cloaking their magical signatures. Darby found herself relaxing slightly, the exhaustion still there but tempered by the company and the food and the sense that maybe, finally, they were getting somewhere.

They ate in companionable silence for a few minutes. Then Topaz stopped mid-page.

"Wait," she said through a mouthful of chicken. She swallowed hastily. "What about this one?"

Darby leaned over, squinting at the page. "The Null Field Spell?"

"Yeah." Topaz read the description aloud. "Creates a protective bubble of magical 'silence' around a working space to prevent outside magical interference during delicate spellwork." She looked up, and Darby could see the idea forming in her eyes. "It's basically a magical clean room. Keeps external magic out so whatever you're casting doesn't get contaminated or disrupted."

"Okay," Darby said slowly. "I think I see where you're going with this."

"Yeah, what if we cast it as a personal ward instead of around a space?" Kara's excitement was building, making Darby's exhaustion start to lift. "A bubble that moves with us. If the bracelet's detection magic can't penetrate the null field, it never registers that we're there."

Darby felt something click into place in her mind. She scooted closer to Kara and Topaz, leaning in to read the spell in the grimoire still open in her lap. "That could actually work. The bracelet is actively scanning for magic, right? But if we're inside a null field, there's nothing for it to detect."

"Exactly. We're not hiding our magic, we're just putting it behind a wall the bracelet can't see through."

They all looked at each other, and Darby felt tentative hope rising in her chest for the first time all day.

"Let's try it," she said.

They cleared space on the coffee table, moving the containers of half-eaten food to the kitchen. Darby reached for the stolen bracelet, where she'd left it sitting on a folded dish towel. The buzzing rattle against the table surface had started to drive her crazy hours ago, so she'd needed to muffle the noise. When she picked it up, the gentle buzz pulsed against her palm, and she could see its sickly orange glow even in the lamplight.

The sight of it made her stomach clench, but she pushed the fear aside. They had work to do.

The Null Field Spell was complex, more intricate than the spells they'd been practicing up until that point. It required precise gestures and carefully measured intention. The spell itself warned that too much force and the field would be rigid, impenetrable even to their own magic. Too little and it would be as useful as tissue paper.

However, the real challenge was adapting it to be mobile. The original spell was designed to be anchored to a physical space, tied to the walls and boundaries of a room. They needed it to move with them, to treat their bodies as the boundaries instead.

Their first attempt guttered out before it even formed, the magic slipping through Darby's fingers like water. The second collapsed in on itself with a faint fizzle. The third sent a wave of pressure through the apartment that made her ears pop painfully.

"This is harder than I thought," Darby muttered, rubbing her temples where a headache was starting to build.

"The spell needs an anchor," Kara said, frowning at the grimoire. "Something solid to tie it to."

Darby's hand went to her throat, fingers finding the malachite pendant Sage had given her. She never took hers off. The pendant helped focus her magic and kept her centered.

"What if we anchor it to these?" She held up the pendant. "We already wear them all the time. They're already tied to our magic."

Topaz's eyes widened. "That could work."

They tried again, and this time Darby focused on the pendant. She poured her intention into it, imagining the null field anchored there, radiating outward from the stone.

The magic responded differently this time. It felt contained and personal, instead of a room-sized barrier. It was something close to her skin, encapsulating her magical signature instead of erasing it.

But when Darby opened her eyes, the bracelet was still glowing.

They worked for hours, making small adjustments, tweaking the phrasing, changing how they channeled the magic through the pendants. Darby's back ached from sitting on the floor, and she'd chewed her thumbnail down to the quick without even realizing it. The lo mein had long ago grown cold, and the soup dumplings sat abandoned, their skins beginning to dry out. Finally, Kara called a break, and they took a few minutes to put the leftovers away.

Returning to their spots on the floor by the coffee table, the apartment grew dark around them as they worked. None of them bothered to turn on more lights beyond the lamp beside the couch, which cast everything in a warm amber glow.

Darby felt herself starting to spiral. They were so close, she could feel it, but close didn't mean anything if they couldn't actually make it work. And if they couldn't figure this out, then what? Never leave the apartment again? Wait for the Torch Bearers to track them down one by one?

"Let's try it again," she said, her voice hoarse. "There's got to be a way to make this work. We're so damn close. I can feel it."

Topaz nodded, then hesitated. "Wait. The wording. We've been saying 'within these bounds' like the original spell, but that's for a room."

Darby looked down at the grimoire, then at her pendant. "What if we say 'upon this anchor' instead? We're tying it to an object, not a space."

"That could work." Kara's eyes brightened. "On three?"

They each took a breath, hands closing around their pendants. Darby watched Kara center herself and tried to do the same, pulling all her scattered energy inward.

"One, two, three."

They spoke the modified spell together, their voices overlapping, the words careful and precise. Darby focused on the pendant in her hand, pouring her intention into it, feeling the null field anchor there and radiate outward.

She could feel Kara and Topaz doing the same beside her, their magic working in tandem.

Darby kept her eyes on the bracelet, watching with desperate intensity. She held the magic, maintaining it through the pendant instead of letting it dissipate.

The orange glow flickered.

Darby's breath caught in her throat.

The glow pulsed again, then dimmed. The vibration that had been a constant presence since they'd started slowed, stuttered, and finally stopped.

The bracelet went dark.

For a long moment, Darby couldn't move. She just stared at the dark face of the bracelet sitting on the coffee table like it might be playing a trick on them, like it would suddenly roar back to life and prove this had all been wishful thinking.

"Did we—" Kara started, her voice barely a whisper.

"I think so." Darby's heart was hammering. "The spell should be embedded in the pendants now. Anchored to the stone."

"So we don't have to keep it active?"

"Not if it worked right." Darby reached for her pendant, unclasping it. Her fingers reluctant to remove it from around her neck. "Here. Take this to your bedroom. That's far enough away that the bracelet should detect me if the null field isn't working."

Topaz removed her pendant as well, handing it over. Kara took all the pendants and walked down the hallway. Darby and Topaz stayed at the coffee table, watching the bracelet and holding their breath.

It stayed dark and silent.

Then, as Kara crossed the threshold into her bedroom, the bracelet blazed to life. The orange glow cut through the dim lamplight, and the angry buzz made Darby jump.

"It's working!" she called down the hall. "Come back!"

The moment Kara stepped back out of her bedroom, the bracelet went dark again. She handed Darby and Topaz their pendants back.

"Holy shit," Darby breathed, clasping it back around her neck. "It actually works."

Kara dropped down onto the floor beside them and pulled Darby and Topaz into a fierce hug. They held on for a moment, all of them shaking slightly with exhaustion and relief, then Darby pulled back and started laughing.

"We did it!" Topaz said with a squeal. "We actually did it."

"We did." Kara put her own pendant back on. "Though we'll

probably need to renew the spell occasionally. I'm not sure how long this spell will last."

But reality dampened Darby's elation almost immediately. "We still don't know if it works in the real world, though. What if there's something we haven't thought of?"

The thought sobered them. Kara looked at the bracelet, lying on its side on the table, and Darby saw her own anxiety reflected in her roommate's face.

"We're going to have to test it," Kara said quietly.

"Yeah." Darby picked up the bracelet, dark and inert in her hand. "But not tonight. Tonight, we get some sleep. Tomorrow, we figure out how to walk around Medeon and test our pendants against witch-detecting bracelets."

"I'll text everyone," Kara said through a yawn. "Tell them to come over first thing tomorrow morning. We'll need to cast the spell on their pendants as well."

"Good idea," Topaz said. She pushed herself up from the floor with a groan. "Jesus, I'm too old to sit on the floor for hours at a time."

"You're twenty-eight," Darby said, grinning. "Better start looking at nursing homes now. I've heard those waiting lists fill up early."

Topaz shot her the finger with a tired grin. "Yeah, but I just pulled a double shift at the coffee shop, followed by two hours at the venue, and then an impromptu spell marathon." Topaz stretched, her back cracking audibly. "I should probably head back to my place and get some actual sleep."

"Thanks for staying," Darby said, meaning it. "We couldn't have figured this out without you."

"That's what coven sisters are for." Topaz grabbed her flannel from where she'd draped it over the arm of the couch. "Text me tomorrow once everyone's here and you've done the spell on the other pendants. I want to be there when we test this thing for real."

"Will do," Kara said, already looking half-asleep where she sat on the floor.

Topaz headed for the door, then paused with her hand on the knob. She looked back at them, her expression unreadable in the amber lamplight. "Hey. Thanks for earlier. For what you said about the show."

"We meant it," Darby said. "You're going to kill it."

"Yeah, well. Guess we'll find out." Topaz's smile was crooked, vulnerable in a way she rarely showed. "Night, guys."

"Night," they called back in unison.

The door clicked shut behind her, and Darby heard Topaz's footsteps in the hallway, heading to her own apartment. The sound faded, leaving the apartment feeling suddenly quieter and emptier.

Kara hauled herself up from the floor, groaning at the stiffness. "I'm taking a shower. Try not to destroy anything while I'm gone."

"No promises," Darby called after her.

She started cleaning up the chaos, needing something to do with her hands while her mind raced. The grimoire sat on the coffee table, and she placed the bracelet beside it, staring at it for a moment. The weight of what they'd accomplished, and what they still had to do, settled over her like a physical thing.

Later, when Kara emerged from the bathroom with wet hair and fresh pajamas, Darby was curled up on the couch with her phone, reading the messages from the group.

"Topaz wants to test it tomorrow after work," she said without looking up. "Ivette, too."

"Makes sense. Safety in numbers." Kara settled onto the opposite end of the couch, tucking a throw blanket around herself.

"Jazmin offered to be a lookout, but she's got classes tomorrow afternoon."

They sat in silence for a moment. The apartment felt different now – not safer, exactly, but like they'd managed to take back some small measure of control. Outside, the wind howled against the windows.

CHAPTER 33

*D*arby sat at a table by the window of the coffee shop across from the Beacon of Light church, nursing what had to be the world's most expensive cup of plain black coffee. She had a paperback open in front of her – some thriller she'd grabbed from Kara's bookshelf – and made a point of turning a page every few minutes to maintain the illusion that she was actually reading. The glamour she'd cast made her look like a middle-aged woman with graying hair pulled back in a severe bun, the kind of person who probably had strong opinions about homeowner association rules. She'd added reading glasses on a beaded chain for good measure, which made it easy to peer over the frames at the church entrance without being obvious about it.

At the table next to hers, Ivette and Kara sat together looking like college study buddies. Ivette had glamoured herself to look like a student with jet-black hair and too much eyeliner, hunched over a notebook. Kara had gone for an ethereal waif look with platinum blonde hair and multiple nose piercings. Papers and highlighters were spread between them as if they were cramming for finals. They'd positioned themselves with a clear view of the church's entrance.

And then there was Topaz.

Darby had to bite the inside of her cheek to keep from laughing every time she looked at her. Topaz had decided, for reasons known only to her, to glamour herself as a gangly teenage boy with aggressive acne, greasy hair, and an oversized hoodie. She was hunched over her phone, pretending to doomscroll through social media with the glazed expression of someone who'd been staring at a screen for too long.

"Stop looking at her," Ivette muttered without moving her lips. "We're all supposed to be strangers."

"I can't help it," Darby whispered back. "She looks like she's about to ask someone if they play Fortnite."

"Focus."

Darby took another sip of her overpriced coffee and returned her attention to the church. They'd been here for almost two hours, watching people come and go. Most were older folks, the kind who probably attended every service and brought casseroles to potlucks. But there were younger people too, families with kids, a few high-school-aged kids who looked like they'd rather be anywhere else.

And then, finally, Darby saw them.

Three men emerged from the church's front entrance, and even from across the street, with the afternoon sun in her eyes, she recognized them. The thin one with the sharp features was Rick, the man whose bracelet was currently in her purse. He had his left arm in a cast that looked fresh, the white plaster bright against his dark shirt.

The stocky one beside him looked equally beat up. He was sporting a black eye visible even at this distance, and he was moving with the careful stiffness of someone with bruised ribs. The third man was the only one Darby hadn't seen before. He was bulkier than the other two, with a receding hairline and the physique of a man who spent a lot of time at the gym.

"That's them," Darby said quietly, her pulse starting to quicken.

Ivette's eyes darted up from her notebook, then back down. "I see them."

The three men stood on the church steps for a moment, talking. Rick gestured with his good arm, and even without hearing the words, Darby could tell he was upset about something. The shorter one shook his head, and the gym-rat put a hand on Rick's shoulder like he was trying to calm him down.

"I can't tell if Rick's wearing a new bracelet," Darby said, squinting. The cast made it impossible to see his left wrist, and his right wrist was covered by his jacket sleeve.

"The other two are, though," Ivette said. "Look at the big one's wrist."

Darby focused, and yes – there it was. A leather cuff wrapped around the man's left wrist. It looked exactly like the one they'd stolen from Rick. The bearded man had one too, though his was partially hidden by his sleeve.

Topaz's chair scraped loudly as she stood up.

"What is she doing?" Ivette hissed.

Topaz was heading for the door. Before Darby could stop her, she pushed through the coffee shop door and out onto the sidewalk.

"Shit." Darby was already standing, grabbing her purse. "Come on. We're her backup."

Ivette touched Kara's shoulder as she stood. "Stay here and keep an eye out. If anything goes wrong, you'll see it first."

Kara nodded, her knuckles white where she gripped her highlighter.

The weather had finally embraced winter, kicking off with the kind of damp chill that got into your bones. Darby pulled her sensible wool coat tighter around herself.

The three men had started walking down the sidewalk, still

huddled close together and talking. They weren't paying attention to their surroundings, too caught up in their conversation. Rick was gesturing again, his cast making the movement awkward.

Darby and Ivette hung back, keeping about fifteen feet behind Topaz, who was walking with her hands shoved in her hoodie pockets, head down like any teenage boy who'd rather be playing video games than existing in public.

The men were maybe thirty feet ahead of Topaz now, walking in a tight group. Darby could feel her heart hammering. This was it. The moment of truth. If the null field spell didn't work, if their glamours weren't enough, those bracelets would light up and then—

Topaz picked up her pace, angling her trajectory to intersect with the men.

"She's going to bump into them," Ivette breathed.

"I think she might be insane," Darby said, shocked and impressed by her friend's fearlessness.

Darby took a slow breath, readying the words of the Unraveling spell in her mind. She stuffed her hand into her pocket, fingers closing around the little baggy she'd prepared that morning – a confusion spell, simple but effective. If things went sideways, she could use that instead of something more aggressive. Better to leave the men dazed and uncertain than nursing more injuries and looking for revenge. Her other hand found her pendant through her shirt, the stone warm against her fingers.

Topaz was almost on them now. The men still hadn't noticed her, too absorbed in their heated conversation. Darby caught a few words – something about "still hurts like hell" and "should've stayed home" – before Topaz collided with the stocky man's shoulder.

Darby swallowed a surprised gasp.

The man stumbled, his conversation cutting off mid-sentence. Rick and the buff man both turned, startled.

"Oh my god, I'm so sorry!" Topaz's voice had gone up an

octave, taking on that squeaky quality of a teenage boy whose vocal cords hadn't quite finished changing. "I wasn't looking where I was going, I'm such an idiot—"

Darby stared at the leather cuff on the stocky man's wrist. Her breath caught in her throat.

The bracelet stayed dark.

No orange glow. No telltale buzz. Nothing.

Topaz was still apologizing, making a show of dusting off the man's jacket. "Are you okay? I didn't hurt you, did I? I'm really sorry, I was texting and not paying attention—"

"It's fine, kid," the man said, but his voice was tight with irritation. He shrugged off Topaz's hands. "Just watch where you're going."

"I will, I'm sorry, I'm really sorry—"

"We said it's fine." Rick's voice was sharp and dismissive. He looked at Topaz the way someone might look at a particularly annoying insect.

The muscular man's bracelet was visible now; his jacket sleeve having ridden up when he'd moved. It too was silent and dark.

Topaz backed away, still apologizing, then turned and practically skipped down the sidewalk. Just before she reached the corner, she turned around and looked directly at Darby and Ivette.

Her grin was so bright, so triumphant, that Darby was surprised the men didn't feel the force of it at their backs.

Then she disappeared around the corner.

The three men shook their heads and resumed their conversation, already forgetting the clumsy teenager. They started walking again, heading in Darby and Ivette's direction.

Darby forced herself to stay calm, to maintain her placid expression, to not do anything that would draw attention. She fished her phone out of her purse and pretended to check it, angling her body slightly away from the approaching men.

As she got closer, she kept her eyes on the buff man's bracelet.

The stocky man was rubbing his shoulder where Topaz had bumped him, looking annoyed.

Darby tracked the bracelets on their wrists with quick, furtive glances, counting down the closing distance between them in her head while maintaining the careful illusion of a middle-aged woman minding her own business. She opened her purse and put away her phone, using her movement to mask her glances.

The men passed them without a second glance.

Darby glanced over her shoulder at their bracelets, her heart in her throat.

The men kept walking, their voices fading as they moved down the street; the bracelets on their wrists stayed inert.

Darby looked at Ivette.

"It worked," Ivette said quietly. Her voice had a note of wonder in it. "It actually worked."

"Let's go find Topaz before she combusts from excitement."

They hurried to catch up, finding Topaz pacing back and forth at the corner, her teenage boy body almost vibrating with excess energy.

"Did you see?" she said the moment they were close enough. "Did you see? They didn't light up at all! Not even when I was literally touching one of them!"

"We saw," Darby said, feeling a grin spreading across her face that probably didn't match her middle-aged woman glamour at all. "You were brilliant. Absolutely brilliant."

"I know!" Topaz threw her arms up in celebration, and the gesture looked so ridiculous on the gangly teenage body that Darby finally let herself laugh.

"Come on," Ivette said, but she was smiling too. "Let's get back to the coffee shop before someone sees us and wonders what we're up to."

They walked back to the café together, and Darby felt something light and bright blooming in her chest. Hope, she realized. Real, genuine hope.

The null field spell worked. The glamours worked. They'd been within feet of Torch Bearers with active detection bracelets, and the bracelets had registered nothing.

When they pushed back through the coffee shop door, Kara looked up from her papers, her glamoured face carefully neutral. But her eyes were questioning.

Darby gave her the smallest nod.

They ordered another round of coffee – Darby's treat, since they were celebrating – and reconvened at the window table.

"That was incredible," Kara said quietly, leaning in so her voice wouldn't carry. "When Topaz bumped into them, I thought I was going to have a heart attack."

"Join the club," Ivette said. "I'm pretty sure I stopped breathing."

"But it worked." Topaz's grin hadn't faded at all. "We're officially undetectable."

"As long as we wear our pendants and make sure to maintain the null fields," Darby added, because someone had to be the voice of caution. "We can't get careless."

"I know, I know." Topaz waved a hand dismissively. "But let me have this moment. We just walked right past witch hunters, and they had no idea."

Darby raised her overpriced coffee in a toast. "To being undetectable."

The others raised their cups.

"To being undetectable," they echoed.

They sat there for another hour, watching the church, taking notes on who came and went, starting to build a picture of the Beacon of Light's patterns and routines.

Darby felt like she'd reclaimed something. Every moment they sat there undetected, every person with a bracelet who walked past without noticing them was a small victory.

And right now, Darby would take every victory she could get.

CHAPTER 34

*D*arby couldn't believe the day of Topaz's show had finally arrived.

The coven had hardly seen Topaz all week. She'd been a ghost; texting in the group chat at odd hours with updates about rehearsals running late, sound checks that needed re-doing, a wardrobe crisis that had required Darby to come over Tuesday night and help her go through her entire closet twice, trying to find the perfect outfit. Darby had also fielded several late-night calls where Topaz spiraled about the possibility of freezing up on stage or forgetting her lyrics or tripping over a cable in front of hundreds of people.

They'd all arrived with her earlier that evening, squeezing into Kara's car for the drive to the venue with Topaz's equipment in the trunk. Topaz had been vibrating with nervous energy in the front seat, her leg bouncing so hard Darby could feel it from the back. At the employee entrance, they'd hugged her tight. Kara adjusted Topaz's collar, Ivette squeezed her hand, Jazmin pulled her into a bear hug and said, "You're gonna be a fucking legend tonight" with such fierce conviction that Topaz actually laughed.

"She's right. You're gonna kill it," Darby had told her, meaning every word.

Topaz had grinned, but her eyes were bright with unshed tears. "Love you guys."

Then she'd disappeared through the door marked PERFORMERS ONLY, and they'd made their way around to the main entrance.

The concert venue was packed by the time they entered. The air was thick with anticipation and the smell of beer and sweat. Darby felt the press of bodies around her as music from the venue's playlist thumped through the speakers, the crowd restless and waiting.

"Front row! This is gonna be epic," Jazmin announced, muscling her way through the crowd.

They claimed a spot right at the barrier, close enough to see the stage crew making final adjustments. Topaz had texted a few minutes ago: *Almost showtime. So nervous I might puke.*

When Topaz appeared at the side of the stage, visible in the shadows just beyond the curtain, she looked anything but nervous. She wore black leather pants and a deep purple tank top that shimmered under the spill of stage lights, her hair wild and perfect. She caught sight of them at the barrier and her face lit up. They all waved and screamed her name.

She mouthed something that might have been 'Wish me luck' and gave them a thumbs up.

"She's going to be amazing," Kara said softly.

The lights dimmed. The crowd roared.

And then Topaz was there, walking onto the stage with her guitar slung across her back, and Darby's heart swelled so much she thought it might burst.

The first chord rang out – sharp and clean and powerful. Then Topaz began to sing.

She commanded the stage like she'd been born to it. Her voice soared over the crowd, raw and beautiful. Between songs, she bantered with the audience, flashed that brilliant grin, and made everyone feel like she was singing just for them.

Darby couldn't stop grinning. She screamed herself hoarse, jumped and danced and sang along. Beside her, Jazmin was filming on her phone, Ivette was crying happy tears, and Kara was so focused on Topaz she barely blinked.

Near the end of the set, the lead singer of The Velvet Ruins walked out on stage.

The crowd went absolutely wild.

"Holy shit," Jazmin breathed. "Is that—"

Topaz and the Velvet Ruins' frontwoman launched into a duet, their voices twining together, guitars matching riff for riff. Then another song, this one faster and harder, with Topaz's fingers flying across the strings.

When the final note faded and Topaz took her bow, the roar of applause was deafening.

* * *

THEY MET her outside the venue an hour and a half later, all of them still buzzing with adrenaline. Topaz looked absolutely effervescent, bubbling over with happiness. She radiated pure joy.

"You were incredible!" Darby grabbed her in a fierce hug. "I mean it, you were—"

"Radio station people were there," Topaz interrupted, breathless. "And there were definitely some industry people in the audience. Like, actual record company scouts. And the fucking Velvet Ruins said they'd love to play with me again sometime!"

"No way." Jazmin's eyes went huge. "Are you serious? Do you think you might get signed?"

"I don't know, but—" Topaz laughed, the sound giddy and disbelieving. "God, tonight was perfect. This was the best night of my entire life."

They started walking back to the car, talking over each other and reliving their favorite moments. The night air was frigid, but none of them seemed to notice. Darby kept stealing glances at Topaz, seeing her friend in a new light. She wasn't just someone with talent; she was someone on the cusp of something huge.

Topaz's phone buzzed. She pulled it out, still grinning, then stopped walking so abruptly that Kara nearly ran into her.

"What?" Ivette asked.

"Sage just texted." Topaz's grin had vanished. "She spotted graffiti downtown. A torch symbol painted on the side of an old warehouse."

The good mood evaporated like steam.

"Where?" Jazmin asked immediately.

Topaz typed quickly, then waited. A moment later, her phone buzzed again. "She sent the address. It's down by the docks, in the warehouse district."

"We should—" Darby started, but wasn't sure how to finish. Report it? Avoid it? They'd spent weeks preparing, but actually confronting the Torch Bearers felt suddenly, terrifyingly real.

"We should go check it out," Jazmin said, her voice steady. "Right now, while we know where they might be. Just to scout the area."

"I don't know," Ivette said slowly. "Shouldn't we plan this better? Check it out during the day first?"

"I agree with Ivette," Darby said. "We're not ready to just walk into—"

"We're as prepared as we're ever going to be."

Everyone turned to look at Kara. The usually timid member of their coven stood with her shoulders squared, her expression determined.

"Think about it," Kara continued. "Topaz might be on the verge of getting famous. She's going to be way more visible then. There'll be press, social media, all kinds of attention. If the Torch Bearers are looking for witches, she'll be so much easier to find.

We need to deal with this now, while we still have the element of surprise. While we have the upper hand."

Silence.

"She's right," Topaz said quietly.

Darby's hand found Bella's witch ball in her jacket pocket. She rolled it comfortingly between her fingers, feeling its smooth surface.

"Okay," she heard herself say. "Okay, let's go."

They piled into Kara's car, Topaz carefully stashing her guitar in the trunk before sliding into the backseat. She pulled up the map on her phone and they followed it through progressively emptier streets. The warehouse district by the river was a maze of abandoned buildings and rusted chain-link fences. Broken windows stared down at them like empty eye sockets.

Kara pulled to a stop at the end of a dead-end street. The warehouse with the torch graffiti loomed before them.

It was massive, three stories of corrugated metal and crumbling brick, windows either broken or boarded over. And there, spray-painted across the entire side facing them, was a torch. The image was easily ten feet tall, rendered in harsh red and orange paint that looked fresh.

"Jesus," Ivette whispered.

Kara pulled around the corner and parked in the shadows between two abandoned buildings, out of sight from the main road.

Before getting out of the car, they each cast glamour spells, watching as faces shifted and changed – new features, different hair colors, ages adjusted up or down. Strangers stared back at each other from the dim interior of the car. Darby passed around protection oil, and they dabbed it on their pulse points, the scent of herbs and salt sharp in the enclosed space.

They circled the building slowly, keeping to the shadows. There were no lights inside that they could see. And no vehicles nearby. The only sounds were the distant lap of the river against the docks and their own breathing.

"It looks completely abandoned," Topaz said finally. "I want to take a closer look."

She started toward the building before anyone could argue. At the main entrance, a pair of heavy metal doors sagged in their frame. One had been forced partway open, leaving a narrow gap just wide enough to see inside.

Topaz put her face close to the opening, shading her eyes. "It's empty. Completely empty inside."

"Topaz—" Ivette hissed in warning.

But Topaz was already slipping through the gap, disappearing into the darkness beyond.

"Damn it." Kara moved to the doors. "I'll keep watch out here. You two go make sure she doesn't do anything stupid."

"Jazmin, stay with Kara," Ivette said, her tone leaving no room for argument.

Jazmin's face fell. "But—"

"We need someone watching our backs," Ivette said firmly. "That's you two."

Darby exchanged a glance with Ivette, then they squeezed through the opening.

Inside, the warehouse was cavernous and dark. Broken pallets and rusted machinery cluttered the floor. The ceiling stretched impossibly high above them, barely visible in the faint light filtering through the broken windows. The air smelled of rust and mold and the sour tang of old chemicals.

"Topaz?" Darby called softly.

"Over here!" Topaz's voice echoed from somewhere in the back. "No one's here, but I think I found something. It looks like they used this place as a secret meeting spot or something. There's papers and stuff."

Darby's pulse hammered in her ears. A part of her wanted to

turn around and leave, but her feet carried her forward, following Topaz's voice.

They found her in the far corner, illuminated by her phone's flashlight. She stood beside an old metal table covered in scattered papers.

"Come check it out," Topaz called, looking back toward the entrance. "Jazmin, Kara! It's safe! Coast is clear. There's paperwork with some names and stuff on it."

Darby started across the warehouse floor, her footsteps echoing. Behind her, she heard Jazmin and Kara follow, their hesitation fading at Topaz's reassurance. As they drew closer, Topaz looked up at them with a bright grin. A chill brushed the back of Darby's neck, though she couldn't say why.

"Finally," she said, rolling her eyes. "Took you long enough."

Darby tried to take another step closer.

Her feet wouldn't move.

Panic spiked through her. She looked down, saw nothing holding her, tried to lift her foot and couldn't. It was as if her shoes had been glued to the concrete.

"What the—" she started.

"I'm so glad I'm almost through with you whiny bitches," Topaz said.

Then her smile turned cruel.

"$\mathcal{T}$opaz?" Darby's voice cracked. "Wha— What's happening?"

Topaz tilted her head, that cruel smirk still playing on her lips. "I have some friends who want to meet you all."

She pulled out her phone with casual ease, dialing without taking her eyes off them. "Everything's ready," she said into the phone, then paused. "Yeah, all four of them walked right into it." She hung up and slipped the phone back into her pocket. "My patrons are very eager to meet you."

"Patrons?" Darby tried again to move her feet, muscles straining so hard she started shaking. "What are you talking about?"

The warehouse erupted in overlapping voices as Kara, Ivette, and Jazmin all shouted at once.

"Topaz, what the hell—"

"Let us go!"

"This isn't funny—"

Darby spoke a release spell under her breath, feeling the magic build in her chest and rush outward – only to slam against an invisible wall and dissipate like smoke against glass. Her heart hammered, and her ears started buzzing.

With a loud creak that echoed through the cavernous space, the warehouse doors swung open. People began filing in – mostly men, maybe fifteen or twenty of them, talking and laughing like they were arriving at a party. Some clapped each other on the back. They carried themselves like they owned the place.

Darby's blood turned to ice. She recognized Rick immediately, and his two friends. Darby did a double take when she recognized Eugene from the diner in Briarton.

Several of them wheeled in a large ornate table that looked like someone had taken a medical gurney and decorated it with elaborate metalwork and jewels. The thing gleamed in the dim light, completely out of place in the abandoned warehouse.

"What in the hell?" one of her coven sisters screamed. Darby couldn't tell which one through the roaring in her ears.

Darby chanted the unraveling spell, then pulled hard on her plant magic, trying to summon vines to attack. She could feel plant life all around her. Roots beneath the concrete, weeds forcing through cracks in the foundation, even the moss clinging to the exterior walls. All of it was tantalizingly close, but she couldn't reach them. The magic surged through her body and slammed against that invisible barrier, contained within the dome around them.

"Tsk tsk." Topaz shook her head. "Did you really think it would be that easy? You walked right into a magic circle designed specifically to trap witches and contain their power. I've been planning this for months."

Darby's eyes dropped to the dusty concrete beneath her feet. Runes and black lines were traced across the floor in intricate patterns, barely visible in the dim moonlight filtering through the grimy windows.

"How can you do this to us?" Darby's voice broke. "We're friends. We're sisters."

"Sisters?" Topaz scoffed, the sound harsh and ugly. "You're not my friends. You're my marks." She gestured to the men surrounding them. "These gentlemen have the means to get me a record deal. They're my backers, and all I had to do was provide them with power."

The buff man stepped forward from the group, his face all sharp angles in the shadows. "You sprung the trap too soon, Brenda," he said to Topaz, his voice cutting. Why was he calling her *Brenda*? "The coven members needed more time to build their power. If we drain them now, it won't be enough. You promised us fully powered witches."

Rick shoved forward, his arm in a cast. "And you dared to set this up and call us here, as if you think you're in charge!" he shouted at Topaz. "We're calling the shots, not you! You shouldn't have sprung the trap so soon." He thrust his casted arm toward her. "I had to pretend their stupid untangling spell actually worked! They broke my arm! You were supposed to control them. Look at this!"

"We got you the opening slot for the Velvet Ruins," the buff man added coldly. "We introduced you to the right people. And this is how you repay us? By jumping the gun and ruining months of work?"

"They'd already figured out about the other victims," Topaz said quickly. "The coven knew who the Beacon of Light was. They were going to be a problem—"

"No." Rick's voice dropped to something dangerous. "You're the problem. And we're here to fix that."

He pulled a syringe gun from his pocket and pressed it to Topaz's neck before she could react, triggering it in one smooth motion. Whatever was in it worked instantly. Her body went slack, collapsing like a puppet with cut strings. Two of the men caught her before she hit the ground.

"What was that? What've you done to me?"

"A little concoction we've perfected," he said, almost conversationally. "A potion to neutralize witch magic, mixed with a paralytic. Quite effective." He tilted his head, studying her like a specimen. "If we include you in tonight's ritual, when we consume your magic, it will give us enough power."

"No!" Topaz cried, her voice starting to slur. "I'll get you more witches! I'll bring you Sage from the occult store! And the vel—"

"We'll get to her in due time," the thin man said calmly. "But you've become a liability."

"I helped you!" Desperation cracked her voice. "You owe me!"

"We owe you nothing." His smile was terrible. "You're a witch, and we shall not suffer you to live."

"You need me! I can still find more witches! I have the power to detect them!"

"This is the last sacrifice we need. We have enough power now. You're no longer useful."

Topaz screamed as the men carried her to the bejeweled gurney. They strapped her down with practiced efficiency while Darby and the rest of the coven shouted and fought against their magical prison, trying desperately to move, to break free, to do anything.

Darby fumbled her phone from her pocket with shaking hands, trying to dial 911. Before she could hit the first digit, a lasso made of pure light snaked out and knocked the phone out of her grasp, smashing it against the concrete floor.

"Nice try," Rick said, and proceeded to do the same to the other coven members, magical lassos of light snatching their phones one by one.

They threw everything they had – keys, water bottles, wallets, jewelry, whatever they could reach. But with their feet glued to the floor, the items fell short or were easily batted aside. A few of the Torch Bearers swatted things away with their glowing lassos, laughing at their futile efforts.

The group formed a circle around the gurney, their hands raised. They began to chant, their voices rising and falling in unison. The thin man's voice cut through: "A man or a woman who is a medium or spiritist among you must be put to death. You are to stone them; their blood will be on their own heads."

Topaz began to scream.

A glowing wisp of smoke started rising from her chest, pulled upward by the chanting voices. Her screams turned desperate, agonized and inhuman.

Darby's hand wrapped around the witch ball in her pocket, the only item she hadn't thrown at the Torch Bearers. With nothing else to lose and no other options, she pulled it out and threw it as hard as she could outside the magic circle.

The glass orb shattered against the concrete with a sharp crack.

CHAPTER 36

"*I*sabella Rousseau," Darby said, her voice steady despite her terror, "I welcome your spirit into my body."

The impact hit her chest like a physical blow, driving the air from her lungs. A presence flooded into her body and mind – powerful and angry. Her mouth opened, and a voice that wasn't hers came out: "*My* feet aren't bound to your magic circle."

Darby felt the spirit begin building magic, the power different from her own. It was kinetic – raw and forceful. Hoping it wouldn't be the last thing she ever did, Darby pushed all her power toward the spirit. She felt the rest of the coven, except for Topaz, whose screams had turned into gasping whimpers, do the same, their magic flowing into her like rivers converging.

The spirit released it all at once.

A concussive blast exploded outward, knocking every person in the warehouse off their feet. Darby felt the spirit pull partially out of her body – a nauseating sensation – and smudge the writing on the floor with ethereal fingers.

The magic circle collapsed.

Darby didn't hesitate. She instinctively tried the unraveling spell first, but it did nothing against these men. So instead, she pulled on her plant magic, summoning vines that burst through the concrete cracks, swatting and binding as many enemies as she could. But there were too many attackers. The Torch Bearers scattered in all directions, and several of them conjured those glowing lassos of light.

"Split up!" Kara shouted. "Don't let them surround us!"

Rick charged at Darby, a whip of light spinning in his hand. She rolled to the side as it cracked against the concrete where she'd been standing. She summoned vines to trip him, but he leaped over them.

"You witches think you're so special," Rick snarled, advancing on her. "But you're just fuel for our power."

Before Darby could react, she felt Bella use her telekinetic magic to seize a piece of broken concrete and hurl it at his face. A small shield made of light materialized in his other hand, and the concrete shattered against it in a spray of dust. Darby used the time that Bella bought her to summon a thick root that burst up between them, forcing him back. She willed thorns to grow along its length, creating a barrier between them. Then she threw a striking hex at him with everything she had. The spell hit him square in the chest and knocked him off his feet, sending him sprawling backward.

Across the warehouse, Kara faced off against three Torch Bearers at once. She swept her arms outward, and a miniature tornado exploded from her palms, strong enough to whip dust and loose debris into the air. Her attackers scattered in different directions, forcing her to choose which one to focus on. One lunged at her with a knife that glowed with the same orange light as the torch bracelets. She threw up a wall of compressed air that sent him flying backward into a concrete pillar with a sickening crack.

But while she was distracted, another Torch Bearer grabbed her from behind, pinning her arms. Kara slammed her head backward into his nose. He howled and released her. She spun and thrust both hands toward him, fingers splayed. He gasped, eyes bulging, hands flying to his throat as he struggled to breathe. His knees buckled and he collapsed, unconscious before he hit the ground.

Ivette dodged between a few pieces of machinery, electricity crackling between her fingers. Two Torch Bearers cornered her, using their light magic to form a net. She sent a bolt of lightning at the nearest one, but he deflected it with a light shield. The other one used his lasso to wrap around Ivette's ankle and yank her off her feet.

She hit the ground hard and lay there wheezing. The Torch Bearer dragged her toward him, grinning. Ivette slammed both hands into a puddle of stagnant water beneath his feet and sent every volt she could summon through it. His body convulsed and he dropped, smoke rising from his clothes.

Jazmin had created a whip of water that she cracked like a weapon, keeping four men at bay. But they were learning her rhythm, dodging her strikes. One of them hurled a chunk of broken brick that passed straight through her water whip and grazed her cheek. She flinched, losing her concentration, and the whip splashed to the ground. Another rushed her while she was distracted.

"Jazmin!" Darby screamed, summoning a root from beneath the concrete. It burst upward, sharpening to a point as it shot toward the charging man and impaled him. He screamed in agony. Darby ignored it, already searching for the next threat.

Jazmin nodded her thanks and shifted tactics, pulling moisture from the air and forming it into razor-sharp shards of ice. She hurled them at her attackers. Two of them went down screaming, ice embedded in their legs and shoulders, blood spreading across the concrete.

Darby felt Bella's spirit surging inside her, adding power to her own. Together they summoned vines from every crack and crevice, but the Torch Bearers kept coming. One of them –

Eugene from the diner – charged at her with a length of pipe. She threw up a wall of brambles, but he smashed through them, splinters of wood flying.

He swung the pipe at her head. She ducked, feeling it whistle past her ear, and drove her knee into his stomach. As he doubled over, she grabbed the back of his head and slammed it down onto her rising knee. He crumpled, and she dropped him like a piece of used tissue.

But three more took his place.

"There's too many!" Ivette shouted, backing toward the others. Blood ran from a cut above her eye.

"Together!" Darby called out. "Back-to-back!"

The four of them formed a circle, facing outward as the remaining Torch Bearers closed in. There had to be almost a dozen still standing, maybe more. Their light lassos glowed in the darkness, creating a net of power around the witches.

"On my mark," Darby said, feeling Bella's power thrumming through her veins. "Everyone give it everything you've got."

Rick stepped forward from the circle of Torch Bearers, that terrible smile still on his face. "It's over, witches. You fought well, but—"

"Now!" Darby screamed.

Kara snapped her palms outward, releasing a burst of air so sharp it hit like a sonic punch. Jazmin hurled needles of ice at all the men, the frozen shards slicing through the air. Ivette sent lightning arcing after them.

Bella's power rose up within Darby like a tidal wave, seizing every loose object in the warehouse and turning them into weapons. Darby felt the telekinetic force whip outward, bombarding the Torch Bearers with a storm of projectiles.

And Darby summoned every plant within a hundred yards.

The warehouse exploded with vegetation. Vines burst through the concrete floor like erupting geysers, wrapping around legs, arms, throats. Roots tore through walls. Greenery spread across every surface in seconds. The Torch Bearers' light magic flickered and died as they were overwhelmed by the sheer volume of plant life.

Some tried to fight free, but Ivette hit them with electricity, the current traveling through the wet vines like a conduit. The few who slipped past Darby's vines were caught by Kara's wind, sent tumbling across the room like leaves in a storm. The few who broke loose found themselves on ice-slicked floors, their feet sliding out from under them, bleeding from hundreds of needle-like cuts from a barrage of ice shards.

Darby kept the vines coming, relentless, binding the Torch Bearers to the floor, the walls, to each other. She felt their struggles weakening, heard their shouts turning to whimpers.

When the last of them stopped fighting, she let her magic settle. The warehouse was a jungle now, green growth covering every surface, bodies wrapped in nature's grip.

Some of the Torch Bearers were unconscious. Others groaned weakly. A few didn't move at all, and Darby didn't let herself think about whether they were breathing.

Jazmin sprinted to the gurney where Brenda lay strapped down. "She's not breathing!" she screamed. "She's not—"

"It's too late." Bella's voice came from Darby's mouth, strange and hollow. "The Torch Bearers already consumed her spirit and life force. She's gone. There is nothing to bring back."

Kara looked around wildly, still panting. "What do we do?"

Darby felt something shift inside her, like a door closing. She could feel the softer parts of herself – the woman who'd cried over her divorce, who'd worried about affording rent, who'd wanted nothing more than to rebuild a quiet, normal life – receding into shadow. That version of herself would hesitate, would look for another way, would try to find mercy even for monsters.

But mercy wouldn't keep them alive. Kindness wouldn't protect her coven.

She pushed those gentler instincts away deliberately, feeling them dissolve like morning fog. In their place, something harder crystallized. Something cold and certain and utterly ruthless.

Darby took a deep breath and spoke with her own voice this time. "We send them a message. No one leaves here alive."

Kara and Ivette stared at her in shock, their faces pale in the dim moonlight.

"Darby—" Kara started, her voice shaking. "We can't just... we can't murder them."

"They were going to murder us," Jazmin said fiercely. "They've murdered dozens of witches. They were going to eat our magic and life force and—"

"But if we kill them, we're no better than they are," Ivette cut in. Her hands were trembling. "There has to be another way. We could call the police, or—"

"And tell them what?" Darby asked. The coldness in her own voice surprised her. "That a group of men tried to magically drain our life force? They'd laugh us out of the station. Or worse, they'd lock us up."

"We can't leave any of them alive," Bella's voice added through Darby's mouth. "They know who you are, thanks to Brenda. They know where you live. They won't stop trying to kill you. They'll hunt you down one by one until you're all dead."

Kara pressed her hands to her face. "There has to be another... I don't want to be a murderer."

"Then I'll carry it," Darby said quietly. "This is on me. I'm making this choice. But we don't have time to debate it. Either we end this now, or we spend the rest of our lives running."

Ivette looked at Jazmin, then at Kara, then back at Darby. Her expression crumbled for just a moment. "If we do this... there's no going back."

"I know." Darby met her eyes steadily. "I can live with this. But I won't live in fear, and I won't let them kill any more of us."

A long moment of silence stretched between them.

Finally, Kara lowered her hands. Her eyes were red, but her jaw was set. "I can pull all the oxygen out of the warehouse," she said quietly, her voice barely above a whisper. "Knock them out first. Make it... make it quick."

"And I can start an electrical fire," Ivette said, her voice hollow. "Burn the whole place down. Destroy any evidence."

"We can't leave Topaz – Brenda – whoever she was." Jazmin's voice broke. "I know she betrayed us, but I can't just—"

"Of course not," Ivette said immediately. "We'll bring her out with us."

They unstrapped Topaz's body from the gurney and carried her outside together, stumbling into the cold night air. As they set her down gently on the ground, Bella began to speak through Darby's mouth again. "I was part of a coven that Brenda set up, one just like yours. After I watched the Torch Bearers consume my coven sisters' magic and life force, I astral projected my spirit out of my body before they could take it. I've been an untethered soul ever since, watching Brenda do this to other women. Over and over."

"Brenda?" Darby managed to say with her own voice. "She told us her name was Topaz."

"Brenda McAllister. The only witch to survive the Briarton Garden Club fire."

"Then who did we talk to on the phone?" Kara asked. "That wasn't Topaz."

Ivette shrugged, gesturing to the warehouse. "Probably one of those Torch Bearers. They were in on it the whole time."

"Let's finish this first, and then we can figure out how this all happened," Darby said, waving her hand at the warehouse.

She turned toward the building and felt nothing – no horror at what they were about to do, no guilt, no hesitation. Just a cold, crystalline certainty. These men had murdered how many women? How many covens had Topaz led to the slaughter?

Darby pulled vines from every crack in the pavement, every

weak point in the building's structure. They responded eagerly, as if they too wanted justice. The vines wrapped around the doors, the windows, the walls, creating a living cage that would ensure no one could escape.

Kara lifted her hands and pulled the air out of the warehouse in one long, steady draw. The building gave a muted groan as pressure shifted, and the vines inside trembled, tightening around the unconscious bodies they held. Within moments, the interior went still.

They waited a few long minutes, watching for any sign of movement. Nothing stirred.

Only then did Ivette flick her fingers and spark the electrical fire. The flames caught immediately, licking hungrily over the walls and the vines Darby had wrapped around the building. Jazmin pulled moisture from the air itself, leaving the plants bone-dry. Darby hardened them, turning the vines into perfect kindling. Kara fanned the fire with precise bursts of air, directing it inward, making it burn hotter and faster.

The warehouse quickly became an inferno.

Orange and gold light blazed against the night sky, casting dancing shadows across the empty street. The flames reflected off the Taskequan River beyond, turning the water's surface into liquid fire. Heat rolled toward them in waves, and Darby could hear the building groan and crack as the fire consumed it from within. Smoke billowed upward in thick black columns.

Glass exploded from the windows with sharp cracks, shards raining down onto the ground. The roof buckled with a thunderous groan, metal beams twisting and collapsing inward. Support columns gave way one by one, each collapse sending up fresh plumes of sparks and ash into the night sky.

Jazmin stood with her hands raised, using her water magic to contain the blaze, creating invisible barriers that kept the flames from spreading to the neighboring buildings. Sweat beaded on her forehead from the effort and the heat.

In the firelight, Darby's coven sisters' faces looked transformed. They were no longer the friends she'd made just months ago, but something harder. Something forged. Kara's jaw was set, her eyes reflecting the flames as she maintained her air magic. Ivette's expression was grim but resolute. Jazmin's face was streaked with tears, but her hands never wavered.

"We need to move back," Darby said. Kara and Ivette helped her carry Brenda's body deeper into the shadows of a nearby alley. Jazmin followed, retreating from the firelight into the darkness where they couldn't be seen.

They stood together in the darkness and watched the warehouse burn, and Darby felt the weight of what they'd become settle over her like a cloak. They were killers now. Murderers.

But they were alive.

"What will you do now, Bella?" Kara asked.

"I don't know," the spirit said softly. "Find somewhere nice to haunt, I suppose. My body was destroyed years ago."

They watched in silence as fire consumed the warehouse. In the distance, sirens began to wail.

"We need to leave," Ivette said urgently. "Before they get here."

"What are we going to do with Topaz's – with Brenda's body?" Jazmin asked. "Just leave her here?"

Darby thought about the book she'd read on possession and spirits, an idea forming. She looked at Brenda's body on the ground, then at the warehouse burning behind them.

"Actually," she said slowly, "I have an idea of where Bella's spirit can go."

EPILOGUE

*T*hree weeks later, Darby stood at the kitchen counter, tossing a salad with more force than strictly necessary. The repetitive motion helped calm her nerves – something she'd been doing a lot of lately.

She couldn't stop thinking about what Rick had said to Topaz in those final moments before everything went to hell. *"This is the last sacrifice. We have enough power now."* Enough power for what? What had they been building toward? What ritual or spell required the life force of dozens of witches?

The questions circled in her mind like vultures, but there were no answers to be found. The Torch Bearers were ash, and their secrets had burned with them. Maybe it was power just for power's sake, she told herself.

She'd watched the old movie theater for a week after the fire, using different glamours, hoping to learn something – anything – about the organization. But no one who came or went wore the telltale bracelet. Just regular employees and church members as far as she could tell. Then, a week later, the facility shut its doors permanently. A "For Lease" sign appeared in the window, and just like that, any trace of what had happened there was gone.

Whatever the Torch Bearers had been planning, whatever dark purpose had driven them to murder coven after coven, it was lost now. Part of her wondered if there were more of them out there. But she didn't know how to find those answers, and honestly, she wasn't sure she wanted to.

Her dreams had been consumed by that night. The warehouse. The flames. The choice she'd made.

The fire had burned hotter and longer than any natural blaze should have. When they'd finally left that night, there had been nothing but ash and a few bits of twisted metal framework. Even the concrete foundation had been scorched clean.

Intellectually, she knew they'd had no other option. Those men had been a threat; not just to her coven, but to all witches. Their actions had backed her into a corner, forcing her to make an impossible choice. It was survival, pure and simple.

She was glad she'd been the one to push for it. Neither Kara nor Ivette had the kind of soul that could carry that weight without breaking. They were too soft, too good. And Jazmin was still in high school, for god's sake. That was too heavy a burden for any of them to bear.

But knowing all that didn't stop Darby from seeing the flames every time she closed her eyes. Didn't stop her from wondering if there had been another way, even though she knew there hadn't been.

The worst part, in a way, is that she would make that choice again. Without a second's hesitation.

"Easy there," Kara said, pulling an enormous lasagna from the oven. The cheese on top was perfectly golden and bubbling. "You're beating up that lettuce like it personally wronged you."

"Sorry." Darby set down the wooden spoons. "I'm just—"

A brief knock at the door cut her off.

"Come in!" Darby called, glad for the interruption.

The door opened and Bella stepped inside, her movements still slightly uncertain in Topaz/Brenda's body. Her dark hair was pulled back in a simple ponytail, and she wore jeans and a sweater that looked brand new, probably because they were. She'd confided to Darby that she couldn't bring herself to wear Brenda's clothes. She'd already stolen her body and her life; wearing her clothes felt weird and wrong. Plus, they weren't Bella's style at all. Starting over meant starting from scratch.

"You don't need to knock, Bella," Kara said, grabbing oven mitts. "You're part of the coven now."

"I know." Bella closed the door behind her, ducking her head slightly. "I think I'm still just getting used to everything." She paused, then took a breath. "Actually, there's something I wanted to say. You should all start calling me Brenda. Since that's who I have to be from now on."

The apartment went quiet for a moment. When they went through Topaz's belongings after the attack, trying to piece together who she really was, they found several fake IDs – Topaz Johnson, Brenda McAllister, Melissa Sterling, and Rachel Brennan. But they'd also found a passport and real ID that said her actual name was Brenda Wright.

Darby met Kara's eyes, then nodded. "Okay. Brenda it is."

Brenda's shoulders relaxed slightly. "Thank you." She moved further into the kitchen, leaning against the counter.

"I've been wondering," Darby said. "Those articles on my computer. How did you finally manage to do that? To actually open the tabs?"

Brenda let out a long breath. "Years of practice. *Years.*" Her voice was tight with frustration. "Do you know how maddening it is to watch covens get picked off one by one and not be able to do anything about it?" She looked down at her hands – solid, real hands that could actually touch things now. "At first, I could barely interact with the physical world at all. Moving a pen an inch felt like lifting a car. It took me half a year just to learn how to flicker a light."

"So it was just a matter of getting stronger?" Kara asked.

"Getting stronger, learning control, figuring out how to focus what little power I had." Brenda rubbed her temples. "I tried warning the other covens before yours. But whatever I tried wasn't strong enough; they blamed the wind or bad electricity. I even tried writing in steam on a bathroom mirror once – just the word 'danger' – but it faded before anyone saw it." She let out a bitter laugh. "And I spent so much energy just trying to attack Topaz directly. Tripping her, making things fall near her, whatever I could do to ruin her day. But I was too weak, and it was never enough. The small things I could do – they just got dismissed as coincidence or imagination."

"That must have been awful," Kara said softly.

"It was torture," Brenda admitted. "By the time I got strong enough to actually control a mouse, to click and open those tabs, I'd been practicing for years. Building up my strength bit by bit. And even then, it drained me completely. I couldn't do anything like that again for days afterward."

She pushed away from the counter, wrapping her arms around herself. "At least now I can actually *do* things. Even if everything about this feels completely weird and wrong."

"You saved us," Darby said quietly. "If you hadn't opened those tabs, we might not have figured it out in time."

Kara nodded. "You did everything you could with what you had. That's all any of us can do."

Brenda's eyes looked suspiciously bright, and she opened her mouth to respond when Ivette emerged from the living room, where she'd been setting up plates on the coffee table. "Bella! How was the café?"

The relief on Brenda's face was obvious. She cleared her throat and managed a small smile. "I'm finally getting the hang of things, but it's been weird. So many people will say something or discuss an event that I have absolutely no idea about. I just smile and nod a lot."

As Brenda talked, Darby found her mind drifting to something else they'd learned in these past three weeks. Something Brenda had told them early on, when she'd still been adjusting to having a body again.

The grimoire. Topaz had planted it for them to find. She'd made Jazmin think she'd stumbled across it in that library office, but she'd orchestrated the whole thing from the beginning. She'd snuck it onto the pile of books when Jazmin's back had been turned.

They'd told Jazmin, of course. She'd deserved to know that her proudest moment – finding that grimoire – had been staged. She'd taken it hard, been quiet for a few days. But she was resilient. They all were. They'd had to be.

They'd also found out that Topaz's true affinity had been magic detection. She'd worked hard at fire magic, practiced until she was skilled enough to convince them it was her true affinity. Her real ability was sensing dormant witch magic in people. She'd spent years searching and finding people with potential.

She'd found each of them, moved them around like pieces on a chessboard: getting them all into the same apartment building, ensuring they'd meet and become friends. Then she'd planted the grimoire where Jazmin would find it, knowing they'd all unlock their powers together.

A coven built from scratch with magic she'd helped unlock. Then she helped them grow stronger, to strengthen their magic. Just so there would be more power for the Torch Bearers to eat. That had been her game from the start.

Every moment of their friendship with Topaz had reframed itself in Darby's mind over these past weeks. The helpful advice. The concerned questions. The way she'd always seemed to know just what to say. It had all been manipulation.

Darby pulled herself back to the present as Brenda exclaimed, "Oh, I almost forgot! This was sitting on your welcome mat." She held up a deep burgundy envelope.

Darby took it, frowning. The envelope was made of heavy,

expensive-looking paper. No address on the front, but there was a golden wax seal stamped with what looked like a scepter over a shield.

"What is that?" Jazmin asked, coming out of the bathroom.

"I don't know." Darby broke the seal and pulled out the contents. The paper was thick cardstock, the kind that practically announced its own importance. She started scanning the letter, her eyes widening. "What the f—"

"What?" Ivette cut in. "What is it?"

Darby started reading aloud: "To the Medeon Coven: This letter serves as official notification that the Michigan Conclave has received reports of an incident involving your coven on December 8th within Medeon city limits. Your presence is required at Conclave headquarters to provide a formal statement regarding said incident. The Conclave has intervened in the police investigation and ensured no connection will be made to your coven. However, this intervention does not absolve you of the requirement to appear before the Conclave Council to provide your account of events.'"

She paused, her throat tight. So someone knew what they'd done. Of course they knew.

That explained why Darby hadn't heard anything on the news. She'd seen a brief report on a fire in the warehouse district, but she'd kept expecting to see something about human remains or at least a report mentioning all the now missing church members from the Beacon of Light Ministry. But there'd been practically nothing. Just a routine warehouse fire, for a building slated for demolition anyway, with no injuries reported.

This 'Conclave' had made it all disappear. Which made Darby think that the coven now owed them something.

She continued reading: "Furthermore, you are advised that per Section 3, Article 12 of the Conclave Charter, all practicing covens within Michigan state lines must register with the Conclave to receive official recognition. Registration is mandatory for all covens and must be completed within thirty days of this notice.'"

She pulled out a registration form, scanning it quickly. It looked like any government form she'd ever seen – bureaucratic and impersonal. The first line stopped her cold.

"It's asking for a coven name."

Silence fell over the apartment. They'd never really talked about what to call themselves. They'd just been... them. A group of friends who'd stumbled into magic and somehow survived.

Jazmin's face broke into a slow grin. "I know what we should call ourselves…"

ACKNOWLEDGMENTS

Thank you to the incredible people who helped bring *Asphalt Coven* to life. My beta readers – Amira, David C, David Woolf, Frank, Jillian, Joanne, Paige, Pam, Rachael, Rachel, Susan – deserve a special shout-out for their sharp eyes, honest feedback, and boundless patience. Your help made this book more magical.

A quick note on the setting: I usually base my books on real places – I love sharing corners of the world that have captured my heart. But for this book and what I have planned for the coven, no real place quite fit. So, despite Asphalt Coven sharing the same world as Sophie Feegle, Medeon is entirely fictional. Consider it a love letter to gritty cities everywhere, distilled into one that exists only in these pages.

As for the character Topaz... Yes, I named her that because she wanted to be a 'rock' star. Yes, that's the whole joke. I regret everything.

To everyone who's supported me, encouraged me, or simply listened to me ramble about witches for far too long – thank you. This book exists because of you.

ABOUT THE AUTHOR

Gwen DeMarco is an avid reader, coffee snob, sailing enthusiast and a lover of all things nerdy. Gwen loves to write paranormal romance novels with a focus on the weird and wonderful.

Gwen is happily married to her high school sweetheart and has two teenage children. She can often be found with her nose in a book and a glass of wine or mug of coffee in her hand.

Sign up to her mailing list and receive a **free** copy of a novellas: one from the Kingdom of Erishum Trilogy and another from the Sophie and The Odd Ones series.

To learn more, please visit my website and sign up for my mailing list to receive updates at www.GwenDeMarco.com

ALSO BY GWEN DEMARCO

Sophie Feegle Series

Sophie and The Odd Ones

Portents and Oddities

Odd Times for Sophie Feegle

Against All Odds

Odds and Ends

Auras & Embers Series

Gideon Bean

Spirit Marked

Witches of Kirra Cross Series

Asphalt Coven

Kingdom of Erishum Trilogy

The Mudlark

The Gutter Shrike

The Dying Wilds

*9 7 8 1 9 6 3 9 0 6 3 7 0 *